VOICES IN
AN EMPTY ROOM

VOICES IN AN EMPTY ROOM

FRANCIS KING

LITTLE, BROWN AND COMPANY
BOSTON   TORONTO

Although this is a work entirely of fiction, I must make grateful acknowledgement to *ESP: A Scientific Evaluation* by C. E. M. Hansel (Macgibbon & Kee, 1966) and to *Trance Mediumship* by W. H. Salter (SPR, 1950)

FIRST AMERICAN EDITION

LIBRARY OF CONGRESS CATALOGING IN PUBLICATION DATA

King, Francis Henry.
  Voices in an empty room.

  I. Title.
PR6061.I45V6 1984   823'.914   84-14400
ISBN 0-316-49348-1

PRINTED IN THE UNITED STATES OF AMERICA

To
Diana Petre,
staunchest of friends

At rare moments one thinks that one hears a murmur of voices from behind the locked door, but one knows that, if one were to succeed in battering it down, one would find only an empty room.

George Meredith,
in a letter to Alfred Sutro

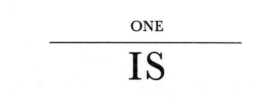

ONE

IS

Sybil goes into her study, then comes out of it again and hangs over the door handle a printed notice which says DO NOT DISTURB. The notice came from the Hilton Hotel in Stratford-upon-Avon but, since all her life she has been obsessively honest – returning to a newspaper shop because she has inadvertently taken away two copies of the *Guardian* after having paid for only one, burdening other passengers with the responsibility of handing over her fare to the conductor after she has alighted from a bus, and scrabbling in her purse for the odd coppers to make up the exact sum which she owes to some friend – it was not she who filched it but her brother Hugo.

'Oh, Hugo! I can't take that!'

'Well, I don't know what else you can do with it – unless you want to post it back. You're always complaining of your staff and girls bursting in on you. If you think "Do Not Disturb" sounds too peremptory, you can always write "Please" before the "Do".'

Although it is four years since Hugo gave her the notice and five months since his sudden death, she feels uneasily guilty whenever she has it in her hand. In precisely the same way, she feels uneasily guilty if she has some sausages from Cullen's in her shopping basket when she goes into Tesco's. No one from the Hilton is going to say to her 'You stole that sign from us', any more than anyone from Tesco is going to make the same accusation about the sausages. But the uneasy guilt remains. 'You're too honest,' Hugo used to tell her, just as, many years ago, in an attempt to explain to her the painful mystery of why no one had ever wished to marry her, he told her, 'You're too beautiful.' Too honest, too beautiful: was it possible to be either?

When a girl or a member of the staff sees that notice, she at once retreats. Sybil is writing. What she is writing, no one knows; but that she is writing is beyond all dispute. The general assumption is that, after her lifetime collaboration with Hugo on a new edition, eleven volumes in all, of Meredith's Letters, it must be about Meredith. 'More admired than read' is Sybil's verdict on Meredith's poems and novels. The same might be said of those eleven volumes.

Sybil has had a long and wearisome day. She woke too early, as she often does now. Then she began to think, with what was a physical ache behind her sternum and across what Henry, a friend of Hugo's, once called, half in irony and half in admiration, her 'noble brow', of the brother, so profoundly loved and so passionately grieved, who died as a result of a stupid and tragic accident. A stupid and tragic accident: that is how the coroner described it and that is how she thinks of it. But perhaps Hugo himself might not have cared for that phrase. In life, he might have said through the mysticism which wafted about him like a gaseous cloud, no event is stupid and accidental.

After she had dragged herself off her bed, with that recurrent sensation that all her bones are hollow, the marrow somehow shrivelled up, and had gone through the routine of morning prayers, there had been a trying session with the young architect, so brilliant and so self-willed, about the side chapel to be dedicated to Hugo and to be financed out of the money that he left her; then a no less trying meeting of the Governors, followed by a luncheon party for them; and, finally, a lecture, at which she had to introduce the speaker, a novelist whose works she had not merely never read but whose name, to the surprise of the English mistress who had invited him, was totally unknown to her.

She takes out the pad of foolscap paper from the drawer of her desk. She unscrews the top of her broad-nibbed fountain pen. She gazes out of the window, its curtains undrawn, at the croquet hoops on the lawn. Sometimes, at this hour in the summer, the mistresses emerge to play croquet. But if they see that the lamp on her desk is lit, they shake their heads at each other, shrug shoulders and retreat. The writing, whatever it is, must not be disturbed.

Sybil feels the imminence of happiness. All day, she has had to choose her words so carefully, concealing some things from the architect and other things from the Governors and never giving away anything of importance to the staff and the girls. Never for a moment has she been wholly spontaneous and wholly herself. Now she is free.

The pen pecks at the paper, with the side of its nib, leaving a single, wavering scratch. It strikes at it again, more firmly. She half-closes her eyes, her breath becomes heavy and even, as though in slumber. The pen tries one word, another, then another, with pauses between, until suddenly, as though the engine of a car had at last, after repeated pressure of the accelerator, coughed and spluttered into life, it begins to speed along the lines. Sybil is writing fast. She is writing far faster than Meredith, with his enormous output, can ever have written.

She is writing what, to Meredith or to any of her staff or to any of her girls would seem to be gibberish. She writes on and on.

Audrey dreads Sybil's visits, even more now than when Hugo was alive. 'I can't do with intellectual women,' she would say to Hugo; but it is not so much Sybil's intellectuality as her perspicacity with which she cannot do. People opaque to themselves rarely care for those who have the ability to see through them.

'Dear Audrey!' Sybil clambers out of her Mini and throws her arms around her sister-in-law. 'How are you? Let me look at you.' The elongated, grey-haired, still beautiful woman and the small, blonde, plain one stand each holding the other by the forearms, as though in preparation for a wrestling match. It is, as always on such occasions, Audrey who first gives in and lets go. 'Is everything all right?' Sybil asks, as though she has already assumed that everything is all wrong and has come here to right it.

'Oh, yes, fine.'

The house is a large, mournful Georgian one, with an unkempt lawn in front, littered with the children's toys, and straggling hedges all around, shutting it in claustrophobicly. On the other side of the hedges are the sheds and hutches for the goat, the pony, the donkey, the two cows, and the innumerable hens, guinea-pigs and rabbits which always seem to be needing the attentions of the vet. The cows go dry, because Audrey has forgotten either to milk them herself or to get one of the boys from the neighbouring farm to do so. The eggs tend to be found by the children under the hedges, after they have lain there so long that, when they are cracked, their yolks are a metallic green and they stink of sulphur. It is impossible to cook or even kill one of the rabbits because the children make such a scene.

Audrey was once a dancer. Then she met Hugo, who, to the surprise of his friends and to the consternation of Sybil, married her. Everyone assumed that Audrey would continue with a career already so successful; but she decided that, no, she wanted only to be a wife and mother. She persuaded Hugo to sell his flat in Beaumont Street in Oxford and to move into the country, and she began to collect the animals on what she referred to as 'the farm'.

'It's not real, Hugo,' Sybil would protest to him. 'None of it.'

'The animals seem real enough to me, when I have to pay the bills for their food.'

'It's all a performance. This little townee from Crouch End or Tufnell Park or wherever it was, sees herself as an

12

Oxfordshire countrywoman. But there's something sick and sickly about it all.'

That Sybil could speak like this to Hugo about his wife, and that Hugo should not be angry, were indications both of their closeness to each other and of Hugo's distance from Audrey.

'Even the children aren't real.'

'Oh, yes they are! You should hear them scream.'

'I do hear them scream. Whenever I stay here.'

'Well then!'

'They still are not real. Those are screams in a nightmare.'

Now the two girls, one five and one three, their hair so blond that it looks almost white, come out to greet Sybil. They hope that she has brought them a present but on this occasion she has forgotten to do so. It has been difficult to remember anything other than what she has to tell to Audrey.

The younger girl, Betsy, wanders off, pulling behind her a horse on wheels, which wags its tail as it jerks across the gravel. The older girl, Angela, who so much resembles Hugo that merely to look at her gives Sybil a pang, says, in that coaxing, wheedling way of hers, 'Oh, Aunt Sybil, haven't you brought us a surprise? You promised.'

Sybil wants to say: No, the only surprise that I've brought is for your mother. But she shakes her head, genuinely sorry and ashamed, 'I meant to stop at the toyshop in Woodstock. But my mind was on other things.' Other, far more important things. The child still gazes up at her, with Hugo's long-lashed, pale blue eyes and Hugo's way of resting the tip of his tongue on the overfull upper lip of his half-open mouth. Sybil cannot stand it; and the child mysteriously intuits, in the manner of children, that Sybil cannot stand it. She continues to gaze at her aunt, in this slow, subtle torture. Sybil opens her bag and then her purse inside it. Only notes. She jerks out a pound. 'This is for the two of you,' she says. 'Remember. For Betsy as well. Half and half.'

'Half and half,' Angela repeats, though the division does

13

not seem a fair one to her and she certainly will not observe
it. 'Oh, thank you, Aunt Sybil!' She gives one of the little
bobbing curtsies that Sybil finds so affected and twee, but
that always delighted Hugo.

'You shouldn't have done that,' Audrey says. She is not
being polite; she means it. People, she has been brought up
to believe, should not give each other money as presents. It
is, she has been brought up to believe, the easy way out.
Best of all is to give people presents made by oneself. It is for
that reason that last Christmas she gave Sybil a handknitted
purple jumper at least two sizes too small for her and the
Christmas before that some home-made chutney, with
mould whitening the surface under the waxed paper.

'She's so like Hugo. It always gives me quite a turn.'

'Do you think so? Everyone says she's so like me.'

The two women begin to walk slowly towards the house,
as though each shrank from the closer proximity to each
other which going inside will enforce on them. In the hall,
Audrey seats herself on a chest and pulls off first one
Wellington boot and then the other. Underneath, she is
wearing coarse Army surplus socks. The chest is a Jacobean
one. It would have pained Hugo to see Audrey squat on it,
just as, vicariously, it pains Sybil. Audrey pulls off her beret
and her hair, blond and dishevelled, tumbles out from under
it. It is scarcely believable to Sybil that this is the girl whom
she first met, in the Long Bar at Covent Garden, dressed in
a trouser suit of soft, honey-coloured suede, her hair
cropped, with obviously expensive artistry, close to her head.

Sybil slips out of her coat and then, feeling the chill of
the house, wishes that she had not done so. 'Audrey is such
a wonderful manager,' Hugo would say. By that he meant
that she would enforce the economies that he was too sybar-
itic to enforce. But perhaps now, Sybil thinks with genuine
compassion, the economies are really necessary. Audrey has
probably already mishandled the money, as she will go on
doing. She is the sort of person who saves two hundred

14

pounds on the heating bills and then loses two thousand on some daft investment.

'I've baked a cake,' Audrey says, as though she were announcing something unusual; but Audrey is always baking cakes, just as she is always baking the hard, gritty loaves of which, whenever she visits the school, she brings two or three as offerings for Sophie. 'A carrot cake,' she adds. 'We've had a glut of carrots. I sometimes think that old Mason planted nothing else in the vegetable garden.'

The two women go into the kitchen, where Audrey examines the Aga. 'Bugger!' She often swears now that Hugo is not here to chide her gently, as she used often to swear before she married him. 'I think it's gone out. I must have forgotten to fill it.'

Sybil feels a terrible, unwilling pity both for her incompetence and her self-delusion of competence. 'Let me see,' she says.

'But you don't know anything about these things, do you?'

'Yes. Something.' Hugo used to say that Sybil knew something about everything; and, in doing so, he always seemed to Audrey to be implying that she herself knew nothing about anything.

Sybil soon has the Aga blazing once more. 'It wasn't out,' she says maddeningly. 'But you had both those dampers shut.' Audrey has never really mastered the dampers, now that Hugo is dead. She leaves them to Mrs Pratt, the daily.

The tea is to be a nursery one at the long, rickety kitchen table, once a highly polished dark mahogany when Audrey bought it at an auction but now bleached – an act of vandalism to Sybil – to the colour of whisky with too much water in it. Hugo hated nursery tea. He would put an arm round Audrey's shoulders and say, 'Look, love, why don't you give the girls their tea here and Sybil and I will take a tray to the drawing room and have a cosy little chat.' But Sybil can hardly take a tray to the drawing room by herself, even though she would be glad of a cosy little silence.

The carrot cake at first tastes delicious, as it crumbles

under Sybil's strong, white teeth. But then she is aware of something spongy and tough. She chews on it, she goes on chewing on it. Eventually she swallows. It is a piece of carrot.

The younger of the girls, Betsy, is less well mannered. She pulls a piece of carrot out from a corner of her mouth between finger and thumb and holds it out to her mother. 'What's this, Mummy?'

'Put it down,' Audrey hisses. 'If you don't like it, leave it.'

'But what is it, Mummy?'

'It's a piece of carrot,' Audrey tells her. 'Now eat it or put it down, but shut up!' She turns apologetically to Sybil, 'Those carrots were terribly woody. I wondered if they would do.'

Sybil says nothing. She thinks, as she has often thought before, how awful it would be to have children. For many years Hugo shared her view. 'Night after night,' he would tell people, hoping to shock them, 'I go down on my knees and thank the Almighty for having at least spared me the burden of children.' Then suddenly he married Audrey, on a whim as it seemed; and it seemed to be another, even more eccentric whim when he fathered first the one girl and then the other in quick succession.

'Remind me to give you some of my gooseberry jam before you go,' Audrey says. She wishes that she did not always sound as though she were trying to placate her sister-in-law.

'Thank you,' Sybil says, but she has no intention of reminding Audrey. She knows that gooseberry jam.

The children give up on their slices of the cake and are each handed a Mars bar, which they clearly much prefer. Sybil thinks that she would rather like to have one herself; but she does not ask and Audrey does not offer. Audrey chatters on and on, with a lot of nervous giggling and clearing of her throat and a lot of those 'sort ofs' and 'you knows', which caused Hugo so much irritation. What she mostly chatters on and on about is the village; and the village is of absolutely no interest to Sybil, as it was of absolutely no interest to Hugo.

'May I get down, Mummy?'

'Yes, you may. When you've wiped the chocolate off your mouth.' Sybil has the familiar, maddening sensation that, yet again, Audrey is playing a part for which, unlike Odette or Giselle, she has no aptitude.

'May I get down too, Mummy?'

'Yes, dear. But wipe your mouth too.'

The two girls wander off, the older one unwrapping the pound note which she has screwed up in the pocket of her pinafore and showing it to the other.

The women are alone, with the Aga roaring beside them. Sybil gets up, half closes a damper and then sits down once more. She says, 'I didn't come just to see how you were making out.'

'No?'

'I've had a strange experience. Strange. Encouraging.'

Audrey has already guessed, with the same panic which overcame her when she thought that the Aga had expired, the nature of this experience. It is to do with Hugo. Oh, why can't Sybil leave him in peace and leave her in peace too!

'You know what we always promised each other?'

Audrey nods, her panic growing. 'Whichever of you died first . . .'

'Would find some means, any means, to get in touch with the other. Yes.' Sybil closes her large, green eyes under their beautifully arched eyebrows and presses fingers to her temples, as though she had started a headache. 'Well, I think he has. Has found the means. Has been in touch.'

'Oh.' Audrey feels sick. It is all such nonsense. Hugo died, in Brighton, in a manner which has always seemed to her mysterious and frightening. They brought his shattered body back here to the village and Father Jessop buried him in the churchyard. Later, there was a memorial service in the

17

college chapel, when everyone present seemed more eager to condole with Sybil than with her. Finis.

Sybil nods, 'Yes. I'm sure he's come through.'

'But you thought that once before,' Audrey cannot resist telling her, partly although and partly because she knows it will annoy her.

What happened was that, soon after Hugo's death, Audrey and Sybil went to Chichester, leaving the two girls in the charge of Audrey's mother, to see Bernard Shaw's *On the Rocks*. Originally, the plan had been that Sybil and Hugo would go, since Audrey did not like to leave either the girls or the animals and, in any case, was not, as she put it, all that certain that she was all that keen on Shaw. But then, after Hugo's sudden death, Audrey agreed to use his ticket and his reservation at the hotel.

The evening over, the two women went to bed in their adjoining rooms, and each fell asleep. But before she fell asleep, Sybil, unlike Audrey, who tried not to think about him, made herself think, with intense concentration, about her dead brother. She was woken by a strange sound of jangling, at once awesome and thrilling. She lay in the dark, listening to it, vibrating on and on, until the conviction came to her: 'It's Hugo. It's his way of getting through to me.' After a while, she got up, pulled on a wrap and, trembling with a mixture of excitement and terror, knocked on Audrey's door.

There was no answer and, so having knocked for a second time, Sybil vigorously turned the handle. It was typical of Audrey, in whom a protected, middle-class upbringing in the suburbs had implanted a natural trust, not to have turned the key. It was also typical of Audrey, in whom the same upbringing had failed to impose any sense of order, to have left her suitcase, the lid open, on the floor of the entrance, so that as Sybil hurried forward in the darkness, calling 'Audrey! Audrey! Audrey!', she stumbled over it with an even louder 'Bugger!' Audrey, who had been snoring peacefully – it was that snoring that Hugo had used, soon

18

after their marriage, as a pretext for not sleeping in the main bedroom with her, but in the dressing room by himself – sat up with a start. 'Who is it?' she asked, in a tone of curiosity rather than of alarm.

'Me. Sybil. Audrey, come at once! To my room! Come on!'

'Why?' Audrey rubbed an eye with the back of her hand. 'What's going on?' She reached over and switched on the bedside lamp.

'Don't ask questions! Come! If you don't hurry, it might stop.'

'What might stop?'

But Audrey began to climb out of her bed, revealing, to Sybil's surprise, that she was wearing absolutely nothing. Sybil grabbed her C & A wrap off a chair and flung it to her.

'Quick!'

In Sybil's bedroom, the two women stood side by side. Puzzled and sleepy, Audrey yawned, stretching one arm above her and then the other and wriggling her shoulders. 'Listen!' Sybil hissed. Both of them then listened. Audrey, whose cheeks had been flushed by sleep, visibly paled. The jangling was getting louder and louder and more and more frenetic, until it filled the whole room.

'What is it, Sybil?'

'The sign,' Sybil whispered. 'Hugo's sign.'

Audrey, her head on one side and a hand cupped to an ear, listened again. Then she walked briskly over to the built-in cupboard in a corner of the room and pulled open the door. The dress which Sybil had worn to the theatre was all that hung in it. All the empty wire coat-hangers were shaking against each other.

Sybil tried to make some connection between Hugo and coat-hangers. Why should his spirit choose to agitate coat-hangers as his sign to her? Then, with the shock of a blow to the solar plexus, she realized that Audrey was giggling.

Yes, giggling; she was one of those women who did not laugh but giggled.

'Audrey!'

Audrey pointed upwards to the ceiling. 'One of those bookies and his floozy must be at it. Well, good luck to them!'

It was race-week at Goodwood, so that, when the two women had returned from the theatre, they had found the bar of the hotel full of plump, jowly men in unbuttoned, fancy-coloured shirts sprouting grey hair at their wide-open necks and of stringy, sunburned, bangled women with cleavages even more striking. One of the men was apparently called Mr Pymm (or Pym) and, since he was squiring two women, with identical loud, husky voices and identical wigs, seemingly spun out of wire-wool, there was a lot of noisy joking about Pimm's No 1 and Pimm's No 2. An unattached, middle-aged man, with drooping eyelids and drooping moustache, asked Audrey, as she and Sybil were buying their drinks, 'Had any luck today?' Audrey at first looked affronted; then she realized that he must be referring not to what he had assumed to be her profession but to the races. If she explained to him that she and her sister-in-law were in Chichester not for Goodwood but for a play by Bernard Shaw, he would no doubt think her 'toffee-nosed' or something equally uncomplimentary; so she gave him her sweet, girlish smile and said No, she was afraid not, she never did have any luck, in fact she was the most unlucky person in the world. Later, he had come over to their table, glass in hand, to ask if he might join them; but Sybil had replied chillily that they were about to go to bed – even though it was at least twenty minutes before they actually did so.

Now Audrey can see from the exasperated expression on Sybil's face that she should not have referred to the incident of the coat-hangers. Sybil wishes to forget all about it, just as Hugo wished to forget all about the occasion when, entertained to a buffet lunch by some of Audrey's ballet colleagues at a flat in Cornwall Gardens, he had first become feverishly

excited about a 'vision' which he had experienced, alone on
the balcony, of a horse-drawn carriage circling the square
below, and had then sunk into embarrassed despondency
when Audrey, not yet his wife, had pointed out that it
belonged to Dunn's, the hatters.

Sybil opens her capacious handbag, with its tortoise-shell
clasp, and takes out a sheaf of papers scrawled over in her
handwriting. She puts the papers on the kitchen table before
her and then covers them with a hand.

'I've told you of my writing?'

'Writing?' Audrey thinks of Meredith, and of Hugo's
repeated but always unsuccessful attempts to push her
through one of the novels.

'Automatic writing.'

Audrey nods. Oh, lordy, lordy!

On the day after the wedding of Audrey and Hugo, Sybil
developed trigeminal neuralgia in so ferocious a form that
no pain-killers could relieve it. Her doctor, who was also the
school doctor, infuriated her by suggesting, in what she
called his 'usual smart-aleck way', that her symptoms might
be psychosomatic in origin. When she persisted in returning
to him, he wearily proposed either a specialist or
acupuncture. Meanwhile, Hugo and Audrey had returned
from their honeymoon in Greece and Hugo came up with a
proposal of his own. A fellow member of the Institute of
Paranormal Studies, in constant pain after a motor accident,
had received remarkable relief from a psychic healer with
the unfortunate name of Cocke. Sybil had consulted the
healer, who, on the first of her visits, went into a trance and,
on the second, whether intentionally or accidentally, put her
into one. After that second visit the pain abated. Cocke told
her that, if it returned, she should think herself back into
the trance during which she had been healed. The pain did
not return but, slumped at her desk one night, a blank piece
of paper before her and a pen in her hand, as she wished
that Hugo, away at Harvard, were with her to advise her
on the Meredith lecture ('Modern Love and The Modern

21

Voice') which she was preparing to deliver at the Royal Society of Literature, she once again involuntarily slipped away into a trance. When she came to, in a state of exaltation, she found that the piece of paper and several pieces below it had been covered; but what she then read was not the beginning of her lecture but seemingly random words, phrases and sentences. She and Hugo subsequently spent many excited hours interpreting these supernatural effusions and others like them. Sybil, they both decided, was a natural medium.

'I feel that, at last, Hugo is coming through. Oh, I've had vague inklings that things in my script must have derived from him, but now I'm certain, absolutely certain. Read this, for example.' She pushes one of the sheets across at Audrey and Audrey frowns at the passage down the side of which Sybil has drawn a single thick line in red ink.

. . . Impotently, imperfectly, imperishably. Immortal. With Life and Death I walked. I want to. Try to. Must. So difficult. You have had that dream. One wishes to move, cannot, Wishes to speak, cannot. Or that other dream. One moves, no one sees one. One speaks, no one hears one. I want to. Try to. Must. She says, I wish only to die. Wish. Only. If only. The secret of the shrouded death. But not, not by lifting up the lid of the white eye. Fire to reach to fire. A yonder to all ends . . .

Audrey finds it hard enough to read anything other than the *Daily Express* or a cookbook. She takes a long time to read this brief passage, and at the end she looks up at Sybil, who has been watching her intently, with bewildered exasperation.

'I don't get it,' she says.

Sybil has long since decided that there is a lot that Audrey does not get. Common clay. But she decides that she must be patient, since further down the page – she points to the words, underlined in red ink – there is written:

. . . Audrey. Tell. Comfort.

'It's his message to us.'

'But I still don't get it.' In her fretfulness, Audrey sounds as though she were on the verge of tears.

'No. I can see that. I can understand that.' Audrey feels at her most uncomfortable with Sybil when she adopts this kind of superior, sarcastic tone. 'Well, let me try to explain, dear. Firstly, there's a poem called "Hymn to Colour" by–'

'Meredith!' Audrey all but shouts, as though in a game of snap.

'Yes, Meredith. Precisely. You know it?'

'No.'

'Well . . . it's an extraordinary poem. Not known to many people. Not known like, say, "Modern Love" or "Love in the Valley".'

Audrey remembers those embarrassing minutes, an endless chain of them, link on link, when she sat perched on the hard edge of her bed in the Athens hotel and Hugo, lying full length, in stockinged feet and underpants, on his next to it, had read to her, in a sing-song voice, almost a chant, first the whole of 'Love in the Valley' and then the beginning of 'Modern Love'. But she had had a tiring and trying day, first jolting out to Daphni with him on a crowded bus, then trekking all the way round the Plaka to find that taverna where he and Sybil had once eaten such a wonderful meal for a song but which now seemed no longer to exist, and then panting up to the Acropolis and listening patiently to his lecture on the vulgarity of the Parthenon ('a garishly painted table with too many legs') as it once must have been. She managed to keep herself from slumping back on the bed, she even managed to keep her eyes from closing. But after suppressing one yawn, which merely made her nostrils dilate imperceptibly, she could not suppress the next and her mouth gaped. Hugo quietly put down the book. 'I'm boring you, I can see. I'm sorry.' 'Oh, no, Hugo, no! Do go on!' But he threw the book on to the bed, as he jumped off it. Audrey reached out a hand, as though she wanted not so much to retrieve the book as to rescue something drowning between them. But Hugo stopped her with

the whipcrack of his, 'No, Audrey, leave it. Leave it, please.'
Common clay.

'Well, of course, I know "Modern Love" and – er, "Love
in the Valley",' Audrey says. She begins to blush, as she
always does after having told what she calls a whopper.

'I'm not going to give you a whole lecture on the poem
or even to attempt a rapid exegesis.' Sybil wants to add: If
I did, I'd be wasting your time and mine. 'But the point is
that the "Hymn to Colour" is a highly complex poem –
complex in its rhythm, even more complex in its imagery –
about Life and Death.' The way she speaks those last two
words endows them with the capitals that they bear in the
text. 'And in that piece of automatic writing which no doubt
struck you as meaningless, there are, remarkably, innumerable references to that poem. "With Life and Death I
walked" – that's the beginning of the whole poem, and it
goes on "when Love appeared". That's his Love for you,
for me, for both of us. For the children too, of course,' Sybil
adds, though this is the first time she has connected them
with that Love. 'Then there's that phrase "The secret of the
shrouded death".' Sybil runs her forefinger, head twisted
round in order to see properly, under the words. 'It's
followed by that reference to "the lid of the white eye". Now
the key passage in the poem is a stanza which runs–'

Sybil gazes out of the window and, in that same sing-song
voice which Audrey found so embarrassing when Hugo used
to assume it, she begins to quote:

> 'Shall man into the mystery of breath
> From his quick beating pulse a pathway spy?
> Or learn the secret of the shrouded death.
> But lifting up the lid of a white eye?
> Cleave thou the way with fathering desire
> Of fire to reach to fire.'

Sybil opens her eyes. 'Of fire to reach to fire,' she repeats.
'That of course, is also a phrase in the script. There.' Again

the pointed, unvarnished nail of her forefinger indicates the words.

'Well!' Audrey exclaims, hoping that this one monosyllable will convey the requisite understanding, amazement and gratitude to her sister-in-law. But Sybil is far too perceptive to be taken in for a moment. The little ninny obviously hasn't a notion what she's going on about.

'To put it briefly, this is a poem about Life subsumed in Death and Death subsumed in Life.' Subsumed? Silly to use that kind of word to a woman so uneducated. 'They are coexistent, each is a part of the other, just as, just as –' the simile, now that she has started on it, somehow embarrasses her '– two lovers are part of each other.' She stares at Audrey, who, discomfited, looks down at the sheets of script, fingering the edge of one of them as though to test its physical reality. Sybil goes on, 'Well, of course, that was what Hugo believed, believed so passionately and so wholeheartedly. For him, Life and Death *were* one.' She pauses, 'Then there's that sentence "She says, I wish only to die." Well, that's clearly a reference to . . .' She stops. A desolate reticence inhibits her from continuing. 'To another Sybil, the Sybil of Cumae. People asked her, "What do you wish?" and "I wish only to die" she replied. Like her, I, too, have wished only to die since Hugo's death.'

'So you think – you think that he . . . ?' Audrey suddenly wonders what the children are up to; she remembers that it is long past the time to milk the cow; she can hear one of the hens squawking from the hedge by the road – presumably she has laid an egg.

'I'm certain of it. You see, Audrey dear, there's something very odd about the fact that this particular poem, of all Meredith's poems, should have come through. And I'll tell you why. You know how Hugo loved to read poetry aloud?' Audrey nods; she knows it only too well. 'In fact, he used to say that that was the only way to read it. Anyway, when I last saw him – when we went to Brighton together and I left him there and then that terrible accident happened – he read "Hymn to Colour" to me during our train journey. There he was, opposite to me in the carriage, in such a state of elation that I thought to myself, Well, if there's such a thing as a truly happy man, then there's one before you! He read the poem so beautifully. I had never fully understood it before – as with so many of Meredith's poems, I felt that there was always one last veil between me and the final, essential meaning. But that veil had been rent. It had disintegrated. Hugo had worked a kind of magic.'

Audrey is now rolling up one corner of the script between a thumb and forefinger. Sybil has an impulse to reach out and slap her hand, as she has seen Audrey herself reach out and slap Betsy's hand, when she is picking the almonds off one of her home-made Dundee cakes. Audrey is also frowning, in the manner of a schoolgirl who has given up all hope of solving an equation but wishes to give the impression that she is still working at it. She heaves a deep sigh.

'Now it's odd, to say the least, that what should have come through is references to a poem in which Hugo's own affirmation of the oneness of the living and the dead achieved so magnificent an expression. But it's even odder that that should have been the last poem that he ever read aloud to me – probably the last poem that he ever read aloud to anyone – on the day on which he died. Isn't it?'

Audrey is silent, her cheek supported on a hand and her eyes still fixed on the script. She seems to be sulking.

'Isn't it?'

Audrey looks up and suddenly, in those eyes which are usually submissive, there flashes a sudden anger. Sybil is as much taken aback as she would be if, on a clear summer day like this, lightning were to fork down on to the table between them. Audrey's lips tremble. Then she says, 'But why do you think it was Hugo who wrote all this?'

'Why do I – ?' Sybil is astounded. 'Well, who else could have written it. Who else?'

Audrey glances fearfully at her sister-in-law. She wishes that she could go out to milk the cow or to call to the children or to look for that egg in the hedge by the road. She swallows. 'You,' she says.

'Me?'

'Well, what I mean is – your subconscious.'

'My subconscious?'

'I mean – this – this writing comes out of your subconscious, doesn't it? And you told me, told me only last week, that not a day, not an hour passes when Hugo's wholly out of your mind. So couldn't it be that . . . ?' Her voice fades away in a diminuendo of embarrassment and dread.

'Couldn't it be . . . ?' Sybil prompts. But, all at once, so intelligent, she feels like a chess-master suddenly checkmated by a novice.

'Well, couldn't it be that you yourself wrote – subconsciously of course – what you wanted Hugo to write? I mean, it's only natural. One wants to believe. One wants proof. Wants that – ' she swallows ' – that consolation.'

Sybil draws air deep into her lungs. Then she puts out her strong, capable hands and draws the script towards her. She smooths out the edge of the sheet which Audrey's restless forefinger and thumb curled up. Then she raises all the sheets and taps them against the table, so that they fall exactly into place. She replaces the sheets in her handbag. All without a word.

'Well, you may be right,' she says drily.

Audrey says: 'I wonder what has happened to the children.' She jumps up from her chair.

Class is over, outside the sun is shining.

TWO

WAS

Sybil often told Hugo that, in her life with him, Audrey was acting out a role in a play. What Hugo never told Sybil was that the play was a two-hander in which he was the other actor. It was not until he was forty-one that they had married each other, so that it might be said that he was late in discovering his vocation; but, once he had discovered it, it was with the realization, common to actors, that he was really far happier being someone else than being himself.

With the exception of Sybil, his senior by two years, women, though he had found them vaguely attractive, had always embarrassed and irritated him. They demanded too much, they responded too fervently. As exemplified by his girl students, they had this inability to move from the general to the particular, to see the trees for the wood. They also smelled odd: not unpleasant but odd, in the way that food can smell odd and so blunt one's appetite. He had had women friends, of course, most of them older than himself and most of them married either to their work or to colleagues of his. But neither they nor he had ever supposed that he would, on a whim as it seemed, suddenly forsake his bachelor life in his one room in college and his two rooms in Beaumont Street, in order to marry someone both so much junior to himself and so much his intellectual inferior.

'Why do you want to do it?' another bachelor don had asked him with a mixture of puzzlement and pique; and Hugo had then replied, 'I suppose that, like Hedda Gabler,

31

I feel my time has come.' But that was disingenuous. For months and months before meeting Audrey, he had day-dreamed, as the middle-aged often do, of the paths which, at each crossroads in his life, the mere choice of other paths had prevented him from exploring. What if he had opted for that job with *The Times*, instead for his fellowship? What if he had accepted that chair in Australia, instead of sticking where he was? What if he had continued with his work on tropes and liturgical plays, instead of devoting all those years to the Meredith correspondence? Above all, what if he had married, had sired children, and had acquired a multitude of possessions? It was this last 'what if' which began to obsess him. Though there was nothing in his life to make him unhappy, he knew that he was not happy; and though his colleagues would certainly maintain that his career had been productive – after all, there were the eleven volumes of the Letters to prove it – none the less, he had a sensation of barrenness.

When he and Audrey were playing Peter Pan and Wendy in their dank Cotswold farmhouse, he would often think to himself, Yes, this is the life – with the inevitable corollary, and that was the death, of those years now behind him. 'I'll bath the baby, dear, you go and put your feet up, you've had such a hectic day. . . . I want to try this recipe for taramasalata, I found it in the *Guardian*. . . . Betsy said the funniest thing, I went into the sitting room and there she was lying, motionless and flat on her back, with her arms outstretched and I asked her, "Betsy, what on earth are you doing there?" and she said, you won't believe this, she said, "Sh, Daddy, I'm Christ on the Cross." . . . Yes, it *does* look rather a peculiar colour, I'll give Dr Duncan a call and ask him to drop in. . . . ' It was with remarkable conviction that he delivered such lines. 'Who would ever have supposed that Hugo would have become so uxorious and domesti-cated?' one of those wives of his colleagues remarked admir-ingly to Sybil as, kneeling on the carpet, Kleenex in his hand, Hugo wiped up some cat vomit. 'There was a time when he would never have allowed a cat into his rooms. And if a cat *had* got in and, horror of horrors, had also vomited, he would have summoned a scout.' But Sybil could not share the speaker's admiration. She found it painful to see this distinguished scholar humiliate himself in so grovelling a manner – for so it appeared to her.

But the actor, however dedicated and however much acclaimed, from time to time craves a respite from his role. Suddenly, at breakfast, Hugo would feel an irritation so intense that it was like a physical eczema, as Audrey dragged herself sleepily back and forth from Aga to table in nightdress, dressing-gown and Wellingtons (she had just returned from milking the cows), the two girls began to flick rice crispies at each other, using their spoons as catapults ('For God's sake stop that, you nasty little brats!') and outside the door the muddily dishevelled sheepdog, Bruno ('Why does no one ever brush or comb him?') was scratching away at the paint. Hugo would make an effort to restrain himself; and then he would say, 'I think I'll pop over to the school for a night or two to see how Sybil is making out,' or else he would sigh that it was really time that he looked in on Henry, the poor chap was so ill and so lonely. Without complaint, but faintly exasperated, like an actress who realizes that her partner must have a rest for a few days and that she must put up with an understudy, Audrey would accede, 'All right, darling. Why don't you do that?' and would then often add, though Hugo did not need this reassurance, 'We'll be perfectly all right on our own.'

It was after such a moment of, metaphorically, stripping off costume, make-up, padding and wig, that Hugo set off on the journey to Brighton which was to have momentous consequences not merely for himself but for many other people, the majority of them unknown to him. He was going to Brighton to visit Henry Latymer, whom he had met when Latymer was ambassador, at the fag-end of a career which had smouldered rather than burned brightly, to a small African state, and Hugo was on a British Council lecture tour. Despite a difference of thirteen years in their ages, the two scholarly, fastidious bachelors, both Wykehamists, at once took to each other, so that, after one night in a concrete shell of a hotel, its air-conditioning defective and its 'mini-bar', proudly advertised in its brochure, erupting cockroaches from its otherwise empty interior when he opened its door, Hugo moved into the cool, cleanliness and tranquility of the embassy. He remembered so well what had first made him take to Henry. There was a cocktail party, given by the British Council Representative after his lecture, and at it this tall, stooping man with a large, beaked nose inflamed at the tip, in a white cotton suit so shrunken that at least two inches of socks could be seen below his trousers, came over, took him by the arm and said, 'Do you see that chap over there? No, not that one, the one who looks as if he were wearing striped pyjamas. Well, that's the Minister of Tourism, believe it or not. And since no tourist has ever been known to visit this benighted country, he asked me for a slogan for some posters which he had in preparation. I came up with "Where every prospect pleases" and I am delighted to say that he used it – without, of course, the five important words which follow.' Henry made the coughing sound, little more than a rustle, as of phlegm, in the back of his throat, that Hugo was later to recognize as his laugh. Though totally unmalicious himself, Hugo admired the neatness of the malice.

Henry eventually retired. Few people asked the question 'What on earth became of old Henry Latymer?' and even fewer knew the answer. But Hugo kept up with him, as he kept up with a number of people who struck others as 'dreary' or 'boring'. The intimacy between the two men was a curious one of calling each other by their surnames, but never by their Christian names, of discussing literature, art, music and, above all, psychical research but never their private lives, and of faintly adumbrating their emotions through the lightest of allusions. Although he was staying with Henry on the weekend after the Thursday on which

Audrey had accepted his proposal (the old-fashioned phrase suits the old-fashioned manner in which the proposal was made), he did not mention it to him; and when, eventually, he sent Henry a wedding invitation, he was surprised neither by his refusal, on the pretext of ill health and the length of the journey from Brighton to Oxford, nor by the munificence of his cheque.

Henry, like many of Hugo's friends, happened to be rich; and when they died, such friends usually happened to leave Hugo, if not money, then an ancient Daimler, a charming little Boudin (Deauville, Les Dunes), six Chippendale dining chairs, a choice item of erotica (*Zephérin ou L'Enfant du plaisir, conte qui n'en est pas un*), a Georgian tea service. But, son of a wealthy banker, who had left him a legacy far larger than that which he had left to Sybil, Hugo did not need such bequests; and, in no way acquisitive by nature, he neither wanted nor sought them. None the less they continued to come to him, as a reward for having seen in the testators qualities of mind or spirit invisible to others.

Henry lived in an early Victorian, semi-detached villa, looking like a wedding cake left out too long in the sun, on a quiet, upward-sloping street above the centre of Brighton. His neighbours had put in baths, bidets and low-level lavatory basins where there had been dressing rooms, had constructed jacuzzi in their basements, and, often at huge expense, had restored period details – a canopy here, some moulding there – destroyed by the vandals before them. But Henry had moved into his house as it was and had left it like that. Worse, whereas everyone else painted their houses cream, and their window-frames and doors black, Henry, through some freak of taste not to be expected of a man with so valuable a collection of nineteenth-century water colours, had opted for a uniform pink, inexpertly applied, so that it looked like strawberry yoghourt, by a jobbing builder whom many thought to have been involved in a subsequent robbery from a neighbouring and far more elegant house.

Henry's wiring was ancient, so that Hugo had only to attach his electric razor by its adaptor to the bedside lamp – there was no socket for an electric razor anywhere to be found – for all the lights to fuse. His furniture was equally ancient, without being antique, so that, having lowered themselves on to a settee or an armchair, his visitors found that they were, in effect seated on the ground. Threadbare carpets were scattered over floors sealed by dust with linoleum over it. The hot water spattered orange out of a high, brass tap into a bath, which looked like a bassinet afflicted with elephantiasis, while a gas geyser alternately coughed and roared. In a cupboard beside Hugo's bed there was a tin chamber-pot. Hugo never had occasion to use it; but he was sure that, had he ever done so, he would have found it still full when next he retired.

Henry was looked after by the woman whom he called 'My invaluable Mrs Lockit'. Henry's neighbours, who were the sort of people familiar with *The Beggar's Opera*, referred to her, among themselves, as Lucy, though no one, probably not even Henry, knew her real Christian name. It was the general opinion that it was certainly Lucy who had found the jobbing builder to paint the front of the house and probably she who had chosen that nauseating pink, the colour of so many of her hats. Lucy lived in the basement, the curtains of which she usually kept drawn, even though extravagant loops of thick nylon net would, in any case, have prevented anyone from peeping in.

It was Mrs Lockit (or Lucy) who opened the door to Hugo. 'Oh, Mr Crawfurd!' She managed to sound surprised, as she always did when Henry had a visitor. On one occasion when Hugo arrived at the house, she even went on 'Fancy seeing you!', making him wonder, until Henry appeared, whether he had come on the wrong weekend.

'And how are you, Mrs Lockit?'

'I've made a stew for you both, a goulash really, and an upside-down cake,' she announced as though in answer to his question. The day was Saturday and on Saturday

36

evening she went to her sister in Portslade. 'You've got a new suitcase, I see. Very smart.'

'How observant you are!'

Mrs Lockit replied airily, 'Yes, people often tell me I'd have made a good detective. Nothing escapes me.'

There was something ominous in the way in which she said that. It made Hugo feel uneasy, as he had often felt uneasy, for no known cause, in the presence of this middle-aged, gypsylike woman, with her wild eyes and twitching mouth and her habit of pressing her hands into the sides of her stomach, as though in a vain attempt to establish the seat of some mysterious pain.

'Who is – or was – Mr Lockit?' Hugo once asked Henry, to receive the reply, 'Haven't a clue, old boy.'

'And how did she come to you?' Hugo pursued.

'Rang the bell, that's how. Said she'd heard I was looking for a housekeeper. But I can't think whom she can have heard it from, since I'd told nobody. Perhaps she has that thing you're always going on about.' He clicked his fingers in a pretended effort to recall a phrase perfectly familiar to him.

'Extrasensory perception.'

'That's it.'

'Sir Henry's in the garden. Would you be wanting to go up to your room first or to go straight out to him?'

'Oh, I'll go straight out to him.'

Hugo put down his suitcase and Mrs Lockit, head on one side as her fingers again palpated the sides of her stomach, examined it once more. 'Yes, nice. Very nice.'

Henry, who now spent much of his time sleeping, since there was little else to do, opened his eyes as Hugo approached the deckchair in which he lay stretched out. 'Ah, dear fellow!' He got up, his panama hat tilted over his forehead, so that the brim all but touched the inflamed tip of the nose which made his neighbours suspect, with no justification, that perhaps he was a secret drinker. Then he gripped Hugo's wrist with his left hand, exerting surprising

37

strength, while his right squeezed Hugo's right in a lengthy handshake. It was the only expression of affection that he allowed himself. 'Did you have a good journey?'

'Fine.'

'I'm sure you were extravagant and travelled first class.' Though so rich, Henry never travelled anything but second.

'I'm afraid I did.'

'And took a taxi?'

Henry derived the same excitement from Hugo's extravagances as a prude from the behaviour of a libertine.

'No, that I didn't. I walked.'

'Mrs Lockit thought that we might have our tea out here in the garden, since it's so hot.'

'A splendid idea.'

Mrs Lockit was wearing one of her hats, bought at the Oxfam shop, when she appeared dipping and swaying between the rosebeds, as though in a dance. This did not mean that she was about to go off. She sometimes wore a hat even when she was 'doing the outside toilet' (as she would put it) or serving up what she would call 'dinner' even if it consisted only of scrambled eggs on toast and a carton of yoghurt for each of them. 'Who's going to be mother?' she asked.

'Oh, Mr Crawfurd, Mr Crawfurd,' Henry said. The less that he had to do these days, the less he wanted to do.

Hugo was by now so low in a deckchair that he had to get to his feet to pour out the tea from the much higher wrought-iron table, rusty and in need of a coat of paint, that stood between them. 'Three lumps and milk in first?'

'Ah, Hugo, that's what I like about you, that's what I like about you. You always remember.' Henry took the cup held out to him. 'Silly, snobbish people, who say the milk must go in last. The people next door, what are they called? – yes, the Gascoynes – they were quite affronted when I asked for milk in first.'

Hugo, back in his deckchair, his cup beside him, nibbled at a biscuit, scattering crumbs into the creases of his shirt and jacket. He looked impressive like that, since, when he was seated, there was a less obvious discrepancy between on the one hand the grandeur of his head, with its brown, deep-set eyes and high cheekbones, on which out of some odd vanity, he allowed the grey hair to sprout, and on the other the fragility of a body which dwindled, as in a fairground mirror, towards its extremities. He was happy. He could be himself for a while.

Henry stirred his tea, with a tinkle of stainless steel on Denby ware. Upstairs in the attics and downstairs in a basement storeroom, there were tea-chests and cupboards full of valuable silver and crockery inherited from grandparents, parents, aunts, uncles and cousins by this last wintry branch of a once burgeoning tree; but Mrs Lockit had given her verdict, she couldn't do with all that stuff, it was more trouble than it was worth.

'Tell me,' Henry said. 'What's the news from over there?'

'From over there? From where?' Hugo understood perfectly well what Henry meant but he preferred to pretend not to do so. His friend's irony did not offend him, since he knew that it concealed a genuine, passionate interest, even if one which he had always shrunk, with a kind of spinsterly dread, from openly satisfying.

'From the Other Side.' Hugo put the phrase in inverted commas.

'Well, interesting things are happening. They keep on happening. We've got several investigations under way at this moment.' When Hugo said 'we', he meant the Institute of Paranormal Studies, of which he was a former President and now a member of the Council.

'Tell me.' Henry was like a customer saying to a shop assistant 'Show me.'

'Poltergeists?' the shop assistant offered.

'Ah, poltergeists! Pubescence!'

'As you say, pubescence.'

Hugo began to describe the strange happenings on a council estate in the East End of London, and, as he did so, it was as though, in a vision, he was reliving his whole visit there, tremendously speeded up. There was the mother, Mrs O'Connor, a Liverpool Irish Roman Catholic, whose husband had left her, just walked out on her, vanished, with no warning, no goodbye, leaving her with the two kids, a teenage girl and a little chap. Hugo could hear her wan, plaintive voice and he could see her chapped hands – she worked in a City diner, washing up most probably – gently stroking her forehead. She was at her wit's end, she couldn't go on living in this place. But the council and most of the neighbours thought that she was inventing everything in order to get moved. Why should she want to invent such things? She was as happy here as she was ever likely to be, given the circumstances. It was so unfair. She couldn't sleep easy at the best of times, she was a martyr to these headaches, blinding they were, she was having one now. And all through the night there would be these bangings and crashings, furniture actually falling over, a chair, even the wardrobe in the room of the girl, and these zigzag flashings, as though lightning were streaking from room to room. It was more than flesh and blood could bear.

It was at that precise moment in her narration, delivered in the calm, remote voice of someone who has suffered a recent and catastrophic bereavement, that the saucepan hurtled past Hugo's left ear, slammed against the wall and then bounced off it to roll across the floor, with an interminable jangling, as of a discordant carillon of bells.

'Christ!' He was simultaneously shocked and delighted by so energetic a display of what, he was in no doubt, was psychokinesis.

Mrs O'Connor merely sighed. 'There it is again,' she said. She might have been referring to an overloud record player in the flat next door.

At the moment that the saucepan performed its mysterious levitation, a shrivelled child, boy or girl it was hard to tell from the matted blond curls which clustered around cheeks the colour of lard, appeared beside Hugo, a much-dented model of a vintage Bugatti car tucked under one arm.

'This is my younger one,' Mrs O'Connor said, leaving Hugo to pick up the saucepan, which had come to rest against an overflowing rubbish-bin. 'Sean.'

Sean began to whimper, pulling out of shape what was usually a pretty, if girlish, mouth. 'It's started again, mam! Mam, I'm frightened.'

Mrs O'Connor put her arm round the child and hugged him to her. 'Oh, my head! It's so bad, I can hardly make out your face, Mr, Mr . . .'

'Crawfurd.'

'Mr Crawfurd.'

'Well, as I was saying, we've had the health officer here and a social worker and the probation officer that's been keeping an eye on our Madge since she had her little spot of trouble. Oh, and someone from the council, about whether to move us or not. And, of course, all the newspaper people and your lot from the Institute of Whatever It Is. There was also this psychalist, speciatrist, *psychiatrist*—' at last she got it right '—who said he thought it was all the older one and that the best thing would be to separate the two kids and put her into care for a time. Well, I'd not stand for that.'

'No, of course not.'

'Anyway, come into the lounge, Mr Crawfurd, if you're sure you couldn't do with a cup of tea or Nes.' She had suddenly roused herself at the thought of that psychiatrist who wished to see her family split up. Her tone was no longer wan, it had an almost bossy strength to it. 'Come along, Sean.' Her arm was still around the child, who gazed up at her with that look of premature experience so common among children of the slums, out of his peaked, wizened face. 'We'll go with the gentleman into the sitting room.' As she crossed to the kitchen door, propelling Sean before her, she sighed, 'Oh, what a relief! My head's almost gone. Like after a thunderstorm.'

She preceded Hugo down a narrow passage, its wallpaper

scratched and torn and, up to three or four feet, scribbled over with variously coloured crayons. There was a door ajar and, as he walked past it, Hugo could not resist peeping in. He saw clothes scattered on the floor, a wall covered with huge blow-ups of pop stars and, sitting on an unmade bed, facing out to him, the solemn face of a girl, in a wrap-around tartan skirt and white blouse, her skinny legs and feet bare, of – well what? eleven? twelve? – staring not at him, but at something just above his right shoulder with a morose intensity.

'What an attractive room!' Hugo said automatically, as he tried to erase from his mind that somehow disturbing image of the child on the bed, elbows on knees and face in hands, as she stared out at that thing which might have been perched, an invisible bird, rat, monkey, on his shoulder.

'Yes, it is nice. My hubby – him that's left me – was a joiner. He made me all these lovely fitted cupboards. He was so happy making them, night after night he'd come home from work and he'd settle down to more of it. You'll tire yourself out, I'd tell him. Have a little rest. Leave it until the weekend comes. But he was like that, we'd just moved in after waiting, oh, years, for a place of our own, and he wanted everything to be just right. And then–' the boy, squatting on the floor now, the model of the vintage Bugatti held in a hand, was gazing up at her, as though this were an often-told, ever-fascinating fairy story '–then he vanished. Just like that. Never came back from the place where he'd been working. I went there, of course, had a word with the foreman, had a word with one of the bosses. But they was in as much of a fog as me. Said he'd asked for his cards, just like that, and taken off. They'd no complaints against him, none at all. He'd not been in trouble. An excellent worker, that's what the foreman told me and the boss bore it out. At first, of course, I thought that maybe he'd had an accident or lost his memory, one hears of people losing their memories, not knowing who they are or where they are or anything, doesn't one? But then I noticed that

42

certain things had gone, his razor, his pipe, clothes, not all of them, some of them, and, oh, all his fishing rods and tackle. He must have got them out secretly, me never noticing. . . . Well, I know what you want to ask. Was there another woman?'

She looked directly at Hugo, on the other side of the table from her, and he gave a little start, as an absent-minded pupil does when aroused by the teacher. 'Yes, oh, yes,' he said.

'That's what everyone wants to ask and everyone is too polite to do so. Well, the answer is no. As far as I can give an answer. But of course—' she huddled into herself now, her arms going across her breasts, her hands on her bony shoulders, and her face drained of its animation '—who knows? How can anyone ever know?'

. . . Henry, who had been listening to all this intently, his head pressed back into his deckchair, his panama hat tilted over his nose and his eyes shut, now sat up and scratched at an ankle, pulling down a hand-knitted sock, bought from Homebound Craftsmen, in order to do so. 'Extraordinary!'

'Yes, extraordinary,' Hugo agreed. 'I only wish I'd more time to spend with the family. Of course, it's the classical situation for poltergeist phenomena. An unhappy family, the unhappiness is tangible. It's so tangible that, as the President of the Institute has put it with his unerring flair for a cliché, you can cut it with a knife. A child on the verge of puberty. A little boy who suffers from epileptiform convulsions – yes, I learned that later – and a mother who has migraines, with those common premonitory symptoms of partial blindness, flashing lights and tingling of the extremities. Interestingly, she always starts a migraine just before the phenomena take place.'

'Suggests some excessive discharge of electricity.'

'Or of energy of some kind. Quite. Well . . . Oxford is a long way from East London – especially if, like myself, one doesn't drive. And it's been an unusually busy term, what with one of the other Eng. Lit. men on a sabbatical in the States and the eleventh volume going through the press and first one of the girls and then the other getting impetigo, God knows from where. And so I've not really been able to devote all the time I'd have liked to an investigation. That's been in the hands of Bridget Nagel.'

'Bridget . . . ?'

'You met her once, some time ago. We were having a weekend conference down here on metal-bending – remember? – and I brought her to lunch. I also brought that Japanese, Otani or Utani, who has devised or claims to have devised a method of recording electrical signals around the bodies of metal-bending subjects. Something to do with the transient conduction paths between the body and a receiving electrode.'

Henry nodded. He remembered the Japanese, a clever little monkey; he did not remember the woman, who must have bored him.

'Poor Bridget has been through a particularly tough time. Her father was killed in the Battle of Britain – and, though she was only a child at the time, that's how she first became interested in parapsychology. Then, only a few weeks ago, she heard that her husband, a journalist with the Task Force, had been killed in the Falklands. So this fascinating case has come at just the right moment, to distract her. She's a remarkable woman. I'm very fond of her.'

The sun was now low and Henry, abnormally sensitive to cold, gave a little shiver. 'A goose must have walked over my grave,' he said, struggling out of his deckchair. 'Either I must get myself a rug or we must go in.'

'Let's go in then.'

As they passed the open door to the kitchen, Hugo noticed that Mrs Lockit, motionless by the open window, was gazing intently out at their deckchairs and the used tea things on the table beside them. For some reason, he was once again reminded of the child, seated on the narrow bed of the South

London flat, her eyes fixed on something invisible above his shoulder.

Eventually, Hugo went up to his room to unpack his things. Among the underclothes, shirts and socks, there was a bottle of Amontillado from Berry Brothers as a present for Henry, and a pack of Tarot cards as a diversion and consolation for himself. He pushed the clothes into drawers lined with ancient, yellowing newspapers, felt between the sheets to see if they were as damp as he feared (they were) and then, on an impulse, took the cards out of their box in order to do a reading. But he had no sooner laid out the first three of the cards, when there was a knock on the door and Mrs Lockit, still in her hat, burst in before he had had time to tell her to do so.

'Oh, I'm so sorry, Mr Crawfurd. I came to turn down the bed. I hadn't realized you were in here.' Never, on any of the occasions when Hugo had stayed with Henry, had Mrs Lockit ever turned down the bed.

'Please don't bother about it.' It was on the bed that he had been laying out the cards.

Mrs Lockit gazed down, the brim of the pink hat almost touching her shoulder, as she turned her sombre, passionate face sideways. 'Patience?'

'Patience?' For a moment, he had imagined that she was counselling him to be patient, since the first cards were all so bad. 'No, oh, no. Tarot.'

'Fortune telling?'

'Yes. I find it helps to clear my mind if I give myself a reading. I don't often do it for others. Just for myself.'

Mrs Lockit continued to stare downwards. Hugo almost expected her to say 'Jack on queen' or 'Six on seven'. But instead, 'I couldn't help hearing,' she uttered.

'Couldn't help hearing?'

After a peculiarly unpleasant meal of gristly beefburger and sodden chips in the buffet of the train, Hugo had been suffering from wind, so that, as soon as he had reached the privacy of his room, he had indulged in the relief of farting.

Could Mrs Lockit possibly have heard and have now arrived with either a complaint or the offer of a remedy?

'What you and Sir Henry were saying in the garden. I was at the kitchen window, trying to draw a breath of fresh air, and you were talking about that London family and those poltergeist phenomena.'

'Oh, yes.' Hugo hoped that his chilliness of tone would convey that he did not approve of such eavesdropping. There were occasions when even the most honourable people could not help overhearing a word, a phrase or even a sentence, but clearly Mrs Lockit had done far more than that.

'I have two nephews,' Mrs Lockit went on, drawing in her chin so that it all but rested on her breastbone. 'Twins. To meet them you'd think they were two of the most ordinary boys in the whole of Brighton. But they're psychic.'

'Psychic?' Hugo involuntarily thrilled to the word, as a man may involuntarily thrill to some such word as pants, knickers, bra, shoe, bottom, chain, leather.

Mrs Lockit nodded. 'No doubt about it. ESP. You mentioned that before you got on to the poltergeists, didn't you? Well, those boys have an extraordinary gift. Someone should investigate it, someone qualified, someone not out for just the sensation. Scientific. Mind you, the whole thing bores them, that's the laugh. They look on it as a kind of parlour trick, to amuse the family and their mates. But between twins . . . well, things go on between twins that defy all explanation. There was that article in one of the Sunday supplements only recently. They traced those twins who'd been separated at birth or as near to birth as made no bit of difference. And there were these two girls, when they were brought together, were found to have exactly the same hairdos and to be wearing the same-coloured dresses; and then it came out that each of them was married to a man several years older than herself, who worked in the rag trade. Oh, and then there were those two men who'd lost the joint of a finger in an accident, not the same finger, one

46

was the little finger and the other the forefinger, but still it makes you think, doesn't it?'

Hugo, previously annoyed by the intrusion, was now delighted. 'Yes, at the Institute we've done a lot of research into ESP between twins. We're still doing it.'

'Well, then!' Mrs Lockit gave one of her rare smiles, such as Henry had only seen when she had backed a Derby winner, a pound each way.

'How old are these twins – these nephews of yours?'

'Twelve, almost thirteen. Oh, they're the nicest, politest couple you could hope to meet. I will say that for my sister. Whatever her faults, she's done wonders with them – seeing the kind of man she's married.'

'And what form does this – er – ESP take?'

'Well, I'd better leave you to find out that for yourself. When you've met them. If, that is, you do want to meet them.'

'Oh, I do, I do. I most certainly do. Can you arrange it?'

'I'm seeing my sister this evening, this being Saturday. Out at Portslade. I expect I'll see the boys, they're not great gadabouts. But if I don't, then of course I can leave a message. You wouldn't mind them calling here?'

'*I* wouldn't mind, no, of course not. But I'll have to have a word with Sir Henry.'

'Oh, I don't think he'll mind. He always falls in with your wishes. No trouble about that.'

'Well, thank you, Mrs Lockit. This all sounds most promising.'

'I don't think you'll be disappointed, Mr Crawfurd.'

Mrs Lockit left, with no further attempt to turn down the bed, and soon after that Hugo, having swept up those ominous cards from the Tarot pack and replaced them in their packet, descended to the drawing room, where Henry, outstretched on the sagging sofa, was asleep under *The Times*.

Hugo failed to arouse him with a cough or with a noisy pushing first up and then down of a sash window on to the street. Then he called his name. Henry sat up, *The Times* slipping to the floor beside him. 'Was thinking,' he said. 'Metal-bending. Metal's grain size.' Henry knew far more about science than Hugo.

'Mrs Lockit's just been telling me about her nephews. Thought they might be worth investigating.'

'Her nephews? Didn't know she had any nephews. She has a sister.'

'And they're that sister's sons.'

'My God!' Henry threw his legs off the sofa. 'Well, what about them?'

'Seems they're sensitives of some kind.' Hugo shrugged. 'ESP.'

'And what precise form does this ESP take?' Henry inquired with quiet irony.

'She wouldn't be specific. But she said she could ask the boys to come here to see me – us. If you had no objection, of course.'

'I find this most odd. She says nothing to me about having any nephews, let alone about their powers of ESP. But you haven't been in this house for more than two or three hours before she confides the whole bang lot to you.' Henry was pettish.

'Perhaps she thought you wouldn't be interested,' Hugo placated. 'She knows by now that the paranormal is of enormous importance to me. Second only to English literature.'

'Oh, you're far more interested in the paranormal than in English literature. I don't think you're really interested in English literature at all. Though I admit that you know a lot about it.' Henry was still piqued.

'At all events,' Hugo said equably, 'shall I or shall I not tell her we'd like to see the boys?'

'By all means let's see them. Why not?' Henry got off the sofa and walked stiffly to the window. The Gascoynes, flashily dressed, were getting into their equally flashy BMW. Thoughts of tea with or without the milk in first passed through his mind. He scowled at them and continued to scowl even when Mrs Gascoyne, catching sight of him, raised a small, plump hand and waved. Then he turned, 'Nothing to lose. No skin off our noses. In for a penny, in for a pound.'

Though they had not discussed the matter, Hugo and Henry had both expected the twins to look exactly like each other; but, as Henry put it with that sly malice which had first attracted Hugo to him, it was a case of 'one pearl and one plain'. The pearl had a startlingly nacreous skin, so delicate that one feared that the slightest blow or jar would chip it. His hair, falling in deep waves over his collar and ears, looked as if it had been sculpted from ivory, so unnaturally pale was its colour and so unnaturally stiff its texture. He had a long neck, around which he was wearing a gold chain with a crucifix visible against his blue-veined skin, just where the flung-open vee of his shirt first came together at a button. The skin round the pale green eyes, with their long lashes, was coloured a bruise-like purple. On his left hand he wore three rings, on his right four, one of them on the forefinger. His name, he said in a husky whisper when Henry asked him, was Cyril, Cyril Creane.

The plain was dark-haired and stout, with the sort of paunch which usually comes from drinking too much beer and the sort of complexion which usually comes from eating too many sweets. The nails on his pudgy hands had been systematically bitten to the quicks and his arms had the appearance of being too long and thin for the stocky torso from which they dangled. Unlike his brother's, his voice had broken. His name, he volunteered, since neither Henry nor Hugo was interested in asking it, was Lionel, Lionel Creane.

Mrs Lockit, who had remained in attendance after ushering them into the drawing room that Sunday morning, said, with evident relish, 'Well, that's taken you aback, I'll be bound!'

'What's taken us aback, Mrs Lockit? I don't think I follow.' Henry spoke with glacial dignity.

'Well, you've only to see the faces on the two of you! You thought that, being twins, they were bound to be alike. Didn't you now? Own up!'

'Well, that was certainly the natural presumption.'

'They're certainly twins. But they're not what you'd call identical twins.'

'No, I can see that. They're not. They're not what anyone would call identical twins. . . . Well, boys, no need to stand. Why don't you sit over there, er, Lionel and you, Cyril, why don't you come over here?' Henry nodded at Mrs Lockit, a clear invitation to her to leave them and to get on with the preparations of the Sunday dinner; but Mrs Lockit, ignoring him, drew up another chair for herself.

Having sat where he was bidden, Lionel violently stuck out his legs and then tweaked at his trousers where they were pinching his crotch. Cyril, dainty and demure, crossed his hands in his lap and his legs at the ankles, leaning slightly forward, as though eager to hear what next these two gentlemen might have to say to him.

'Now tell me,' Hugo intervened, feeling that so far Henry had been taking an initiative not rightly his, 'what precisely is it that you both, er, do?'

The two boys looked at each other. Then Mrs Lockit ordered, 'You tell them, Lionel.'

Lionel bit at what was left of the nail of his little finger and then delicately pinched a fragment from his lip, with the gesture of a smoker removing a shred of tobacco. 'Thought-reading,' he said laconically, applying himself again to the nail.

'Telepathy,' Hugo corrected prissily.

'Pardon, sir?' Cyril leant even further forward in his chair, as though he were deaf.

'That's what we call it. Thought-reading, we call it tele-pathy.' Hugo suddenly knew, as he always knew on such occasions, that he was on to something, something really big.

'Yeah. OK.' Lionel spat out a fragment of nail.

'And what precise form does your telepathy – thought-reading – take?'

Again the twins looked at each other, as though uncertain who should answer. Eventually it was their aunt, her hands resting on the arms of her chair as though preparatory to pushing herself up and hurrying to the kitchen and the already overcooked joint, who spoke up. 'Well, each of them often seems to know what's going on in the mind of the other. But of course that's hard to prove – scientifically, I mean.' She turned, not to Hugo, but to Henry for confirmation and Henry nodded, and muttered, 'Quite, quite.' 'There are so many little things. Like the other day, for example, when Cyril was late coming home from his extra art and Lionel at once said, "He's had a puncture and doesn't know how to mend it" and he set off and there was Cyril pushing his bike along, a long way from home, and he *had* had a puncture. Or the time when Lionel said, it was even hotter than today, "Oh, Auntie, what I'd like most in the world at this moment is an ice-lolly" and I said, "Well, why be so lazy, go out and get one," and, as I said that, Cyril arrived, and, believe it or not, he was carrying two ice-lollies, one for himself and one for his brother. But of course that's not scientific, not really scientific, is it? That might be coincidence. No, what's scientific is the cards, the playing cards.' She looked over to Hugo. 'Like what you were using.' Clearly she had not realized that there was a difference between an ordinary pack and Henry's Tarot one. 'Ace, king, queen, jack, ten. Show Lionel one of those and Cyril can tell you which it is, even if you put him out of sight in another room.'

'Well, that sounds most remarkable.'

'It's not one hundred per cent,' Mrs Lockit went on. 'You wouldn't expect that, would you? But there are far more successes than you or I would score.'

'When can we have a trial?'

Mrs Lockit looked at the two boys. 'Well, not today,' she

said. 'They ought to be getting home for their dinners. But tomorrow. After school.' She looked in turn at the two boys. 'How about that?'

'Yeah, fine,' Lionel grunted. Cyril merely inclined his delicate head on its long, stalklike neck.

A time was fixed and the boys took their leave. Lionel slouched out, hands so deep in pockets that the seat of his trousers was pulled taut across his swelling buttocks. 'Bye then,' he called over his shoulder. Cyril shook hands deferentially first with Hugo and then with Henry. Even on that day of summer heat, the fingers and palm were damp and chilly. His lips moved at each salutation but no sound emerged.

'Well, I'd better see about dishing-up,' Mrs Lockit said, also leaving the room.

Hugo and Henry faced each other, both of them smiling.

'I have a feeling—' Henry said.

'So do I.'

'On the threshold.'

'Of something really rather exciting.'

'What's interesting is that they're not identical twins.'

'Not out of the same egg.'

'All our previous experiments have been with identical twins.'

'This pair couldn't be less identical.'

'I like the one boy.'

'But the other.'

'Dreadful. Spitting bits of fingernail over the carpet.'

'And his shoes needed cleaning.'

As Mrs Lockit, tongue between lips, carefully placed the shrivelled joint on the tablemat in front of Henry, she said, 'I hope you won't mind my mentioning one thing, Sir Henry.'

'Yes?' Henry picked up the carving knife and steel and began to rub the one on the other, with a sound which always got on Hugo's nerves.

'You'll make it worth the boys' while, won't you? I mean, as I said, it's all really a game to them and they soon get bored with it. If you want them to cooperate, over a period of time, well, it would be advisable to make it worth their while.'

'Of course, of course,' Hugo said. He was generous by nature and in any case had been inured to paying the subjects whom he investigated.

Henry was not so sure. 'We hope they're not going to expect too much,' he said, plunging the carving fork into the charred joint of lamb, preliminary to hacking at it.

'Oh, I'm sure not, Sir Henry. They're not greedy boys. It's just that their father's a waster through and through, and such cash as he brings in to that house instead of spending on the horses or the drink has to go to the house-keeping. So the two of them are always short of spending money. Many's the time their poor old auntie's had to slip them a 50p piece – not that I can really afford it.'

Henry waved the carving knife in the air, obviously irri-tated. 'Yes, yes, all right, Mrs Lockit! We'll see them all right. That's understood.'

'I hope you didn't mind my mentioning it, Sir Henry.'

'No, no,' Henry replied, though clearly he had.

Hugo attempted to placate Mrs Lockit as she departed for the kitchen. 'Don't worry, Mrs Lockit. And tell the boys not to worry. I fully appreciate the situation and, of course, we'll pay them for their time.'

Hugo always remembered the principle once enunciated, without any irony, by a previous researcher into paranormal phenomena, S. G. Soal: 'What the investigation does demon-strate is the all-powerful influence of an intense motivation (in this case the love of money) in maintaining scores at a high level over a period of years.'

On the first day, more exciting than any that followed it, Hugo and Henry did not exercise any of the controls that were to become more and more rigid as more and more of Hugo's colleagues were drawn into their investigations.

'They always find it difficult when they're not in a familiar place with familiar people,' Mrs Lockit warned.

'Well, that's only natural,' Hugo said, used to this phenomenon.

Hugo stood in the hall with Cyril, also standing, beside him. In the sitting room off it, the door open but both of them out of sight, Henry and Lionel sat facing each other across the green baize of a card-table. Mrs Lockit moved between the two groups, standing, hands to sides of her stomach with that curious palpating gesture of hers, as she stared fixedly at one or other of her nephews. Hugo and Henry would have preferred her not to be there at all – 'Is there nothing that needs doing for supper?' Henry asked her pointedly at one moment; but at least they succeeded in preventing her from crossing from hall to sitting room or from sitting room to hall while a run was in progress.

'Are you sure you wouldn't prefer to sit?' Henry asked Cyril. It seemed to him, even then, that the boy had the etiolated, sappy beauty of some rare plant kept for too long away from the sun in a potting shed. The veins seemed to be as near to the surface of that nacreous skin as the membranes of an egg to its shell, and the skin itself no less fragile. He was so neat, with his carefully pressed grey flannel trousers and his blazer with the crest of his school on its breast pocket; his slim, highly polished moccasins which looked far too expensive for a boy from a family reputedly so poor; his crisp, white shirt, the collar held together around the hard knot of the tie by a gold or rolled-gold tiepin. Plainly he was nervous, clearing his throat or quietly burping with a maidenly 'Excuse me', or 'Pardon', fingertips to lips, each time that he did so; and this nervousness filled Hugo with a strong, troubling desire, never felt for his own two girls, to protect him and cherish him.

'No, I'd rather stand,' the boy replied in that husky voice of his, little more than a whisper.

'Yes, he finds it easier when standing,' Mrs Lockit

confirmed. Then she remarked, 'Oh, he's breaking out into a sweat. You can see what a strain it is to him.'

Henry himself had just noticed the sheen that had begun to appear on the nacre of the forehead and cheekbones.

'Well, this kind of thing *is* a strain,' he said.

In the drawing room, Lionel lolled back in the chair opposite to Henry's at the table, his legs thrust out, as on the previous day, and one hand deep in his trouser pocket while the other picked at a spot on his chin. Time he started to shave, Henry thought fastidiously, noticing the fuzz of hair above his upper lip and along the line of his upper jaw, as it caught the late evening sunlight streaming through the window.

'All right?' Hugo called.

Henry looked across at Lionel who, still preoccupied by the spot on his chin, nodded perfunctorily.

'All right,' Henry called back.

'Are you ready?' Hugo asked Cyril. Cyril, who had begun to tremble slightly, whispered, 'Yes, sir. Ready.' Hugo felt an impulse to put an arm round his shoulder and say, 'Don't worry, don't fret yourself, it's not all that important,' even though it was, of course it was, important.

'OK. Let's have the first.'

Henry turned over the first of the cards – he and Hugo had put together the ace, king, queen, jack and ten from four packs to make up twenty cards in all – and placed it on the table in front of Lionel. Lionel gave it a glance and then, to Henry's surprise, looked away from it to gaze out of the window into the street beyond. Could the boys have some confederate out there? But the street was empty. In any case, how could a confederate in the street make contact with Cyril, since the hall had no window other than a fanlight? Lionel showed no strain or even deepening of concentration.

Beside Hugo, Cyril's whole body had tensed. The sheen on his forehead had now changed, as though under a magnifying glass, to large drops of sweat. All at once, Hugo was aware of an odour which, from then on, he was always to associate with the boy: not unpleasant but somehow not human and therefore disturbing. Hugo could never really define it to himself but it was akin to the smell of grass recently mown and lying out in the summer sun.

The boy burped, quietly as before, and, as before, put the tips of those heavily beringed fingers to his lips, with a demure 'Excuse me'. Then, 'Jack,' he whispered.

Hugo wrote the number 3 on the sheet of paper on the hall table beside him. He did not know what number Henry had written on a similar sheet of paper in the other room and therefore did not know whether this, the first of the twenty attempts at transmissions, had been successful or not.

'Ten . . . queen . . . queen . . . king . . . ten . . .' The boy was now shivering uncontrollably, his face grey-green under the light filtering down from the cobwebby fanlight. In the other room, legs thrust out, a hand still deep in his pocket and an expression of boredom, even irritation on his face, Lionel glanced for a moment at each card laid down in turn before him and then stared out at the street once again. It was as though all he wanted was to get out there, among the din of cars and the bustle of people, instead of being cooped up in this frowsty, overcrowded room with this decrepit old geezer.

'Right. That's it. Twenty.' Hugo picked up the sheet of paper beside him. He saw Cyril totter and then lean forward, both hands on the hall table, as though about to vomit. 'Are you all right?' He put an arm round the delicate shoulders. 'Steady on!'

'I had a sudden turn. Sometimes it affects me like this.' Cyril straightened, put a hand to his chest. 'I'm all right now, thank you, sir.' The 'sir', used for the first time, surprised Hugo. The adult tone surprised him even more.

Henry, Lionel and Mrs Lockit appeared. Mrs Lockit, her eyes darting hither and thither and her mouth working, came over to Hugo and peered over his shoulder at the sheet in his hand, her breath fanning his ear. He felt a spasm of irritation; he wanted to shout at her 'Oh go away woman!' But he restrained himself, knowing that if there were to be any future with these two subjects, then she would have to share in it.

'He's got most of them right!' she exclaimed. Clearly, she had already examined Henry's sheet.

Henry and Hugo conferred, Mrs Lockit beside them, while Cyril, still exhausted, sat on the hall chair, his head in his hands, and Lionel wandered about, whistling irritatingly under his breath.

'Remarkable!' Hugo said at last.

'Fourteen hits out of the twenty trials.' Henry bared his chipped, yellow teeth in a rare smile. 'Well, boys, that's far, far better than we'd ever dared to hope. You failed with the first four but after that . . .'

'They have to get into the mood of it,' Mrs Lockit said. Then she went on triumphantly, 'Well, now, didn't I tell you they had this amazing gift? But I don't think you and Mr Crawfurd really believed me. Did you now? Be honest, admit it.' Hugo wondered as often in the past, why Henry submitted so meekly to such familiarity. With his staff in the embassy, he had been by turns distant, peremptory and waspish.

'Shall we have another run?' Henry proposed.

'Oh, no,' Mrs Lockit said. 'You can see how this one–' she indicated Cyril, who still sat, head in hands, on the hall chair '–has been affected. It drains him.' She put a hand on the boy's shoulder. 'Doesn't it, love?'

Cyril looked up. The bruise-like shadows under his eyes seemed to have darkened from greenish-violet to dark grey. 'I feel done in,' he said. 'I'd like to oblige but I couldn't, just couldn't.'

'Of course not,' Hugo reassured him. 'We've plenty of time ahead of us. If a subject is exhausted, then his performance always diminishes. No point in pressing you.'

'Thank you, sir.' The boy looked up at him gratefully as he whispered the words.

'I'll take them down to my flat to give them a cup of tea and some cake. They're always hungry after a performance. Aren't you, boys?'

Lionel spoke for the first time since they had all come together in the hall. 'I could do with a fag.'

'I'm afraid neither of us smokes,' Henry said coldly. 'And I never keep the fragrant weed – which, I'm afraid, I also regard as the pernicious weed – on the premises. Sorry.'

'The idea!' exclaimed Mrs Lockit, in an unconvincing performance of being scandalized. 'You know your mother never allows you to smoke. What sort of impression will Sir Henry and Mr Crawfurd get of you? You should be ashamed.'

Lionel stumped down the stairs to the basement without a goodbye. Cyril huskily muttered, 'Thank you' to Henry and then, 'Thank you, sir,' to Hugo, before he followed. Mrs Lockit went last. Before the door shut on her flat, the two men heard Lionel ask in a loud, aggressive voice, 'What about the dough then?' and his aunt tell him, 'Sh! Wait, wait!'

'The dough,' mused Henry, padding back into the drawing room, ahead of Hugo. 'Ah, yes, the dough.' He sank into the sofa and then used his right hand to lift first one leg and then the other on to it, as though they were inanimate objects.

'Well, we knew about that.'

'Yes, but what we don't yet know is how much.'

'We'll have to rely on Mrs Lockit for that,' Hugo replied, though he was disinclined to rely on her for anything.

'Yes, the invaluable Mrs Lockit! But how odd it is that she should have kept these two nephews and their powers secret from me for so long. I can't understand it.'

Had there been any trickery? The two men discussed this possibility, more because, as scientific researchers, they were obliged to do so, than because they experienced any scepticism. Signals? Henry went and stood where Cyril had stood, trembling and sweating, in the hall and Hugo sat where Lionel had sat. They could see nothing of each other reflected on any surface – picture-glass, lincrusta, electric-light bulb. Neither boy had spoken. Henry was sure that Lionel had made no sound of tapping with his feet, much less of clicking with his hands, which had been in his pockets. His breathing had been even.

'Of course, we shall eventually have to examine them under even more rigid conditions, with other people present,' Hugo said.

'Of course.'

They heard footsteps in the hall and then Mrs Lockit saying in her loud, nasal voice, 'Now get straight home, boys! No loitering! I don't want your mother to be anxious.'

'What about the dough then?'

Mrs Lockit's voice, though it sank to a whisper, was still audible. 'Now that's enough of that. I've already told you. I'll have a word with the two gentlemen. You'll get it next time I see you.'

The front door closed.

'Ah, Mrs Lockit!' Henry brought the palms of his hands together and bowed, as though in an Eastern greeting. 'How grateful we are to you. A truly remarkable exhibition.'

'Yes, indeed,' Hugo said. Lionel's mention of the dough for the second time, at the front door, had already made him draw his wallet out of his inner breast pocket, so that he was holding it in his hands. Now he opened it and, Mrs Lockit's wild, dark eyes intently fixed on him, plucked out a five-pound note. Generous, he thought. Overgenerous, thought Henry, who scowled at him and gave his head a little shake.

'Would this be acceptable?' Hugo asked, holding out the note.

Mrs Lockit took it reluctantly, as though it were something soiled, between forefinger and thumb. She dangled it, as she exclaimed, in a troubled voice, 'Oh, Mr Crawfurd!'

Hugo thought that, decent soul that she was, she was over-come by such munificence. But then she drew closer to him, her elbow tilted upwards, as though she were about to give him a nudge. 'I don't know how the boys . . .' She took the note in both her hands and stared down at it, as though examining it for forgery. 'They could earn more than this helping Mr Petrie.'

'Mr Petrie?' For a moment, Hugo supposed that this must be some rival psychical researcher.

'He has the canoes. They lend him a hand from time to time. Two quid an hour – and no travelling, of course.'

'Yes, I see.' Hugo opened the wallet again.

'As I explained,' Mrs Lockit went on, 'it's just a party trick to the boys. It takes a lot out of Cyril, as you could see with your own eyes, now couldn't you? And Lionel, well, he's just bored by it all. So, unless it's worth their while, really worth their while, they just won't turn up again, you mark my words. You can't blame them, that's how it is.'

Hugo sighed. What had been a revelatory, encouraging and exhilarating experience was now becoming squalid. At any moment this gypsy of a woman would be thrusting her palm under his nose and threatening him with ill luck unless he forked out. Ah, well. Common clay, common clay. He drew another five-pound note out of his wallet. Seeing it, Mrs Lockit gave a deep sigh of satisfaction. That was more like it, the sigh clearly said.

'Does that meet with your satisfaction?' Henry asked acidly, as the note changed hands.

'I'm sure the boys will be most grateful. It's not every day that they come to a house like this and meet gentlemen like yourselves and earn some money to give their poor mother.'

Hugo now spent few weekends in Oxfordshire.

'Sorry to have to abandon you and the girls yet again,' he told Audrey one Friday. 'But these developments are so important. We're getting interest not only from people already in the field but from others drawn into it by all the press publicity. There's talk of a television programme and tomorrow I have to show off the boys to a member of the American Society for Psychical Research.' As soon as he had spoken, he wished that he had not used that phrase 'show off'. He was morbidly conscious that, despite all the payments of ten, fifteen or even twenty pounds at a time, he might be guilty of exploitation.

'I had hoped you'd take Minnie to the bull for me. She's just come into season. I'd take her myself but I think that Mr Burton, old-fashioned dear that he is, would be rather shocked. I'll have to ask one of his boys to come and fetch her, even if it does mean a tip of a quid or two.' Audrey knew nothing of the far larger tips that were being handed out to the other boys in Brighton.

'You're sure you don't mind?'

Audrey nodded, biting on her lower lip. Then she said wistfully, 'But it would be nice to have you home for just one weekend – particularly when the weather is so lovely. The girls see so little of you. They're usually about to go to bed when you get home from College.'

'Yes, I know, I know. What is one to do?'

Hugo also had to make guilty apologies to Sybil. Her school was a mere half-hour's run from the farm and, over weekends, one of them had always made the journey to the other, in order that they could confer about the letters. 'You've become so evasive,' Sybil chided Hugo, when he had once again telephoned to tell her that he had posted to her 'a whole stack of material', since he would not be seeing her. 'What are you up to?'

'You know very well what I'm up to.'

'Those Creane boys.'

'Yes. Those Creane boys.'

'When am I going to be allowed to see them perform?'

'You can come to their demonstration next month at the Institute.'

Sybil was not satisfied. She felt, obscurely, that Hugo was keeping the boys from her. 'Couldn't I come with you to Brighton?' she had asked early on in the experiments, to receive the answer, 'Oh, you know what Henry's like.'

'I've always got on very well with Henry.'

'Well, yes . . . But he's getting increasingly misanthropic.' He had all but said 'increasingly misogynistic'. Lamely he went on, 'It's become a business for him to have even one guest.'

'I thought he had a housekeeper. I seem to remember a baleful woman in a large hat.'

'Yes, Mrs Lockit. Aunt of the boys. It's not a question of providing for a visitor. He just seems not to want to have them.'

'He has you.'

'Well, yes, but that's different, isn't it? I mean we're such old friends and, in a sense, we're in this investigation together as partners.' Partners? Hugo recalled, bitterly, that to date Henry had made no contribution to the mounting expenses.

'I scarcely see you now.' Sybil's voice became suddenly mournful and resigned. Not at all her usual self, she might have been Audrey.

'This won't go on forever.'

'Won't it?'

Putting down the receiver, Hugo felt an acute pang of guilt, a spasm of the bowels. It was almost as bad as when he has first broken the news to Sybil that he was going to get married; and what, on this occasion, intensified the guilt was his knowledge that, for some reason still obscure to himself, he did not really want to bring together Sybil and the boys, even though he had been perfectly happy to bring together Sybil and Audrey.

By now, both Cyril and Lionel were, in their separate ways, bored by sitting after sitting. Cyril, though compliant, veered towards tears as an afternoon progressed. Lionel could be cheeky and rebellious – 'Oh, no, Christ no, not another try!' On such occasions Hugo and Henry ceased to resent the continual presence of Mrs Lockit, who was always able to quell him with a stern, 'That's enough of that, my boy. You do what the gentlemen tell you to do.'

To relieve the boredom, Hugo devised other tests. On one occasion, Lionel was asked to draw something simple on a sheet of paper in the drawing room, while Cyril, for once seated instead of standing, tried to reproduce it. On another occasion, Henry produced a series of objects, previously unseen by either boy – pencil, salt-cellar, handkerchief, paperclip, toothbrush and so forth – off a covered tray and Lionel was encouraged to attempt to transmit the image of each in turn to his twin in the hall. 'Nah, can't do that,' Lionel announced of both experiments; and, when he had at last been coaxed at any rate to try, he proved himself right. In the hall, Cyril began to whimper, 'It's impossible, sir, no, sir, nothing's coming through.' After three runs without a single convincing score – when Lionel had inexpertly drawn a cat, Mrs Lockit had, it is true, claimed to see a likeness between it and the sausage-like object produced by Cyril – both these experiments were abandoned. Far more successful was a variation of the original experiment, for which Hugo produced five different targets, a lion, an ostrich, a giraffe, an elephant and a parrot, from a card game played by his girls. (There had been some angry screaming from Betsy when he had announced that he was 'borrowing' the pack.) On each card, he wrote the initial letter of the animal (L, O, G, E, P) and he and Henry used these letters for their recording. At first, the change nonplussed the twins; but after two or three unremarkable runs, Lionel grunted, 'Yeah, OK, I get it now, let's give it another whirl,' and the results from then on proved to be as amazing as with the playing cards.

'It's anything out of the ordinary that upsets them,' Mrs Lockit gave as her opinion.

Hugo nodded. 'A common phenomenon.'

No doubt this was the reason, he and Henry decided, that

the exhibition at the Institute proved to be such a failure. Both boys showed extreme reluctance to make the journey to London and perform in such a large assembly. 'It's only natural,' Mrs Lockit said. 'They're just a couple of ordinary lads – apart from their gift. They don't want to mix with a lot of grand people, scientists and scholars and such like. They're not used to it. With you both it's different, they're used to you by now. But I can tell you that at first I had a real job persuading them to come here.'

Eventually, Hugo's offer of first fifty pounds, then of seventy-five pounds and finally of a hundred pounds, all expenses paid, overcame the boys' reluctance.

In the first-class carriage on the journey from Brighton to London, Lionel spent the hour alternately peering out of the window, that irritating, toneless whistling of his emerging from between his lips, and reading a comic; Cyril, sitting for most of the time on his hands, nervously answered Henry's or Hugo's questions, in between long silences during which he gazed at the reflection of his face, in all its wan perfection, on the window-pane beside him; and Mrs Lockit viciously clacked away at some knitting taken out of a plastic shopping bag, her mouth bunched and her wild, dark eyes squinting from under knotted brows.

There were about sixty people eventually seated in the small hall, once an artist's studio, of the Institute. The day was a sultry one, of alternating brilliance and sudden downpours. Even when there was sunshine, thunder could be heard rumbling about the building. The sunlight, filtering down from the vaulted ceiling through skylights left uncleaned for years, made the atmosphere all but unbearable. The rain, spattering on the glass, was so deafening that even people conversing next to each other found that they had to shout in order to be heard.

While the audience collected, Hugo, Henry, the two boys, Mrs Lockit and the President and the Secretary of the Institute sat in the Secretary's office. Except for an occasional sympathetic glance or smile from Hugo to Cyril, the boys and their aunt, who had resumed her violent knitting, were totally ignored. SWS and REM states, ontological status, ostensible reincarnation, radiesthesia, organic disease relationships . . . As the Secretary, a small woman with coarse grey hair cut in a fringe across a bulging forehead, leaned forward, relentlessly talking, Cyril listened to her, his eyes half-closed, in a semi-trance of bewilderment and apprehension. Meanwhile Lionel gazed about him: at the untidy shelves of books, the used teacups covered in a sour film, the ancient tape recorder, the plaster cast of a pair of hands, the photograph of a genteel, middle-aged woman, her hair parted in the middle, with what appeared to be cheesecloth protruding from her wide-open mouth.

Suddenly, there was a knock at the door and Sybil burst in, her handsome face flushed and beaded with sweat under its thick coating of powder.

'Sybil!' Hugo rose, displeased with her for having disobeyed his instructions to wait until the end of the session before making contact. 'I hope you've found yourself a seat. The hall will be packed.'

'Yes, yes,' she replied impatiently. 'I have a seat. I left my *Times* and a book on it. I don't imagine anyone will take it.'

'We can always place you in the row reserved for committee members.' The Secretary got to her feet. 'How nice to see you, Miss Crawfurd.' Sybil was a member of the Institute. The President, a retired science don from a redbrick university, had also lumbered up. 'Hello, there,' he said in his North Country accent, thumbs hitched in the pockets of the tweed waistcoat which, incredibly, he was wearing under his jacket on a day as hot as this.

'I think it would really be better if you didn't join us now,' Hugo said. Though he knew that he did not want her with them, he could not have given his reason. However, he attempted a pretext, 'It tends to upset the boys if, just before a session, they have to cope with the presence of a stranger.'

Sybil laughed. 'Am I the only stranger?' She looked first

at the Secretary and then at the President. Then she looked at Cyril and Lionel. She nodded and smiled. 'Hello, boys. I'm Mr Crawfurd's sister.'

Lionel stared at her with an unnerving contempt. Cyril all but bobbed to his feet from his chair, as he whispered, 'Pleased to meet you.' Mrs Lockit, whom Sybil had met in the past in Brighton, nodded and went on knitting. Sybil had made no acknowledgment of Mrs Lockit's presence; but that one had always been full of airs and hoity-toity, Mrs Lockit told herself, with a contempt that matched Lionel's.

'This is so exciting,' Sybil said. She looked around her, 'Isn't it?'

Lionel muttered, 'It isn't going to work.'

Before the arrival of the audience, he and Cyril had mounted the narrow stage and inspected the canvas screen, five-foot high and eleven foot broad, set up between two tables as widely separated from each other as possible. Hugo was to sit, as usual, with Cyril, and the President was to join them, as a monitor; Henry, again as usual, was to show the cards, previously shuffled by both the President and the Secretary, to Lionel, with the Secretary as a monitor. It would be the President who would each time shout out 'Next!' Since there had been a suggestion from one of the more sceptical members of the Institute that Mrs Lockit might be involved with the boys in some still undiscovered deception, Henry, as her employer, had been deputed to tell her not to enter the hall. She had taken this badly, muttering to herself, 'Well, fancy that!' 'Blow me!' and 'I could have spared myself the journey.'

Sybil took a handkerchief out of her bag and pressed it to her forehead. The previously musty room filled with the scent, old-fashioned and cloying, of lily-of-the-valley. 'You do all look solemn!'

'Well, this is a serious occasion, after all,' Henry said tartly. He had never cared for Sybil, finding her bossy and opinionated, though there was no doubt, in his opinion, that

66

she was more intelligent than Hugo, and that, but for her, the edition of the Letters would never have been completed.

'Not a parlour game,' Hugo added.

The President looked at his watch. 'Perhaps we ought to . . .'

'Yes, indeed.' Hugo made for the door. 'Come along, boys.'

'Are you sure you'll be all right here on your own, Mrs — er . . . ?' the Secretary asked, as she tried to remember whether she had locked the stamp drawer and the petty-cash box. 'If you get bored, there are some back numbers of our Journal over there.'

'Thank you,' Mrs Lockit replied with aggrieved dignity. She raised her amorphous knitting by its two thick needles, 'I have this to occupy me. But thank you all the same.'

Hugo held open the door and Sybil, head high and elbows close to her sides, her crocodile-leather bag dangling from a wrist, was the first to go through. Henry followed, then the two boys, then Hugo and then the President and the Secretary. Cyril turned to Hugo, his face so puckered and green that it would have been no surprise if he had suddenly vomited, and whispered, 'I can't sir, I can't.' Hugo had often told him to call him Hugo, not sir, to no avail.

'Of course you can. There's nothing to it. Just forget about all those people out there. Just imagine we're back in Sir Henry's house and there are just the five of us.' He took the boy's arm, so fragile that it seemed as if the slightest jar might snap it, and gave it a gentle squeeze. 'I rely on you.'

'Oh, sir!'

Lionel, by now in the doorway to the hall, looked over his shoulder. 'That hall is jam-packed,' he announced. 'They must think us a bloody circus.' Mrs Lockit had insisted that, in spite of the heat, both boys should wear blazers and ties. Lionel now removed his blazer, throwing it over his arm, and loosened his tie. His coarse, dark hair stuck to his low forehead in a number of spikes.

The chatter, reverberating in the high, vaulted roof of the

former studio, now became hushed. Sybil had slipped away to her place in the front row, where she had found a young man in her chair, her book and her copy of *The Times* in his lap. She had quietly but decisively ejected him. The President stood in front of the screen, cleared his throat and began his introduction. 'Good afternoon, ladies and gentlemen. I am glad that so many of you have foregone the pleasures of sunbathing, having a siesta or watching Wimbledon in order to come here. I am sure that you will find it well worth your while. Most of you will have already read – I hope in our Journal but possibly also in the popular press – about the two remarkable twin brothers from Brighton, whom our old friend and Committee member, Hugo Crawfurd, has been so tirelessly investigating during the last months. In his investigations, he has had the assistance, the invaluable assistance, of a former diplomat, a highly distinguished man, not, I regret to say, yet a member of our Institute but none the less a sharer in our interest.' He pointed to his right, where Henry and Lionel had seated themselves at their table. 'Sir Henry Latymer.' Henry half rose and gave a little bobbing bow, as some desultory clapping broke out. 'Now I don't want to waste your time . . .' But whatever he wanted, the President proceeded to do exactly that, for some ten minutes more. He recalled past cases of telepathy; he spoke, more scientifically than Mrs Lockit had done, about the curious, sometimes even miraculous, affinities existing between twins.

Hugo looked at Cyril. His complexion still had the same greenish pallor, the skin oddly scaly. His hands clenched in his lap, the knuckles white, he was biting his lower lip so hard that it was surprising that it did not bleed. First his jaw began to tremble; then one leg, the one closest to Hugo's; then his whole body. He might have been suffering from the sudden onslaught of some tropical fever.

Everyone in the hall was gazing, not at the President, but at the twins; and everyone was amazed, as Henry and Hugo had been at their first encounter, by the physical differences between them.

At last the President ceased, gave a hitch to the baggy trousers which hung low on his ample hips, and said, 'Right then. Let's get on with things.' He walked over to where Henry and Hugo were seated and took the remaining chair, leaning back in it as though to test whether its back would support his weight. Then he called across, 'OK, Sir Henry?'

'We're ready over here.'

'Fine. Then let's have – the first!' He slapped his fist down on the table with so much vehemence that Cyril cringed away with an involuntary, startled 'Oh!'

Henry turned up a card. Lionel, as in the past, gave it only a glance. Then he gazed out, with bored insolence, at the audience before him.

Cyril screwed up his face, shot Hugo a look of terrified appeal and at last, his hand trembling so much that he could hardly write, inscribed the letter 'K' on the sheet of paper before him.

'Next!' the President boomed, his North Country voice echoing in the vault of the ceiling above him.

Henry turned another card.

Suddenly Hugo was conscious of that strange odour which he had originally smelled when he and Cyril had first stood side by side – how long ago it seemed now – under the fanlight in Henry's murky hallway. Oats, Harris tweed, new-mown hay, pot? He now knew the answer to the question which had baffled him. This was the smell of none of those things but of wild, uncontrolled, animal terror. It was far stronger now than on that previous occasion.

It had been agreed that Hugo should address no word to the boy during the session. But he stared at him, willing him, 'Go on, concentrate, write.' Somehow that message must have got through, because at last Cyril's shaking hand managed to inscribe the letter 'T' (for ten).

'Next!'

With that green-faced figure beside him and that smell in

his nostrils, Hugo suddenly felt that the President was some North Country Grand Inquisitor calling for another and yet another torture to be inflicted on a victim. He wanted to put a protective arm round this boy, no, this child, and say, 'That's enough, enough, we're going', but with difficulty he resisted the impulse.

Again Henry turned up a card, again Lionel gave it a glance, and again Hugo stared intently at Cyril, willing him to continue.

Some members of the audience were still glancing, unconcerned, now at the one boy and now at his twin; but others, sensing that terror so close to Hugo, were becoming uneasy. Sybil pressed her handkerchief, heavily scented with lily-of-the-valley, to her upper lip. It was all going wrong, she was sure that it was all going wrong, and she did not know whether to be appalled for Hugo or happy for herself.

This time the letter written by Cyril was so shaky as to be almost illegible. Q? Yes, Hugo decided, it must be Q.

'Next!'

Suddenly Cyril leapt to his feet, knocking his chair backwards. Like a small child, his face screwed up and a knuckle pressed to his mouth, he began to scream, 'No, no, no! No more!'

Hugo jumped up. He put an arm around the boy's shoulders and the next moment felt the boy gripping at him, about the waist, his knees almost touching the floor, as though he were drowning. The blue-veined eyelids fluttered over eyes which showed only their whites.

Sybil rose to her feet, a majestic figure, a necklace of amber swaying and clashing. 'He's fainted. Get him out of here.'

Hugo and the President took an arm each. People were shifting, half rising in their seats, peering, whispering to each other. The Secretary scurried over with a glass of water, most of which she spilled in her haste. Lionel remained seated, staring out at the apprehensive, confused audience with the same look of contemptuous boredom with which he had surveyed them all along.

The President and Hugo supported Cyril, whose otherwise inert body would from time to time twitch disconcertingly beneath their hands, out of the room and into the Secretary's office. Mrs Lockit dropped her knitting and leapt to her feet. 'What's the matter with him?'

'Fainted.' Not used to carrying weights, Hugo had the sensation that his heart was about to burst like an overripe tomato.

'It's the heat. And those crowds, and the strain.' Mrs Lockit delivered this diagnosis while standing over her nephew, now laid out flat on a ragged carpet which clearly had not been swept for a long time.

The blue-veined eyelids fluttered, opened. The green eyes, surrounded by their bruise-like shadows, looked up into Hugo's face. 'Oh, sir, please, sir, I can't sir!'

'No, no. Of course not.' Hugo turned to the President. 'We'll have to call it off. He's in no condition . . .'

'Do you think I ought to call a doctor?'

'No, no. He seems all right now. But it would be folly to try to resume.'

'Oh, that's quite out of the question,' Mrs Lockit intervened.

Lionel was leaning against the jamb of the door, hands in pockets. He now strolled over to where Cyril was still lying, 'Well, you've made a real twit of yourself.'

Cyril smiled up at him, apologetic and embarrassed, as Mrs Lockit commanded, 'Leave him be, Lionel! That's enough.'

At that moment, Sybil hurried into the room, a sheaf of papers fluttering from a hand. To the others she looked troubled and grave but Hugo, who knew her so well, could detect the triumph beneath her manner. 'I thought I'd better rescue these.' She waved the papers in the air. 'Naughty of me, I know, but I couldn't resist taking a peek at them. A complete blank, I'm afraid. Not a single hit. But in this heat

– strange surroundings . . .' She held the sheets out to the President, who took them from her with a mumbled 'Thanks, Miss Crawfurd,' followed by the sententious observation, 'The wind bloweth where it listeth.'

'No one seems to know whether the session is to be resumed or not,' Sybil informed them.

'Oh, dear! I'd better go and tell them. I suppose we could hurry up the tea and biscuits?' The President looked over to the Secretary, who nodded. He then rushed out.

Sybil approached Hugo, where he stood beside the armchair in which Cyril had now been placed, his body slack and his face tilted backwards and sideways, the eyes half-closed.

'Oh, I *am* sorry, Hugo. With so many people present – and that man from the American Society for Psychical Research among them. He was leaving as I came in here.'

Hugo sighed. 'As you very well know, Sybil, the whole history of psychical research is full of these mysterious setbacks. And I should have thought that by now Mark Elstein must know it too. As our President so rightly remarked "The wind bloweth where it listeth". If paranormal phenomena could be duplicated over and over again at will, like scientific ones, then our task would be much easier. Sybil, you *know* all this.'

'Of course, Hugo. But even so . . . well, it must have been disappointing. For you, for the boys.' She glanced down at the fluttering eyelids beside her. 'For all of us.'

Hugo thought: Bitch, bitch, bitch. But he smiled at her and said, 'Let's slip away and get ourselves a cup of tea somewhere else. I don't think we want to mix with all those people in all that heat after a fiasco.'

'I've never been to the Ritz.'

It hardly seemed necessary for Cyril to state this; nor, indeed, to add, 'But I've heard about it.'

'Is it very expensive?' Lionel asked.

'Very,' Henry answered. It had been his idea that they

should slip into the cafeteria at Victoria Station on the way to their train but Hugo had said, 'Oh, no, let's give the boys a treat after all they've been through,' and had then added, to clinch the matter, 'This is on me.'

'Pull the knot of your tie tight!' Mrs Lockit hissed to Lionel, gripping him by an elbow. 'And put on your blazer.' She first tugged at the brim of her hat, a tureen of pale pink tulle with a white chenille rose attached to a side, so that it tilted even more rakishly over one of her thick, dark eyebrows, and then stooped and raised her skirt slightly to hitch at a stocking.

'That walk was a mistake,' Sybil said pettishly. 'Far too hot.'

'We couldn't have all fitted into one taxi,' Henry reminded her.

'What's wrong with two?' she asked.

They found a corner in the surprisingly dim, surprisingly cool Palm Court. 'Now how shall we place ourselves?' Hugo pondered. Meanwhile, blowing out his cheeks, Lionel had slumped down into the most comfortable of the chairs. Mrs Lockit tapped him on a shoulder, 'Out of there, my lad! That's not for you.' Reluctantly, he rose.

'Sybil, why don't you go over there? Then it will be easy for you to pour.' Hugo pointed to the seat vacated by Lionel. 'Henry there. Oh, and Mrs Lockit–' he had purposely ignored her until now '–I was forgetting about you. Why don't you sit there?' He pointed to a chair so flimsy that he had hopes, vain in the event, that it would collapse beneath her weight. 'Lionel here.' The chair was a gilt upright one. 'And Cyril and I can squeeze ourselves on to this settee.'

'Indian or China?' the waiter inquired.

'Oh, China,' Sybil answered. Then she looked around at everyone else, 'China all right?'

'Can't abide the stuff,' Lionel pulled a face. 'Don't like tea of any kind, China least of all. What about a Coke?'

'That could be managed, sir.'

'Would you also like Coca-Cola, Cyril?' Hugo was solicitous.

Cyril shook his head and said, so quietly that he was hardly audible even to Hugo next to him, 'I'd like to try the China tea. I've never had China tea.'

'There's nothing like a cup of piping-hot tea to cool one down, is there?' Mrs Lockit leant forward confidentially to Sybil.

'And we certainly need cooling down,' Sybil replied, noticing how the sweat had darkened the mauve fabric under Mrs Lockit's armpits.

Henry gazed up at the ceiling. 'Haven't been here for years,' he said. 'Not since the war, I should think.'

Mrs Lockit laughed, 'That dates you, Sir Henry.'

'Everything dates me now. I've reached that age.'

Lionel examined the sandwiches which Hugo held out to him. He took one and then hurriedly, before the plate could be removed, took another. 'These look as if they'd been made for a dolls' tea party,' he said.

Mrs Lockit glared at him, 'Sh! You eat what's offered to you and no remarks, *if* you don't mind.'

Henry laughed. 'He's right, you know. Ridiculous price to have to pay for three or four mouthfuls.'

'One doesn't pay only for the food,' Hugo reminded him.

'It's the atmosphere,' Mrs Lockit agreed, daintily picking up a sandwich and nibbling at a corner. Then she tried out a word which she had never used before, 'The ambience.'

Sybil put her still beautiful head, with its thick grey hair springing away from her noble forehead, back in her chair. 'How disappointing that all was,' she sighed. Hugo had hoped that she would not again refer to the exhibition.

Mrs Lockit said staunchly, 'Oh, there'll be other times. Won't there, boys?'

Cyril gave the brave smile of an invalid receiving a brisk assurance from a doctor on his sick bed. Lionel, meanwhile, having already swallowed a whole glass of Coca-Cola, a number of sandwiches, an eclair, a florentine and a macaroon, jumped to his feet and began to move off.

'Where do you think you're going?' Mrs Lockit shouted

after him, so loudly that even people seated at the other end of the Palm Court, teacups or sandwiches half raised to their mouths, stared over at this wild, gypsylike woman.

'Only be a moment.'

'I expect he wants to excuse himself,' Mrs Lockit said. 'All that Coke, gulped down in a single go.'

Cyril had by now revived sufficiently first to look around him and then to hazard to Hugo, still beside him on the sofa, 'I suppose it must be terribly expensive to stay here.'

Hugo agreed that it was.

'Have you ever stayed here?'

'Mr Crawfurd stayed here on the first night of his honeymoon.' Sybil leaned over, her hands clasped. 'He could have caught a late flight to Athens,' she added, in the tone of someone remembering a grievance by now obscure to everyone else but still vivid to the speaker. 'But he preferred not to. He preferred to spend a night at the Ritz.'

'It would have been extremely tiring to set off at once.'

'You could have used my flat.' Sybil had a small flat in a block in High Street Kensington.

'I wanted to give Audrey a treat.'

In its courteous, clipped way, the conversation was becoming increasingly acrimonious.

'And was it very expensive – staying here, I mean?' Cyril pursued.

'Of course it was,' Sybil answered, before Hugo could do so.

'Gosh, I'd love to stay here. Even if only for one night.'

'It was for only one night that Mr Crawfurd and his bride stayed here,' Sybil said.

'Did they bring you breakfast in your room?'

'I rather think they did. Though I don't think Audrey – my wife – appreciated it. She likes to get up for breakfast.'

'I've never stayed in a hotel.'

'I'm sure you will do one day.'

'I could never afford it.'

'You never know.'

They went on talking about hotel life until Lionel,

preceded by that maddening, toneless whistle of his, saun-
tered back into the Palm Court, his hands in his pockets.
To Mrs Lockit's demand, 'Where have you been, I'd like to
know,' he answered, offhand, 'Just exploring.' Shortly after
that, Henry looked at his old-fashioned watch, the rolled-
gold so much worn away from it that its colour was now a
silvery-grey streaked with yellow, held it out to Hugo and
declared, 'We'd better be on our way. We don't want to
miss the six thirty-seven.'

'It's an awful lot of money,' Cyril whispered as he watched
Hugo remove note after note from his wallet, to pay the bill.

'Oh, don't worry about that.' Hugo was touched by the
solicitude of the tone.

Outside the Ritz, Henry pointed, 'We can catch a bus
from there. What about you, Sybil? How are you going?'

'Oh, I'll take a taxi. I'm going to spend the night at the
flat. Well –' she smiled at them all, at once gracious and
formidable '– thank you for such an – an interesting
experience.'

'We'll arrange another exhibition for you soon. Just for
you. All those crowds . . .'

'Thank you, Hugo. Yes, that would be . . . nice.' She
nodded coldly, her eyes moving from one of the faces before
her to another. She knew that she was hurting Hugo but
she wanted to do so, as for some obscure dereliction or
betrayal. 'Well, goodbye all.'

There was a ragged chorus of goodbyes, as a taxi swerved
to a halt beside her upraised arm and, with a speed and
dexterity belying her fifty years, she then jumped aboard it.

'Don't you think that it would be a good idea to try to
squeeze into a taxi ourselves?' Hugo suggested.

'No.' At that, Henry at once began to hobble off towards
the bus stop.

'One lump or two?' Henry was asking not about sugar but
about ice.

'As many as you can spare,' Hugo answered with an irony lost on his friend.

'A wasted day. And a waste of money. I can't think why you wanted to take them to the Ritz. They'd have much rather had a hamburger at one of those Mcdonald places.'

Hugo smiled into the glass that Henry had handed him. 'Cyril enjoyed it, at any rate.'

'Little snob.'

'Not at all. I found that – that awe of his really rather touching.'

'I found it really rather – awful.' Henry gave that dry, susurrating laugh of his, which was so like a cough.

There was a loud knock at the door and, as usual, Mrs Lockit burst in before anyone had had time to answer. 'Well, I've seen that lot off,' she announced, in precisely the same tone, briskly triumphant, and in precisely the same words with which she would announce that she had dealt with a couple of Jehovah's Witnesses, two nuns collecting for the blind or canvassers for a local election. 'They were worn out, even Lionel, and you can see how tough he is. Which reminded me . . .' She came further into the room, brown hands pressing into sides and her teeth bristling large and sharp as she smiled at them. 'You haven't forgotten, have you?'

Henry stared at her, his pale grey eyes as cloudy and chilly as a winter sky. 'Forgotten?'

'What you promised. The boys.'

'No, I have it here,' Hugo said; and again, as on a previous occasion, Henry pulled a face, frowned and shook his head at him, even as the wallet was being opened. On one side of the wallet there were miscellaneous five and one-pound notes; on the other side there were five twenty ones. Mrs Lockit hovered hawk-like above. Hugo drew out the five twenty-pound notes, folded them in two, and handed them to her.

'That's very kind of you, Mr Crawfurd. The boys will be happy.'

'And they bloody well ought to be happy!' Henry exclaimed as soon as Mrs Lockit had shut the door behind her.

'It's what we promised.'

'I don't see why we should deliver if they fail to do so.'

It was, in fact, only Hugo who had 'delivered' to Mrs Lockit but, careless about money and tolerant of the idiosyncracies of his friends, he forebore to point this out.

'That wasn't their fault. They tried, they failed. They'll succeed on some other occasion.'

'A hundred quid seems an awful lot of money,' Henry grumbled, as he had grumbled so often before.

'Yes, I know. It *is* an awful lot of money.' Hugo thought guiltily of his refusal to buy Angela the bicycle for which she had been asking – 'You'll have to wait for your birthday,' he had told her. 'But there it is. If we were conducting tangible instead of intangible experiments, we'd still have to spend money. Probably even more.'

Henry sipped his sherry, his inflamed nose hanging over the glass. Then he looked up. 'I hope this whole thing isn't becoming an obsession with you.'

'An obsession?'

Henry nodded. 'It seems to be taking over more and more of your life. I foresee the danger that it might, well, obliterate it.'

'I thought you shared my enthusiasm.'

Henry sipped again. 'Up to a point, up to a point.'

'I'm still waiting to see the boys show their paces,' Sybil suddenly said to Hugo when, seated side by side at the wide partners' desk in her study, they were going through a recently discovered letter written by Meredith to one of his neighbours. ('Alas, Friday will not be possible for me, nor indeed will Saturday, dearly though I should like to see you. I shall be away, taking a cure . . .')

'We've had some remarkable sessions recently. After that fiasco.'

'So I gather.'

'I'll have to speak to Henry.'

'Oh, I can't do with Henry. He's such a terrible old woman. And so stingy!'

'Henry and I are conducting the investigation as a team. You know that.'

'Why don't you bring the boys to London for the day?'

'I suppose I could do that.' Hugo was reluctant. 'But you know how that turned out last time.'

'I don't mean a demonstration in front of a lot of people. Informal. Just you, me, them.'

'And Mrs Lockit?'

'No, not Mrs Lockit. I can't take that woman.'

'Well, it might be possible.'

'Try. Do try. I'm going to be in London next Saturday and Sunday.' Ever since the fiasco at the Institute, Sybil had had an obsessive craving – totally irrational, she had told herself – to see the twins once again. Unlike Hugo, she was as much fascinated by Lionel as by Cyril.

'I'll have a word with Mrs Lockit.'

'Have a word with the boys. Wouldn't that be better?'

Hugo gave Sybil a smile of fraying patience. 'They're not adults, Sybil. It's not for them to decide whether they make trips to London or not. In theory, their mother decides. In practice, Mrs Lockit decides.'

'Sinister creature!'

'I don't know why you say that.' But secretly Hugo agreed with her. There was something baleful about Mrs Lockit, even when she was at her briskest and jolliest.

'Those boys are rather sinister too,' Sybil mused, wondering to herself if that was why they fascinated her.

'Rubbish. They're perfectly harmless and ordinary.'

'An ordinary boy of – what – twelve, thirteen? – doesn't wear a ring on his forefinger.'

'No, these days he'd more likely to be wearing it in his ear,' Hugo retorted sarcastically.

'And that other boy. So gross and grubby.'

'I don't have to tell you, with all your experience of psychical research, that the people who have the most remarkable psychic powers are often those who seem to be furthest from spirituality. Eusapia Palladio by all accounts was a ghastly old bag. Lecherous, smelly, greedy, ignorant, cunning. And yet she was probably the greatest of them all.'

'The greatest medium, or the greatest fraud?'

Hugo laughed. 'Both.'

It was, as Hugo later put it to Sybil, a 'tricky business' to get Mrs Lockit's assent to the boys' journey up to London without Henry or, more important, herself; and, surprisingly, it was a hardly less tricky business to get Henry's.

'Oh, I don't know about that,' Mrs Lockit said, bunching her mouth and screwing up her eyes, as though making some calculation in mental arithmetic. 'I don't know if their mother would agree to that. They're only kids still. And you know what London is like these days.'

'I'll be with them all the time. I won't let them out of my sight for a moment. And my sister will be with us.'

'I don't see why your sister doesn't want me,' Mrs Lockit challenged, with sudden belligerence. But she knew perfectly well: 'that one' had taken against her from the start.

'Of course I'll make it worth your – their – while,' Hugo said, adopting Mrs Lockit's constant euphemism. 'A trip to London for a sitting involves much more than a sitting in this house. So naturally . . .'

Mrs Lockit at once became more pliant. 'I suppose they can come to no harm with you to keep an eye on them. And I don't really want another journey up the smoke – not in this weather, thank you.'

To Hugo's surprise, Henry's initial reaction was as unfavourable as Mrs Lockit's.

'The boys are used to the two of us. It's always been like that. If I'm not there, it just may not work. You know very well that if, in this field, one varies the conditions of an experiment in the smallest degree, it can end in disaster. Look what happened at the Institute.'

Henry nodded. 'The conditions there might have daunted adults. But if Sybil and I and the two boys conduct some tests together – with no one else taking part – I don't really think . . .'

'Do what you like, do what you like!' Henry cried pettishly. 'But I can't see why Sybil doesn't make the journey here. Far simpler.'

'Because you've never asked her.'

'Good God, I don't have to *ask* her. She's only to ask herself.' And quite capable of doing so too, he almost added.

'She'd by shy of doing that. Embarrassed.'

'Shy! Embarrassed? Sybil!' Henry was scornful.

When Hugo and the two boys arrived outside Sybil's door, repeated ringing of the bell failed to produce an answer.

'You must have got the date wrong,' Lionel said, as he examined the nameplates on the other front doors on that landing.

'No, I haven't. Perhaps she's been held up. It's unlike her to be late. Never mind.' He searched in his pockets. 'I have a key.'

'Did she give that to you?' Lionel asked.

'I'd have hardly stolen it,' Hugo replied.

On the hall table of a flat which to Hugo always seemed to be as unfitted to contain Sybil's effulgent presence as a pinchbeck setting for a diamond, a note had been propped up against a pile of books:

Hugo. Sorry. Tried to ring Henry's but he said you'd already left. Have had to help Madge out urgently – emergency op, St Thomas's. Back by about six. Cakes in tin. Love, S.

Madge was the games mistress at Sybil's school. Could the op. have been so much of an emergency as to justify the absence? Were there not ambulances and taxis? Hugo was annoyed, sensing that, in some subtle way, this was his sister's way of avenging herself on both him and, more important, the boys.

He pulled out the watch which, attached to his lapel by a gold chain, he kept in his breast pocket, and glanced at it.

'Does that watch chime?' Lionel asked, momentarily interested.

'No, I'm afraid not.'

'Mr Petrie's does.'

'Well, we've almost two hours free. My sister must just have left. Shall I make you some tea?'

'Nah.' They had both drunk Tizer on the train. 'But what's all that about cake in a tin?'

'You can have some of it.'

The three of them went into the neat, bare kitchen, where Hugo lifted down the tin and eased off its lid.

'Cripes! Fruit cake! Wouldn't you have known?' Lionel was scornful.

'Well, it's take it or leave it.'

Both boys decided to leave it. They also decided to leave the petit beurre biscuits that Hugo found in another tin.

'We could go to Holland Park,' Hugo suddenly said, remembering how, in their by now remote childhood, Sybil and he used to go there to feed the birds and squirrels.

'A *park!*' Lionel was scornful.

But Cyril said eagerly, 'Oh, yes, sir, I'd like that.'

'We could feed the birds there. And the squirrels.' He cut a thick wedge of cake, found a used paper bag in the dustbin and began to crumble the cake into it between his fingers. The two boys watched. He would have to tell Sybil that they had eaten some of the cake. But what if the boys should then reveal the lie? Oh hell! Never mind.

'Is it far?' Lionel asked.

'No. Five minutes.'

'Walking?'

'Well, I'm not going to take you in a taxi.' Increasingly the boy had begun to get on his nerves.

Cyril kept close to Hugo's side, as though afraid of the traffic that roared and squealed by them, along Kensington High Street. But Lionel kept either running ahead or loitering behind. When he loitered it was usually to stare into some shop stocking electronic equipment. Soon, Cyril began to break out into a sweat which beaded his full upper lip and gave a ghostly shimmer to the pallor of his forehead.

'It's huge,' Cyril said, gazing over the railings between the woodland and the cement path up which they had climbed. Then he pointed: 'Ooh, look! What's that?' High in the branches of a tree, a jay looked down, unwinking at them.

'A jay.'

'Is it dangerous?'

'Dangerous! Of course not. But it's shy. You rarely see them in the park. It steals the eggs of other birds. It even eats the nestlings.'

'Horrid thing!'

'Yes, jays are rather horrid.'

Lionel ran back to them. 'What's that building over there?' He indicated a roof shimmering in the sunlight.

'The Commonwealth Institute.'

'I've heard of that.' At first it seemed unlikely, but then he went on, 'Some of the senior boys were taken on an expedition there. Can we go?'

Hugo shook his head. 'We've come to see the park. Haven't we?'

'*You* have,' Lionel retorted. 'I want to see that Institute place!' He hurried on for a few paces, head lowered, and then turned, 'Tell you what. You go to the park, I'll nip down there. I'll meet you by these seats. OK?'

Hugo hesitated. He had repeatedly assured Mrs Lockit that he would never let either of the twins out of his sight; but to have Lionel out of his sight and Cyril alone was an irresistible temptation. 'Oh, very well.' Again he fished his watch out of the breast pocket of his suit. 'It's now five-fifteen. I suggest we meet here at six. All right? You've got a watch have you?'

Lionel held out his wrist to show that he had. 'Analogue quartz,' he said. Hugo supposed, bitterly, that it was his money which had paid for it.

In the green space in front of the youth hostel, there were a lot of large women in doubtful charge of small dogs and a lot of small men in no less doubtful charge of large ones. 'Toby, come here, come here at *once!*' 'No, leave, leave, *leave!*' 'Naughty dog! Naughty, naughty, naughty!' 'Midas – heel! Heel!' A huge sheepdog, wagging his tail, romped up to Hugo and Cyril and then, having sniffed at Cyril's ankles and hand, jumped up on him. Cyril let out a squeal. 'Midas! What did I say? Heel!' The tiny, elderly man in a white suit and panama hat, a cane in his hand, looked scornfully at Cyril from eyes as hard and bright as chips of mica. 'I've always been afraid of dogs,' Cyril explained to Hugo. 'Ever since one nipped me on the Front. Not bad, mind. But the place went septic and it took a long time to heal.' He stopped and held out his hand. 'You can see the scar.' Hugo raised the hand in his and peered down at it. There was a tiny, upraised squiggle at the base of the thumb where the skin was even smoother and whiter than that which surrounded it.

'That's the youth hostel over there. And that's all that's left of Holland House. I can so well remember watching it burn as a schoolboy home on holiday. During the war that was. My mother and father lived quite near where Sybil now has her flat . . .' He went on to tell the boy how the firebombs had rained down on to London and how, only twelve at the time, the same age as Cyril, he had felt no fear at all of them. 'I couldn't believe that anything could happen to me. And neither could Sybil. We'd refuse to go down to the shelter, our mother and father had terrible difficulty with us. Eventually they whisked us off to the country –

when we weren't at school in the country anyway. Now I'd be scared stiff if I found myself in an air-raid.'

'I'd have been terrified,' Cyril said.

On the other side of Holland House, on an expanse of grass singed yellow by the sun, there were bicycles, half-naked people hurling frisbees, kicking footballs at each other or lying beside or on top of each other, children climbing trees, and transistor sets blaring. 'Oh, dear, how all this has changed!' Hugo exclaimed. It was something that he now found himself remarking more and more frequently.

'You'd think they'd be ashamed,' Cyril said primly, turning his head away from a near-naked couple, squirming on top of each other. Then he added, 'It's the same on the beach. People just strip off there not caring what you can see.'

'Oh, I don't mind about the nudity. That's fine as far as I'm concerned. But the crowds, the filth, the noise! Let's go along here. I'll show you the peacocks.'

The bird enclosure was surrounded by people, many of them foreign and many of them, like Hugo, clutching paper bags. A peacock was strutting around an insignificant peahen, its fan clicking and its beak opening and shutting as though in a serenade inaudible to human ears.

'I've seen one of those only once before,' Cyril said. 'At Chessington with my auntie.'

'Beautiful, isn't it?'

The peacock screeched and screeched again, making Cyril start. 'But its voice is hardly beautiful.'

Now an emu strutted over, bedraggled and drab, and, head tilted sideways, fixed Hugo with a single, mournful eye. Hugo got out some cake-crumbs and held them out on his palm. Cyril retreated. The emu gobbled the cake-crumbs with a rocking of head on sinuous neck. 'He might bite you,' Cyril warned.

Hugo laughed. 'Oh, I don't think so. He wouldn't find me edible.'

They walked on, along winding, baked paths, deeper and

deeper into the woods. Like a corpse deliquescing in the sunlight, an old man lay stretched out on a bench, with his boots and an empty cider bottle beside him. His mouth was open, his face was seamed with dirt, the nails were like talons on his bare feet. A couple, the girl's head on the boy's shoulder, wandered towards them. A man with the wire of a deaf-aid dangling from an ear, held a hand full of bread-crumbs up into a tree and called, 'Come, come, come!' But no bird came.

'Look – a squirrel!' Hugo touched the boy's arm. 'Let's see if he'll come and take an almond. There ought to be one or two in the cake.' He peered into the paper bag and then brought out an almond. He held it out between finger and thumb. Seated on his haunches, in a jagged patch of sunshine in the centre of shade, the animal gazed at him tremulously wary. Then he raced to a tree and ran a few feet up it. He hung there, head downwards, his sides heaving. Still he watched. Then he descended the tree and scampered up another one, even closer. Suddenly he ran down that tree, zigzagged through the grass, and stopped, snout upturned to them, in the grass on the other side of the wooden palisade against which they were leaning.

'He's like a rat,' Cyril said, retreating.

'Sh! Don't make a noise. Don't move.'

They stood still. Then the squirrel ran towards one of the posts of the fence, raced up it and sat motionless on top. Hugo extended his hand, with the nut, towards him. The squirrel seemed about to flee; then he edged along the fence, cautious step by step, opened his mouth, seized the nut. He retreated along the top of the fence, leaping from stake to stake. Halting on one sufficiently far from them, he raised the nut between his two front paws and began contentedly to nibble.

'He's eating it!' Cyril exclaimed, amazed.

'Yes, he's eating it.' Hugo's tone was dry; but he was suddenly moved by the boy's tone of wonder, absurd though it was, in a way that he was never moved, only irritated, by the same tone of wonder when used by the girls.

'May I try?'

'Of course.'

Hugo handed Cyril an almond from the bag. Cyril held it out in his palm. 'I hope he doesn't bite.'

After some hesitation, the squirrel scampered back along the top of the fence, put his front paws on to Cyril's cold, moist palm, lowered his head and took the almond. Cyril, who had squeezed his eyes shut at the moment of contact and drawn his body in on itself, gave a gasp of amazement. 'He took it from me! He took it from me!' Hugo all but said, 'Why not? He's hungry. And he's used to people.' But, not wishing to spoil the pleasure of this strange, timorous child, he merely confirmed, 'Yes, he took it from you.'

'May I try again?'

'Why not?'

Hugo turned over the crumbs in the paper bag and found another almond. The boy held it out. The squirrel, seated on the post, eyed him beadily. Then he whisked down the post and loped off into tangles of grass and stunted bushes. The boy remained standing there, the almond on his palm, with a look of consternation. As he did so, a blue tit skimmed down from a tree, snatched up the nut and was off again. The boy was astounded, 'What was that? What took it?'

'A tit. A blue tit, I think. They're even tamer in the winter. They sit on one's palm – like the robins.'

'I want to come here again. It's wonderful.'

'Well, there's no reason why you shouldn't. I'll bring you when next you come to London. But what about Preston Park? There must be birds there. There may even be squirrels.'

'I've never been there,' Cyril replied. Amazing.

'But it's not far from you.'

'Isn't it?'

'Or you could go to the Downs.'

'My uncle – the one in the Army – took us there once. But I don't remember birds.'

'There must have been some.'

They began to walk away to where the trees were even thicker and the contrast between sun and shade even more pronounced. 'There are no dogs here,' Cyril said.

'No. People have to keep them on the lead in this area. Not that they always obey.'

Cyril raised his palm and examined it. 'It's funny, that scar,' he said. 'A small dog, a small bite. A long time ago. But I suppose I'll have it always.'

Hugo took the hand and again looked down on that tiny, upraised squiggle, even whiter and smoother than the flesh around it. Then, after a furtive glance about him, he raised the hand to his lips and, on a crazy impulse, put his lips to it.

The boy's mouth fell open. 'Why did you do that?' he asked in a tone which Hugo, panic-stricken now, tried to interpret. Annoyance? Shock? Pleasure?

He forced himself to laugh, as though at a joke which the boy had failed to see. 'To make it better of course.'

The green eyes, large and moist, stared into his, as Cyril stroked the palm of the hand which Hugo had kissed with the fingers of the other.

'We'd better go back. Otherwise Lionel will wonder what has happened to us.' Hugo still felt fearful.

But then Cyril gave a long, tremulous sigh and Hugo knew, somehow, that it would all be all right. 'Oh, I wish we could stay here forever!'

'So do I. But there it is. Lionel will be waiting for us and then my sister will be waiting for us. Life sometimes seems to consist of nothing but waiting and being waited for.'

'I wait for the days when we come to you.'

'Do you? Do you really? I thought you found it boring. That's what your aunt always tells me.'

'Oh, *that!* Yes, that's boring now. It's all the same. But I like coming to your house – to Sir Henry's house, that is.'

Cyril gave a small, secret smile – to himself, so it seemed. 'I wish I could live with you in that house.'

'So do I. Perhaps one day . . . Oh, who knows!'

Lionel was not on the bench where they had all agreed to meet, even though it was several minutes past the time fixed. Then they saw him, walking negligently up the path, his hands in his pockets. A dog scampered past him and he must have whistled or clicked his fingers at it, because it stopped, looked back and then raced after him, leaping around him. A middle-aged woman with a red face and a lead round her neck, looked over her shoulder, calling, 'Maisie! Come along! Come!' Lionel stopped, picked up a stick from under a tree and hurled it for the dog in the opposite direction to that in which the woman was walking. The dog raced off. Hugo could see Lionel grinning.

When Lionel arrived, there were burs sticking to his hair and to the seat of his trousers. Hugo doubted if he had been to the Commonwealth Institute, but he was too little interested in what he had been doing – in fact, he had been lying in the long grass of the recreation ground, watching a couple making awkward love – to ask him what it was.

'We'd better get moving,' Hugo said.

'What have you two been up to?'

There seemed to be something in the tone, at once snide and insinuating, which caused Hugo a momentary perturbation. But then he decided that he had only imagined it.

'Couldn't you stay the night and let the boys go home alone on the train?' Hugo often slept on the put-u-up in the small, stuffy sitting room, after he and Sybil had spent a day together in London. But now he shook his head. 'I promised Mrs Lockit. I must take them home.'

'They aren't babies!'

'We'll be all right on our own,' Lionel said. 'Won't we, Cyril?'

Again Hugo shook his head. 'A promise is a promise,' he

said, unmindful of all the promises that he had made to Sybil, to Audrey and to the girls in the recent past and had then heedlessly broken.

Sybil gave a bitter smile. 'Some promises are.'

'Anyway, I hope you're now satisfied the boys do have a quite special gift.'

Sybil would like to have uncovered some evidence of fraud; but she had to admit that yes, they had a quite special gift. Time after time, Cyril, closeted not with Hugo but, at her insistence, with her, in the tiny bedroom, had infallibly guessed the card shown to Lionel by Hugo in the no less tiny sitting room. Admittedly, the doors had been open – 'It seems to work better like that,' Hugo had said – but there had been no way in which the boys could have seen each other for signals to pass.

Of course there was always the possibility – insidiously, it only then suggested itself to her – that Hugo himself was their accomplice. After all, Harry Price and Soal, whom both of them had known and had regarded as incorruptible, had now been revealed each to have manufactured evidence. But she could not believe such a thing of Hugo. All their lives, she and he had longed to believe in the possibility that the so-called laws of nature could, however briefly, intermittently and inexplicably, be suspended; but it was herself, not others, that she wished to convince of this, and she felt sure that it was the same with Hugo. In his years of investigating trance-mediums, psychometrists, metal-benders, water-dowsers and a host of other people possessing or claiming to possess paranormal powers, he had no more been in search of personal glory or notoriety than she had been in her years of automatic writing.

Guilty at leaving her, Hugo said, 'How will you spend your evening?'

Sybil shrugged. 'We might have tried to get tickets at the last moment for *Armide*. You've always wanted to hear it. But never mind. Oh, I expect I'll just sit at home and read.'

'Anyway, I'm glad it was Madge's mother you had to

rush to hospital and not Madge. And glad too that it was not an ulcer after all.'

But in fact, he felt entirely neutral about a colleague of Sybil's for whom he had never cared and an old woman whom he had never met.

As the boys ran down the stairs, in a contest to see who could reach the ground floor first, Sybil touched Hugo's arm before he entered the lift. Thinking of it later, the gesture struck him as one not so much of affection as of warning. But warning of what? 'Take care, my dear.'

'And you too.'

'Oh, I always take care.' She gave a brief laugh.

Hugo looked upwards, through the grille, as the lift descended. Sybil stood above him, handsome and imposing. She looked down. There was a curious look, half of hurt and half of apprehension, on her face.

Henry was not pleased to have Sybil to luncheon; he was even less pleased that she should be accompanied by a dog, and such a smelly and snappy little dog. 'What is it?' he asked, in a tone which suggested that he expected her to answer, 'A giant flea.' In fact, the dog was a Pekinese, belonging to Madge, who had taken her ailing mother away on a cruise and who had asked Sybil to look after him, explaining that the last time that he had been in kennels, he had come home with mange.

Sybil, though not a dog lover, had become attached to Mr Wu. Could it be, she had asked herself with her usual probing ruthlessness towards her own motives and emotions, that she cherished this tiny creature because Hugo, far more remote now than when he had first married Audrey, no longer allowed her to cherish him. She lifted the dog into her lap and, with the tips of two fingers, began to stroke his domed forehead above his bulging eyes.

'I hope he's not soiling that chair,' Henry said. The cretonne of the chair was dull and worn from years of use.

'No. If he's soiling anything, he's soiling my skirt.'

'Such a pretty skirt,' Hugo said placatingly.

Henry got up and went to the window. 'What a lovely day! What a lovely summer! It was a good idea of yours, Hugo, to suggest we should test the boys on the Downs.'

'I didn't suggest it because it's such a lovely day. I suggested it because it seemed to me that it would provide an interesting variation. After all, we've never had them out of doors before.'

'Ah, there they are!' Then Henry's face suddenly darkened with wrath. 'That wretched little brat has tugged a branch off the laburnum.' Hugo did not have to inquire whether the little brat was Lionel or Cyril.

As Henry spoke, the Pekinese leapt off Sybil's lap, rushed to the door, and began a persistent, high-pitched yapping.

'Do you think you could silence that dog, Sybil?' Henry asked spikily.

Sybil smiled. 'I doubt it. He's been taught to be a watchdog and dogs, like people, find it difficult to unlearn what they've been taught.'

'Oh, shut up!' Henry shouted at the dog, in an attempt to impose this unlearning. But the only result was that the dog began to yap at him instead of at the drawing-room door.

When Mrs Lockit entered to announce her nephews, she gave the still yapping dog a sharp kick. At that, the dog, instead of biting her, as Sybil had hoped, at once retreated under Sybil's chair. 'The boys are here.'

'Yes, we saw them from the window.' Henry wondered whether to mention the laburnum branch, now abandoned on the pavement; but he decided not to – it would only put Mrs Lockit into one of her moods and she might then take a day off on her usual pretext of 'an upset tum'.

Hugo rose. 'Well, we might as well get moving. Are you coming, Mrs Lockit?'

'To tell you the truth, Mr Crawfurd, this whole lark is beginning to get on my wick. No, I'll leave you all to it. I've got my hair to wash.' Mrs Lockit, otherwise so grubby, seemed always to be washing her thick, coarse hair, often appearing, not in one of her hats, but with a towel wrapped, like a turban, about her head.

Hugo was relieved.

'You will take care that that animal doesn't *do* anything, won't you?' Henry said, as they all climbed into his huge, ancient Daimler – Sybil in front with the dog, Hugo and the boys behind.

'Mr Wu doesn't *do* things in cars. He doesn't even do them on pavements. Do you, Mr Wu?' Sybil put her head down and kissed the Pekinese on one of his silken ears. 'Mr Wu is excessively well brought-up.'

Henry grunted. Then he clashed the gears noisily, as he changed up.

'Doesn't this car have automatic transmission?' Lionel leant forward to ask.

'No, I am afraid it does not.'

'I don't imagine automatic transmission had been invented when it was made,' Sybil murmured. Henry was even more infuriated when he heard Lionel snigger. But the day was so beautiful, with a sky of eggshell blue and a slight breeze making the tops of the trees tremble as the car lumbered up to the top of the hill on the way out of Brighton, that, as so often, his mood abruptly changed. He began to reminisce. 'The first car I ever owned was a Morris Cowley, bought for me by my father as a reward for getting a First in Greats. Not new, secondhand – it had belonged to some chappie, a solicitor I think, who had managed to get himself killed in it – or, rather, out of it, since he was flung out on his head in an accident and the car was hardly damaged. Funny, I'd not now want to own a car in which someone had kicked the bucket but then I thought nothing of it. It was an open car, that was why he was thrown out so easily. No seatbelts then, of course. It had a dickey, that car. Sybil here and Hugo will know what I mean by a dickey, I'll be bound. But you two boys won't, you'll never have seen one.

No, it's not a false front for a DJ.' He glanced over his shoulder at the two boys, giving that dry, brief laugh of his which sounded like a cough. The boys no more knew what was meant by a DJ than by a dickey. 'A dickey was a kind of folding seat at the back of a car. When I was in the States, they called it "a rumble-seat". Yes, that was what they called it. A rumble-seat. Can't think why.'

He droned on; everyone stopped listening to him.

Hugo, who knew by now that Cyril liked nougat, produced some, specially bought, from his pocket, and held it out silently first to his pale, beautiful darling, his throat so slim and fragile as it emerged from its open collar and his eyes so wide and liquid under the arching brows, and then to the beastly little thug beyond him. Cyril broke off a small piece, which he began daintily to nibble, holding it between thumb and forefinger. Lionel broke off a large one and stuffed it into his mouth, chewing noisily.

'How does this spot strike you?' Henry asked.

Miraculously, there were no cars, no people. A track led off the road, over a stile and then straight ahead, chalky white on billiard-table green, over a hump of the Downs. The sky seemed extraordinarily close above them, the air extraordinarily thin and sharp.

'You'd better bring your sweater,' Hugo said to Cyril with the solicitude which had come to irritate Sybil so much. 'It's quite chilly up here.'

'Nonsense,' Sybil said. 'Once we begin walking, we'll be sweating.'

Cyril looked pained, not so much because she had contradicted Hugo as because she had used that word 'sweating'. Even his mother and his aunt would have been careful to say 'perspiring'.

As though in defiance of Hugo, Lionel not merely left his pullover behind but, after a few steps along the path, unbuttoned his tartan shirt and pulled it off, placing it over his shoulders and knotting the sleeves. His torso, the muscles

94

well-defined and the skin a bluish white, was not that of a pubescent boy but of a grown-up navvy.

'Have we all the impedimenta?' Henry asked.

'All the what?' Lionel sniggered. 'What does that mean?'

'The cards, the pencils, the paper.' Henry's mood darkened as abruptly as previously it had lightened.

'They're all here,' Hugo reassured him. He shook the carrier bag that he was carrying.

Sybil strode out, not on the path, but over the springy turf, even though it was still saturated with the rain of the previous day. Both Henry and Hugo, unknown to each other, felt a grudging admiration for her vigour and health. Her cheeks were glowing, her eyes bright. Mr Wu bobbed along, now just in front of her and now just behind, making the snuffling noise of someone with a bad head-cold and without a handkerchief.

Eventually Henry stopped. 'This seems a good spot.' Ahead of him was a brow of the Downs. 'No habitation, no people!' He turned to Hugo. 'I suggest you and Cyril go up to the top over there and I'll stay down here with Lionel. Sybil can go with you and wave her scarf each time you're ready for the next card. How's that?'

'Fine,' Hugo said. 'Come along, Cyril.'

Sybil noticed that, as so often now, her brother was completely ignoring her. Bitterness rose within her, corrosive as water-brash.

'Oh, I mustn't forget the cards and your sheet,' Hugo turned back to say. He inserted a hand into the carrier bag.

'What distance would you say it was from here to the brow?' Henry asked.

'A hundred and fifty, two hundred yards? Anyway, I'll pace it out. Far further than we've ever attempted before.'

'I hope it'll work,' Cyril said anxiously.

'It'll work if you believe it'll work,' Hugo jollied him along, a hand on his shoulder.

Hugo, the boy, Sybil and the dog began to make for the brow of the hill before them. At one point, Mr Wu placed his flattened muzzle against a rabbit hole and seemed, like the fox in the story of the Three Little Pigs, determined to huff and to puff until he had somehow blown it apart. 'Come along, Mr Wu!' Sybil ordered sharply. 'Leave that alone!' Mr Wu scampered after her, his muzzle covered in earth. Soon she was far ahead of the other two; and there then came to her an absurd, irrational desire simply to walk on and on, not stopping at the brow of the hill, and so eventually to walk out of this particular experiment and all future experiments with the boys – and even perhaps out of Hugo's life. But she resisted it.

'Gorgeous,' Hugo panted, joining her where she stood, the wind whipping her skirt about her magnificent legs and tossing her thick mane of hair, black streaked with grey. He shaded his eyes and stared downwards to where, far off, the sea glittered under a sky so strangely near. 'Now let me get things out.' He removed from the carrier bag the clipboard, paper and pencil. He turned to Cyril, 'Which would you prefer to do. Sit or stand?'

Cyril, visibly nervous, as always before a session, dithered for a moment. Then he said, 'I think I'd like to stand.'

'Of course they can see each other from up here. Indoors, one arranges it that they can't. They could make signals.' Sybil talked as though Cyril were not with them.

'Well, that'll be your job,' Hugo replied with an irritation beyond his ability to control. 'You'll have to watch very carefully, as I shall do, to make sure no signals pass. What sort of signals did you have in mind?'

'Do I have to tell you? You have much more experience of psychic research than I have. Hands. Legs. Even eye-movements. You've not forgotten that woman investigated by Houdini, have you? She and her accomplice could speak volumes to each other merely by fluttering their eyelids.'

'I don't think the boys can see the fluttering of each other's eyelids over a distance like this. But, yes, you can watch for that too,' he added sarcastically.

Sybil unwound her scarf from her neck and gave it a shake

at Mr Wu, who ran forward in an attempt to snatch it in his jaws. 'Oh, Mr Wu, Mr Wu!' she laughed. Hugo, who did not care for dogs, only for cats, thought her behaviour silly. What would her pupils think if they could see her?

'Now you stand here, Cyril. And I'll stand here beside you. And Sybil can go up on to that mound over there and wave her scarf when we tell her. All right, Sybil?'

'Aye, aye, sir.' Sybil gave a mock salute, arm stiffly raised and legs at attention.

Cyril licked his lips, emitted a ladylike little cough and followed that, as so often during sittings, with a quiet burp behind the raised fingertips of his right hand. 'Pardon,' he said. Areophagia: suddenly, the word arrowed, unsought, into Hugo's mind, much as, he supposed, the denomination of a card arrowed into Cyril's.

'All right. Let's have the first, Sybil.'

Sybil raised an arm and the fine, beige cashmere scarf streamed away from it. She waved the arm back and forth. Then Hugo saw Henry turn up a card and show it to Lionel. Cyril drew his brows together, in intense concentration. His body was trembling slightly and, as in the past, the old sheen was glistening on his forehead.

Then yap-yap-yap. Mr Wu, who had been seated on his haunches, leapt up, his ears cocked. Was some walker about to appear? Hugo looked around him but the whole landscape lay deserted. 'Oh, do tell that dog to shut up!' he shouted at Sybil.

'Mr Wu! Come here! Come!' Mr Wu reluctantly moved towards her. 'Naughty!' He now began to slide along the ground. Then, having reached her, he rested his head on one of her shoes.

'Sorry, Cyril. Did you get that?'

'I – I think so, Hugo.' By now, Cyril had learned to address Hugo by his Christian name. A large drop of sweat trickled off the end of his nose and fell on to his shirt. 'Queen,' he whispered. Hugo lifted his clipboard and wrote a 'Q' under the column headed One.

'All right, Sybil. Let's have the next.'

Sybil, Mr Wu still resting his head on her shoe, raised the scarf in the air to be tugged by the wind. Far away, a tiny Henry moved towards an even more tiny Lionel. Henry's arm went out, presumably with the card. Sunlight flashed on his gold-rimmed glasses, mended at one side with some grubby Elastoplast.

There was a silence, as Cyril clearly strained himself, his jaws tense and his eyes half closed. Then, again, Mr Wu began to yap, in an ever-increasing frenzy. 'Mr Wu!' Sybil shouted. But, as she did so, the dog shot off, bouncing along the path, towards Henry and Lionel. 'Mr Wu! Mr Wu!' Her voice seemed to wail, as though in lamentation; but the wind snatched at it and she could only assume that, indomitably bouncing over stones and tussocks, he did not hear her. On and on, he bounced, on his short but powerful legs, his tail an orange plume. Eventually, in the distance, he looked more like a rabbit than a dog.

Suddenly it came to Hugo. He felt a terrible pain behind his breastbone. Dying must feel like this, he thought, the excruciating pain at the centre of one's being, the world tipping sideways, the feeling that all stable relationships with the everyday things around one were on the verge of disintegration. He gazed at Cyril. Cyril opened his mouth, a thread of saliva glistening in the sunlight before the wind snapped it. 'Ten.' Hugo saw, rather than heard, what he said. 'Ten,' the boy repeated.

'Oh, fuck ten!' Hugo swung round. 'That's it,' he said to Sybil.

Sybil was astounded that the trivial annoyance of the dog should have affected her brother so deeply. 'Oh, don't be silly. I'll go and get him and put him on the lead.'

'He'll bark just the same. That's it. Come on. Come on, Cyril!'

She had heard him often enough speak with that roughness to Audrey, the girls and even to herself, but never to the boy. Hugo began to stride towards Henry and Lionel,

from time to time tripping, as though he were walking in
darkness, over the same tussocks and protruding stones over
which the gallant little dog had bounced. Sybil looked across
at Cyril, who was standing motionless, his eyes fixed, wide
open, on Hugo's retreating figure. Suddenly she felt sorry
for the boy, as she had never thought that she would do.
She shrugged at him, gave a nervous smile. 'Well, we'd
better go too. No point in waiting here. But what a lot of
fuss about nothing.'

She began to walk off; then, glancing over her shoulder,
saw that, instead of accompanying her, the boy had
remained on the same spot, as though petrified, that ashen
hair, sculpted around his face, seeming miraculously impervious to the slapping and tugging of the wind which was
sending her own whirling about her. 'Aren't you coming?'
she shouted. 'No use to wait there.' A dread came over her,
like the cloud which at that same moment briefly obscured
the sun. The cloud passed, in seconds as it seemed; the
dread somehow remained.

Suddenly Cyril began to totter, rather than run towards
her, his knees close together and his feet kicking outwards,
as Sybil had so often seen unathletic, booksy girls run at her
school. She waited for him, partly compassionate and partly
contemptuous. What a poor, pitiful creature he was!

As they reached the others, Henry was saying, 'I don't
see why we shouldn't have another go. Sybil could take the
dog for a walk. Or we could put him in the car.'

'No,' Hugo said. His face was anguished and stern; his
left hand was gripping his right arm, just below the elbow,
as though he had fractured it and was trying to contain the
agony. 'Come on. Home.'

Sybil saw Lionel give Cyril a surreptitious glance. Then,
without his realizing, she intercepted a wink, a mere flicker
of the upper lid, and a little smirk. Cyril at once turned his
head away.

In silence they all walked towards the car. Mr Wu was

wholly unconcerned at having disrupted the sitting. He strutted along, head and tail high.

'Perhaps you could drop me off at the station,' Sybil said to Henry, Mr Wu in her lap, as the car moved forward.

'Oh, but you're coming back for a cup of tea, aren't you?' Henry said, out of courtesy and not because he really wanted her to do so.

'No, I don't think so, thank you.' She shut her mouth tight. She was becoming increasingly angry with Hugo, who, she had now decided, had terminated the sitting so abruptly in order to punish her for her presence with the dog. It was all so petty, so childish. She stared out ahead of her.

The car drew up in the station yard and Sybil got out, the dog in her arms. 'Goodbye, Henry. Thank you for my lunch.' She stared at Hugo in the back of the car for a moment, appraising him coolly, before she said, 'Goodbye, Hugo. We'll be in touch.'

'Of course.'

'Goodbye, boys.' She waved the hand which was not holding the dog and then strode off.

'Nasty little animal,' Henry said. He did not really blame Hugo for feeling that they could not go on with all those interruptions from it. 'No discipline.'

Hugo did not reply. The journey continued in silence.

As they entered the house, Mrs Lockit, having heard the engine of the car, appeared from downstairs in slippers and petticoat, her head wound round and round in its turban of towel.

'You're back early,' she said. 'I wasn't expecting you all as soon as this. I can't manage any tea for you until half-past four.'

It was Hugo, not Henry, who answered her. (Cheek! she thought. There were times when he carried on as though he were the master.) 'Thank you, Mrs Lockit. That's all right. I just want to discuss something with the boys.'

Mrs Lockit disappeared down the stairs again.

Hugo turned to Henry, 'Do you mind if I talk to the boys in the dining room alone?'

'Talk to the boys alone?'

Hugo nodded.

'Well. I suppose I've no objection.' But Henry thought it odd, in fact bloody rude.

'Cyril, Lionel.'

Reluctantly, the two boys, Lionel first, went through the door held open for them. Hugo shut the door and then swiftly turned the key in the lock and put it in his pocket. He faced Lionel.

'I'm going to have to look in your trouser pockets.'

'You can't do that.'

'Oh, yes, I can!'

Hugo made an attempt to grab the boy but he darted away, as though in a game. Again Hugo flung out his arms, blundering into a dining chair, while the boy whipped round the table. On the third attempt, Hugo managed to grab Lionel, who first struggled and then kicked out at his shins. Cyril began to emit a low keening, as he stared in horror at their contest. Hearing the commotion, Henry came to the door, tried the handle and began simultaneously to rattle it and beat on the panels with the palm of the other hand. 'What's going on in there? What's all this?' he shouted.

The two bodies, one tall and slender and the other small and stocky, rocked and lurched. An elbow, whether accidentally or on purpose, jabbed Hugo in the testicles; but he was impervious to an agony that would normally have doubled him up. He managed to insert a hand into the boy's trouser pocket in a violent travesty of that tender moment when he had inserted a hand into the trouser pocket of his twin and had felt his childhood throb away, an immediate, fleeting spasm, in his hand. He pulled, at the same moment as Lionel, jerking round, finally managed to fasten teeth, not in his violator's hand as intended, but in his sleeve. 'I thought so.' Dishevelled and panting, Hugo held up his trophy.

It appeared to be an ordinary whistle; but attached to the end was what looked like the bulb of an eye-dropper. 'You bloody little cheats! So that was what I paid for!'

Lionel eyed him with an unwinking contempt, his face red and his breath coming in short, heaving gasps from the exertion of their wrestling match. Cyril had covered his face with his hands. Then, all at once, he was sobbing. The sobs grew louder. They filled the whole room.

Hugo turned on him. He could bear it no longer. 'Stop that!' he shouted. 'Stop it at once!'

Only then did he become aware that Henry was still rattling the door handle, still beating on it with the palm of his hand, still shouting, 'What's going on in there? Open up! What *is* all this?'

Transferring the whistle from his right to left hand, Hugo fished in his pocket for the key, inserted it and unlocked the door. Like wild animals let out of a cage, the two boys, heads down, pushed past Henry, all but knocking him over, and raced down the stairs to Mrs Lockit's flat.

Hugo held up the whistle. 'This is how they did it.'

Henry stared. 'How do you mean?'

'You've heard of a Galton whistle?'

'I don't think so.'

'Well, you've heard of a dog whistle, haven't you?' Hugo was brutal in his impatience, like a master bullying some nit-witted pupil.

'Yes, of course.'

'Well, a dog whistle is audible only to dogs – as a rule. Though some people, young people, can sometimes hear it. A Galton whistle is similar. You can adjust it so that few adults can hear it but it is perfectly audible to children.'

'So you mean . . . ?'

Hugo raised the whistle and then depressed the bulb. 'Hear anything? No. Neither do I. But we're both over forty – as is Sybil. Perhaps someone under forty might just hear something. A child, with normal hearing, like one of those two, certainly could. I pressed the bulb once. That was for ace.' Now he pressed the bulb four times. 'That was four presses. Jack. Simple, isn't it?'

'The little buggers!'

'As you say, the little buggers.' Suddenly Hugo sounded tired and ill. His voice sank away. But he rallied himself, 'Of course, now we understand the fiasco at the Institute.'

'How do you mean?'

'Well, there were young people there – in the audience. So Lionel – I'm sure Lionel was the leader – knew that to use the whistle would be to give away the trick. It was better to accept an afternoon of failure in order, later, to have more success. And more money,' he added with the bitterness of the etiolated child's sperm thin on his tongue.

'Do you suppose that Mrs Lockit . . . ?'

'Oh, I'm sure of it. She may even have thought up the whole idea. But no. Probably it began, just as she said, as a parlour trick, a way of puzzling and entertaining their friends. I wouldn't be surprised if there isn't a Galton whistle in the lab of their school. One of their teachers may even have demonstrated it. It's a common enough piece of equipment.'

'And Mr Wu –'

'Heard it. Thought you were whistling to him.'

'Clever Mr Wu.'

'As Sybil and Madge are always saying – clever Mr Wu. Just as Siamese-owners always think that their cats are cleverer than other cats, so Pekinese-owners always think that their dogs are cleverer than other dogs. Perhaps they are.'

'What shall we do now?'

'What can we do? *La commedia è finita*. That's that. What you do about Mrs Lockit is your own affair.'

Henry pondered. 'She suits me so well. I doubt if I could find anyone better.' He frowned unhappily down at his unpolished shoes.

Hugo was sure that his friend could find someone better; but he was not going to interfere.

'Oughtn't we to try to get the money back?' Henry ventured.

'Pointless. No. Let's just quietly wash our hands of the whole silly business.'

Something disturbed Henry. He peered for a time at the white face before him, as though repeatedly trying to bring it into focus, before he said, 'But you'll have to publish something in the Journal.'

Hugo had not thought of that. 'I don't know,' he mumbled.

'But you must. You can't let people accept for real what we two now know to have been fraud.'

'Yes, but . . . there are complications.'

'Complications?'

'Difficult to explain.' Hugo sank into a chair. 'Let me explain some other time. I have to think – have to think . . .' He swallowed that bitterness, with an effort of the will, in order not to have to spew it out. 'Let me think.'

'Very well.' Henry was already guessing; soon he would have guessed. He would be neither surprised nor shocked. He went over to his friend and put a hand, swollen because of the heart condition from which he was suffering, on to his shoulder. 'A nip,' he said. 'That's what you need. A nip of brandy.'

Hugo shook his head. 'No, what I need is to be alone. Lie down. My room.' He got to his feet, like someone recovering from a fainting spell. 'I'll be all right. In a moment or two.'

'Yes, have a little zizz. This has been a shock to you. You've put so much into this business. Far more than I have.' Henry spoke without any consciousness of the money, hundreds and hundreds of pounds, which Hugo had put into it. He spoke with little consciousness of the flood of suddenly undammed passion.

Hugo climbed wearily up the stairs, drew his curtains and then, without even taking off his jacket, shoes and tie, threw himself on the bed. The sheets, the pillowcases, smelled strangely sour. He had never noticed that before. He lay on his side, a hand under his cheek, and stared at the cheap, old-fashioned wallpaper, of ships, innumerable ships, on and on and up and up, bobbing on sunlit waves. Of course, Cyril had not conceived the plan, could not have conceived the plan. It was that dreadful Lionel or that even more dreadful woman. Poor Cyril, so timorous and pliable. The self-pity which he had been feeling, like some endless throbbing within him, now became a pity for the boy. Like himself, the boy had been a victim. 'Your mother needs that money. It'll make all the difference in the world to her. And to you. You've got to think of her, you've got to think of yourself.' He could hear the insistent, insidious voice and he could see the looming gypsy presence. Then Lionel would chip in, nasally gruff, 'Don't be such a twit. He's rolling in it. And he *wants* a miracle. He wants it!'

Hugo groaned, rolled over on his back, covered his eyes with the back of a hand.

Suddenly, like the lunge of a spear beneath the heart, his own words came back to him: *La commedia è finita.* Did that mean that he would never see Cyril again? It could only mean that.

There was a knock at the door.

Hugo sat up on an elbow, his usually neat, grey hair sticking up in tufts, one side of his face creased. 'Henry?'

But it was Mrs Lockit who entered, not bursting in as she usually did, but like some thief in the night.

'Mr Crawfurd.'

'Yes, Mrs Lockit.'

'The boys have told me.'

'Yes, Mrs Lockit.' He could think of nothing else to say to this now terrible and terrifying woman.

'I think you're being foolish.'

He gave a bitter laugh, like a sob in the back of his throat. 'I've *been* foolish, Mrs Lockit. No longer.'

'Well, I wouldn't disagree with that either,' she said, amazing him with her calmness and self-confidence. She approached the bed. 'You want to continue with the experiments.'

'No. I don't want to continue with them.' He spoke with contemptuous harshness, but he also felt a strange foreboding.

'The boys will miss that money.'

'I'm sure they will.'

'You wouldn't wish to harm them.'

'I have no wish to harm them. I just do not want to see them any more.' (Not see Cyril any more? What was he saying?)

'So they've served their purpose.'

'In retrospect, I don't think they ever served their purpose. They merely served their own ends.'

Mrs Lockit stared down at him, as he sat, head in hands on the bed. The eyes were narrowed in that face so dark that it might have been Indian. 'I thought that Cyril had served his purpose.' Her voice was sickly and sickening in its insinuation.

Hugo turned his head aside and away from her, his breath exhaling on a deep, shuddering sigh. She loomed over him, seemed to envelope him like a miasma off a swamp. 'I don't know what you mean.'

She gave a snort. 'I think you've made a fool of yourself, Mr Crawfurd. If you'll forgive me saying so.' Fastidious as he was about the use of language, Hugo felt a compulsion, absurd at such a moment, to correct her, as he might correct one of his students, 'If you'll forgive *my* saying so.'

'Yes, I've made a fool of myself – or allowed those two boys to make a fool of me.' He laughed, 'It took a dog to show me.'

'I didn't mean that.' And, of course, in his heart, he knew that she had not meant it. 'Cyril is an odd boy. Not like his twin. Well, you saw that for yourself, appreciated it. Given the right chance, he might do something with his life. But life will never be easy for him, as it'll be for Lionel. It's never easy for that kind.' She put out a hand and picked up his hairbrush, the silver crest tarnished on its back, from the dressing-table against which she was now leaning. He rebelled against the idea of those grubby hands touching anything so intimate, as he had not rebelled when, in Sybil's flat – Sybil away at her school, Lionel sent off to a cinema, three pounds in his pocket – those long, feeble fingers had held the brush and had gently and repeatedly drawn it across the fine, ashen hair. 'You'll want to go on helping him, won't you? Even if there's nothing more that he can do for you.'

There was no mistaking the true meaning of what she was trying to say to him, as she picked at a hair lodged in the bristles of the brush and pulled it out between finger and forefinger as though it were a length of thread she was drawing from a needle. Her tongue, sharp and red, appeared between her teeth.

He thought: Oh, Christ, Christ, Christ! How much did this dark, baleful woman know and how much had she guessed? He had been so careful. *'Cyril and I thought we'd go and feed the birds in the Park. But I know that bores you. Would you rather go down to the Odeon if I give you the money?' 'You won't mind, will you, Sybil, if I use the flat tomorrow. I have a group of visiting Americans to see and it'll be difficult for them to get down here, because of their itinerary.' 'This is our secret, Cyril. You must never, ever tell anyone about it. Other people wouldn't understand. They might even try to keep us apart. One day, it'll be different. When you're older. Then we'll have a flat like this of our own and we'll meet in it whenever we want and to hell with everyone else.'* He had been so careful; but, as Mrs Lockit had told him, he had made a fool of himself – or let others make a fool of him.

'I'm always willing to do anything I can to help either boy.'

'Well, as I say, Cyril's the special case. His father's not in a position to do anything for him. Just a drunken lay-about, as you know. Yes, he's a special sort of boy and he deserves a special sort of treatment. If you get my meaning.' The final sentence lilted upwards, vaguely interrogative.

His head still turned away from her, to look out of the window at the mock-orange frothing behind it, Hugo nodded.

Mrs Lockit put down the brush. 'I think we understand each other. I think Cyril can rely on you?' The hands palpated the stomach. 'He'll be happy about that.' She walked towards the door, then turned. 'Oh, what a silly I am, it all but slipped my mind. And I promised the boys. You haven't forgotten the usual, have you?'

'The usual?'

'For their trouble. The ten quid each.'

Hugo all but shouted, 'Go to hell. I'm bloody well not going to fork out my money for being taken for a ride!' But he knew he could not do that, now or in the future stretching ahead of him.

He got off the bed, and put out a hand to steady himself against the edge of the dressing-table, as he felt everything suddenly whirling and darkening, undisciplined particles caught in a maelstrom from which they struggled in vain to free themselves. He put his hand to his inner breast pocket, drew out his wallet. Things steadied, came into focus. Mrs Lockit ran the tip of that sharp, red tongue over her lower lip, watching him. He drew out four five-pound notes, so crisp from the cash dispenser that when he had offered one of their fellows to the girl at the counter in Smith's in order to buy a *Guardian* and *Spectator,* she had produced the old joke, 'Have you just made these yourself?' Such notes often stuck together, but he was now beyond counting them with any care.

'There you are, Mrs Lockit.'

'Much obliged, Mr Crawfurd.' She put her hand on the doorknob. 'I can understand you not wanting to see the boys again, given the circumstances. But it's nice to know you'll continue to take an interest in our Cyril.' As she opened the door he put out a hand, as though to restrain her. 'Was there something else?' She sounded surprised and suspicious.

'I just wondered . . . Tell me . . .' (Yes, yes, he had to know) 'Who was it who originally thought of the idea?'

'What idea?' She peered round the door and down the corridor to make sure that Henry was not listening.

'The whistle, the bulb. Was it yours?'

She laughed. 'Good gracious me. I haven't the education or the brains to think of a thing like that. And Lionel wouldn't be capable of thinking of it. No, it was Cyril. We were all walking on the Front one day and he heard this whistling, kept hearing this whistling. But his mum couldn't hear it, I couldn't hear it, even Lionel couldn't hear it. At first, we all thought it was something in his head. But then he figured it out. It was this woman with a dog. She kept blowing the whistle far out by the sea and, wherever she was, that dog would run to her. Then a funny thing happened, don't ask me why. We waited there, on the prom-enade, to see the woman and the dog come back over the sand and pass us. In fact, I was going to ask her about that whistle, never having seen one like it in all my life. But as they came near to us, the dog – a spitz-like dog it was – suddenly rushed forward and bit Cyril on the hand. It was as though it was angry with him for having discovered its secret.'

Under the gloom of overarching trees, Hugo raised a limp, cold hand and pressed lips to the upraised squiggle, even shinier and whiter than the flesh around it, which made a small boss on the fleshy area just below the thumb.

'So it was Cyril whose idea it was,' Hugo said softly, in a tone of anguished wonder.

'As I say, at first it was just a prank. To take in the other boys at the school – and some of the masters too. And then, well, we played the same prank on you and Sir Henry. It was naughty of us, I know.' She shrugged and smiled, as though that deception and that extraction of money in the past and this blackmail now were of equally small account. 'Are you going to be in to supper?'

'No, I don't think so. No. I have to get back to London. To see my sister.' He had no arrangement with Sybil but it was the first pretext that came to him.

'Oh, that's a shame! I got a rabbit in the market and I've already skinned it for supper.'

He felt an uprising of nausea, as, involuntarily, he envisaged those blunt, tanned hands tearing the fur away from the shiny, bluish carcase beneath it. He gulped. 'I'm sorry.'

Mrs Lockit went out, shutting the door quietly behind her. That he would see her again, he had no doubt. But would it be here? He could not bear the thought of remaining in, or returning to, this house in which he had been so disastrously cheated. He pulled his suitcase out from under the high brass bedstead, opened it and, usually so tidy, began to thrust into it, piecemeal, shirts, socks, shoes, underclothes, pyjamas, dressing-gown, shaving things. He stared down at his hairbrush in his hand. She had touched it, before removing from it that long, ashen hair. Somewhere, on the carpet, the hair would now be lying. He felt an impulse to go on his hands and knees to retrieve it. He threw the hairbrush on top of the things already in the suitcase. He looked around him. Had he forgotten anything? He opened the window, leant out and smelled the overpowering exhalation from the mock-orange on the still evening air. He, Henry and the boys stood under it. 'What's that smell?' It was as though Cyril had never smelled mock-orange in his life. Henry told him. 'It's lovely, isn't it?' the boy said. Henry was irritated, as so often, by his girlishly lisping voice; and he was even more irritated when Hugo reached upwards and broke off a stem for him. The boy held it to his nose, breathing deeply. 'Oh, lovely, lovely.'

Hugo returned to the bed, closed the hasps of the suitcase, and looked around him. Anything forgotten? No, everything remembered, as it would always be remembered, as long as he lived. *As long as he lived.* He went to the door, case in hand, hesitated, and then swiftly made his way along the corridor and down the stairs.

Henry had been waiting for him. He had heard Mrs Lockit go up, he had tried to hear what they had been saying to each other. He knew that something far more terrible had happened than the discovery of the deception and he was beginning to know, without being told, what it was. He felt both a pity and an anger, like a sulky fire attempting to burst forth under damp wood, for this friend who had made such an ass of himself.

'You're not off, are you, dear fellow?'

Henry peered up, the gold rim of his spectacles above his left eye glinting fire from the reflection of late evening sun through the fanlight above him. 'I thought you were going to stay tonight. I thought you were going to give me my revenge at chess.'

Hugo shook his head. He could hardly frame a sentence, let alone utter it. 'Must return. Promised Sybil.'

'She said nothing about seeing you this evening. Why didn't you travel together?' Henry's voice was the stern one of a schoolmaster catching a pupil out in a clumsy lie.

'She had to do something first. She was in a hurry. In any case, I didn't want her here when I – I unmasked the two boys.'

'But you'll tell her about it?' Henry's tone was as sharp as his gaze.

Hugo descended the last step. 'Henry – may I ask something of you?'

'Of course. Go ahead.'

'Henry – please don't say anything to Sybil about – about the deception. Eventually, I'll tell her myself. But don't tell her. And don't tell anyone else.'

'But Hugo, I can't see . . .'

'Please, Henry. I ask it of you. Say nothing. Nothing to anyone. I want you to leave it all to me.'

Henry looked at his friend, whose face had the expression, sickened and stunned, of someone who has just been pulled, unhurt, out of some terrible pile-up. He felt a sudden tenderness, even love, as though the sun had penetrated, by some miracle, through the thick, obdurate shell of an ancient tortoise. He held Hugo's arm, tentatively, above the elbow, then exerted a squeeze. To Hugo it was a terrible travesty of the way in which he himself had touched another arm. 'I'll tell no one,' he said. 'Not to worry. I'll leave it to you.'

'Thank you, Henry.'

Hugo began to walk towards the front door. Then he said, 'I don't think I'll be able to sleep tonight, not after what has happened. I suppose you couldn't spare me some sleeping pills? As you know, I never usually take them.'

'Of course, dear chap, of course.' With a spryness amazing for a man of his age with a heart condition, Henry raced up the stairs. Hugo waited dumbly. Then Henry raced down again, a bottle in his hand. 'Let me give you two. But these are pretty strong, mind.'

Hugo wanted to snatch the whole bottle. Mogadon. Henry had spoken of them only two or three days before. *I suppose you couldn't spare me the whole bottle, could you?* No, impossible. Even if he said that, Henry would refuse. *The whole bottle, old fellow? I'm awfully sorry. But take another one, if you like.*

Hugo took the two pills and slipped them into the breast pocket of his jacket. 'Thank you, Henry,' he said, not knowing whether he was thanking him for all his hospitality during the last weeks or for the two useless pills. 'Good of you.'

'I'll see you soon,' Henry said. There was a pathos in the upward inflection he gave to the words. So many people had moved, a procession drawn by other, more exciting music, out of his life. He did not want Hugo also to move out of it.

'Oh, yes, soon.'

Hugo opened the door, crossed the threshold and then, without looking round, hurried through a cloud of perfume from the mock-orange, ducked his head where the branches of the laburnum trailed above the path, and emerged on to the pavement.

He began to stride out for the station; but then there crowded in on him memories of his face buried in those slim thighs, with their tantalising, vaguely musty odour, of the wretched little dog first yapping and then bouncing off over tussocks and stones, of Audrey saying, 'Oh, not again, not again, we never seem to see you for a single weekend,' of Sybil saying, 'I must say I do find both of them singularly unappealing,' of that hair in his mouth, that earlobe, that choking bitterness, and then that gypsylike woman, hands palpating the side of her stomach, strands of her coarse black hair trailing across her cheek, and her voice reminding him that though the expensive dream had ended, the expenditure itself would never do so . . .

He paused, looking around him at the twee, gimcrack Regency houses, with their brass carriage lamps, glistening front doors, hanging baskets of flowers and extravagant wrought-iron gates. Then, his mind suddenly made up, he turned back. He began to stride, hands in pockets and head lowered, as though in the face of a gale, away from the station. Towards the sea front.

The hotel, when he, Sybil and their parents, had stayed in it before the War, had been rambling and old. Since then, a fire had swept through it, what remained of the historical structure had been ruthlessly demolished, and a gaunt skyscraper had been erected in its place. Henry hated the change but at that moment he could think of nowhere else to go.

'Yes, sir. Of course, sir. It's lucky it's tonight and not tomorrow. We have the conference tomorrow.'

Conservative, Labour, Liberal? IBM, Ciba, BP? Hugo cared too little to ask.

In the clean, bright, boxlike bedroom, far above the promenade, he sat on his bed, his case unopened, and rested his head in his hands. After a while, he patted the breast pocket of his jacket. Two Mogadon. Useless. He and Henry had been talking about death and survival after death, and Henry – who, unlike Hugo, believed that 'we just go out like a light switched off by an invisible, arbitrary hand' (a click of the fingers) – had described how he had procured from Exit a booklet of instructions about 'doing away with oneself as effectively as possible'. One had to swallow a hundred and ten Mogadon tablets, Henry said, his eyes wide behind their thick lenses. 'Can you imagine it? A hundred and ten. And I have difficulty in swallowing a single pill.' Hugo had laughed, 'I suppose that's what coroners call "a massive dose".' Useless. A hundred and ten.

A small refrigerator in a corner of the room suddenly set up a hum, as though to say to him, as discreetly as possible: I'm here, why don't you visit me, I might be able to comfort you. Hugo went over and pulled open the door. He stared at the miniatures. Then he picked up one, Black and White whisky, and unscrewed the cap. He put it to his mouth, swallowed. He picked up another. Another. But though the liquor burned horribly as it went down his gullet, – he felt that he might have been swallowing molten lead, so quickly and so strangely did it seem to solidify on reaching his stomach – none of the expected lightening of mood or blurring of senses followed. The reverse. He felt a dragging within him, so that it was all that he could do not to sink to his knees. At the same time, all his perceptions – of the late evening light slanting through the French windows from the balcony beyond them, of the jazzy, zigzag motif, black on white, of the curtains, of the rush of some distant plumbing – were sharpened to preternatural acuteness. He took another miniature bottle out of the mini-bar, unscrewed its cap and swallowed once again. He looked at the bottle: gin. Standing beside the mini-bar, the bottle to his lips, there came back to him a memory of opening a similar mini-bar in an African hotel and standing back, horrified, as huge, shiny cockroaches cascaded out of it.

The sun was now only a reddening stain, seeping wider and wider across the horizon visible through the windows.

He pulled open one of the doors on to the balcony, then the other. For a long time he stood there, as the traffic, infinitesimally small termites beneath him, crawled, stopped, crawled, with a strange hum, like a far-off wail, arising from it, and the sky and the water began to darken. He felt a mortal sickness, at the thought of the domesticity of his life on the farm, of the tedious hours spent with Sybil over their shared labours, of the wrangles of claims and counter-claims, superstition and scepticism at the Institute, and, above all, of the deception and the separation and the weeks and weeks and months and months and perhaps even years and years of paying out money.

The awning over the balcony hung askew. Some instinct for order, undying when everything else within him seemed to be dying, made him go back into the room and press the electric switch which operated it. The strut that had already descended trembled and then began to rattle as he kept his finger on the switch; the other strut would not move.

That same instinct for order made him pick up the telephone.

'Yes, sir. Can I help you?' A female voice.

'The awning on my balcony doesn't come down properly.'

'What doesn't what, sir?'

Patiently he explained.

'Just one moment, sir.'

'Yes, sir. Can I help you, sir?' A male voice.

Hugo repeated what he had said already.

'I'll send someone up first thing tomorrow.'

'Why not now?'

'I'm afraid it's far too late now, sir. In any case, there's no sun on the balconies now, is there?'

Hugo put down the telephone. He went back on to the balcony. Again he looked out at the darkening sea and sky. After the heat of the long day, a breeze was arising, to make his trousers flap about his legs and untidy his hair. He put both hands to his head, partly to keep his hair from flying about and partly because he felt that everything within it was about to explode.

Suddenly, on an impulse, he hoisted himself up on to the balcony railing, one hand to the strut of the awning which would not descend. He looked down. That strange wail from the traffic grew louder, shriller. Nothing was moving except a single motorcyclist – he could see his yellow jacket – weaving constantly between the stationary cars. 'As soon as he's old enough, Lionel wants a motorbike. I'd be terrified to ride one of those things. Dangerous.' 'Perhaps you'd prefer a car.' 'Yes, I'd prefer a car.' 'Well, when you're old enough, I'll buy you one and you can drive it for me.'

The cars began to move again.

Hugo's body swayed outwards, regained its equilibrium, then swayed outwards again. So easy. Easier, far easier than swallowing all those Mogadon tablets. Let go. Just let go. But at the moment of falling, he could not let go. A hand shot up, grabbed at the awning. The awning held him a moment, then the fabric split and he hurtled down, a streamer of the jolly red-and-white canvas clutched in his fist.

It was clear, the coroner said, that the deceased had been drinking to excess; three miniatures of whisky, one of vodka and one of gin had been found scattered on the floor around the mini-bar. No doubt that excess of alcohol had made him so truculent in his demands that the electric equipment which operated the awning should be repaired, had caused him to try recklessly to repair it himself when told that no one could see to it until the next day, and had resulted in his loss of balance.

Henry sat impassive, his arms folded and his gold-rimmed spectacles low on that nose which, because of its broken veins, made his neighbours commit the injustice of believing that he must be a secret drinker. When Sybil, leaning

forward between him and Audrey, began to sob into a handkerchief smelling strongly of lily-of-the-valley, so far from
trying to give her comfort, he did not even look at her.

'A stupid and tragic accident,' the coroner concluded.

THREE

IS

Despite the coroner's verdict, the manner of Hugo's death obsesses Sybil.

Suicide? Henry testified, the elaboration of his answers, with their qualifications, their parentheses and their anti-quated slang, clearly irritating the brisk, busy coroner, that his friend had seemed quite his usual self, in as far as anyone could be said to be quite his usual self, when he had left the house. No, there was absolutely no indication that anything was worrying or depressing him. One might, indeed, describe his whole mood as jolly, in as far as a man as thoughtful and sensitive as the, er, deceased, was ever jolly. Audrey also testified, her flared electric-blue skirt and pink blouse, open at the neck, making an even less favourable impression on the coroner than Henry's manner had done, that, no, the deceased had had no financial or other worries and, yes, their marriage had been an entirely happy one. But the question remained: why had Hugo taken his leave of Henry, apparently to travel back to Oxford, and then, instead, have installed himself in a room in a Brighton hotel? 'I've no idea,' Henry said. 'None at all. Unless he felt – which he had no reason for feeling – that he had outstayed his welcome with me. When one is a guest, that is always something difficult to decide.'

Murder? Hugo had entered the hotel alone, he had had no visitors, the door of the hotel bedroom had been locked from inside, the distance from one of the balconies to another was approximately eleven feet.

Yet Sybil feels that the truth or at least part of it has still to be revealed. What kind of business could have kept Hugo in Brighton and why should he not have stayed on with Henry, having so often stayed with him for days on end in the past? There is also the mystery of those miniature bottles of spirits scattered on the carpet. Hugo was always abstemious, even ascetic. It is difficult to think of him gulping a variety of spirits neat from their bottles. Sybil recalls a visit which the two of them once paid to an American academic, living in a furnished flat in Crouch End while on a sabbatical. Hugo, with his usual generosity, had taken along from his cellar a bottle of Château La Mission Haut Brion 1971, as an offering. The American, clearly not appreciating its value, said to his wife, 'Look what Hugo's brought us,' and thumped the bottle down on the table already laid for dinner in one corner of the tiny sitting room. Having given Hugo and Sybil the glasses of sherry for which they had asked – 'Lucky I got some in, Valerie and I never touch the stuff' – he had refilled his own and his wife's glasses from a pitcher of Martinis. Hugo had watched their host and hostess for a while; then, able to bear it no longer, he arose, pointed to the bottle of claret and said, in the voice of someone attempting to placate a mugger armed with a knife, 'I think, old fellow, you'd better put that away for some other time.' The American was puzzled; but he did what Hugo told him.

The manner of Hugo's going does not obsess Henry, as it does Sybil; but Henry often thinks about it. Might that plunge on to the roof of a brand-new Volvo 176 have been deliberate, not accidental? Hugo was certainly in a state (Henry's phrase) when he left the house. There was the discovery of the deception, which he had revealed to Henry; there was also something else, to do with the morbid relationship (again Henry's phrase) between himself and that boy, which he had not. Henry guesses that Mrs Lockit may know the answer but he prefers not to ask her since he prefers not to jeopardize the relationship between them. Mrs Lockit is not perfect, far from it; but he does not want anything to come out into the open that might oblige him to dismiss her. For a number of years the two of them have managed 'to rub along together' and though that implies an intermittent abrasiveness, he would not care to make the effort, at his age and in his state of health, of learning to rub along with someone even more prickly. There is also the question of the basement flat. Nowadays one cannot really call one's property one's own. It might be difficult to dislodge Mrs Lockit and the budgie of which Henry has so often heard but which he has never seen, along with all her other possessions, from the basement.

Like baffled detectives in novels and sometimes in real life, Sybil has a compulsion to return to the scene of the crime (or, if the coroner is right, of the accident), just as she so often has a compulsion to return to it in her conversations with Audrey. ('If he told you he'd be staying two nights with Henry, why on earth did he go to the Clarendon? And why didn't he tell you or Henry where he would be?') Often, lying awake on these summer dawns, she sees him, in her imagination, clutching at that awning, hears the awning ripping. She even closes her eyes, her body rigid on her bed, as his body first somersaults and then hurtles down that sheer concrete face.

She goes over and over her automatic writing in search of the key; and eventually she also rings up Henry, convinced that he has a duplicate to that key secreted somewhere about his person. 'Oh, Henry, I have to be in Brighton, over at Roedean, on Tuesday. Examining. I wondered if I could pop in and see you some time in the afternoon.' She is lying, she is not examining at Roedean, though she has done so in the past; and Henry, wily as he is, knows from her slightly breathless tone that she is lying. But though he thinks of her, as he thinks of most women, as 'really rather tiresome', he wants to see her for precisely the same reason that she wants to see him; she must know something about Hugo which he does not know. So he says, 'Yes, of course, my dear. I have a little sherry party that evening. My annual one, for my good neighbours. A rather boring occasion, I'm afraid. But if you'd like to come along, well, I'd love to see you.'

Sybil arrives in Brighton early in the afternoon and she walks down from the station, past grimy little shops selling souvenirs, dusty paperbacks and secondhand clothes, to the Front. She is glad of the keen, blustery wind, since it alleviates the vague nausea from which she has been suffering ever since she settled down to *The Times* crossword in a corner of an empty first-class carriage. There is a luxurious coach with wrap-around windows, net curtains and a German number plate in the courtyard outside the hotel, together with some half-dozen cars. A bored youth in uniform, his hands clasped behind his back, is eyeing a girl who is shaking a tablecloth out of a first-floor window of the house next to the hotel. Either he does not notice Sybil at all or, noticing her, has no interest in her. She stares up at the concrete face, its balconies symmetrically cantilevered, some with their awnings up and others with them down. Over the railings of one of the balconies a bathing-towel, striped green, brown and orange, flaps in the wind. Perhaps, like Hugo, it will suddenly fall; but it will fall far more slowly.

Sybil then examines the paving of the courtyard, as though, after all these months, she expects to see some stain on its surface or even a shadow, like that which, tourists on a trip to Japan, she and Hugo once examined in Hiroshima, each thinking mournfully, though neither said it, 'That's all that's left of someone once as substantial as ourselves.' She wants to go up to the bored youth, who has now lit a cigarette and is surreptitiously smoking it, holding it cupped in a hand (is it possible that in an age as egalitarian as this he is forbidden to smoke on duty?) and to ask him, 'Can you tell me which was the balcony from which my brother fell and where precisely he landed on a Volvo 176, before bouncing off it to the concrete?' But it is unlikely that the boy would be able to enlighten her. She walks on, having learned nothing and, more surprisingly, having felt nothing. On those early mornings when she has lain awake, awaiting the moment when her digital alarm clock begins to buzz, she has always felt so much.

She continues to walk along the front, past serried deck-chairs on which old people lie out, their faces upturned to the sun, past ice-cream stalls and hamburger stalls, with their queues of half-naked trippers, past a pub in which two red-faced Irishmen are having a noisy quarrel. Then she stops and gazes out over the beach. Not many people are swimming today, the wind is far too cold. There is a woman standing, barefoot and motionless in a flimsy cotton frock, a lead about her neck, where the sea meets the shingle. The water laps at her ankles. She puts a hand to her mouth – that is all that Sybil sees – and then a small white dog, separated by a groin, stops rooting in a mound of rubbish left by some picnickers, pricks up its ears and eventually bounds off to join her. Sybil is puzzled. It is as though some kind of extrasensory perception existed between mistress and animal.

She walks on. As children, she and Hugo would wander this beach looking for treasure (as they called it). There would be broken combs, tin spoons, tattered magazines, torn bathing-shoes, cheap toys, halfpennies and pennies. Once, under a deckchair, its seat ripped and sagging, Hugo had glimpsed a set of false-teeth. He wrapped them in his hand-kerchief and together they sought out the lifeguard, immensely excited. But the muscular, middle-aged man, the skin of his bare torso, legs and face the colour and texture of a ginger-nut, received the offering with an indifference bordering on contempt. 'OK,' he said, no more. Who would forget a set of false-teeth? Years later, one or other would refer to that childhood mystery.

125

Henry opens the door. Although it is August, he is wearing a thick double-breasted worsted suit, a stiff collar and an old Wykehamist tie which he has tugged into a small and hard knot. 'Last but not least,' he says, revealing butter-coloured teeth, real, not false. 'I thought I heard the bell. My invaluable Mrs Lockit is getting some ice for someone. Ice with sherry! Well, there's no accounting for taste.' Henry thinks that Sybil is looking unusually pale; Sybil thinks that he is looking unusually flushed.

'Whom don't you know?'

'Everyone.'

Henry looks desperately around the room. 'I think you'll like Mrs Hanrahan. Her daughter is at Roedean.'

Sybil hopes that Henry will not tell this woman, whose tight, flowered dress makes her look like an excrescence of the sofa on which she is sitting by herself, that she has been examining at the school. Maliciously, knowing that Sybil has been lying, he does so; but the woman laughs and says, 'Oh, Sir Henry, you're years out of date. Irene is now in Mombasa.' 'Of course, of course,' Henry says, as though this fact had momentarily slipped his memory.

Mrs Lockit eventually arrives with a tray. There is nothing on it except a number of small tumblers, bought from Woolworth's, half-full of sweet sherry. Sybil takes one, aware that this dark, baleful woman, whom she has never liked, is staring down at her with a peculiar, squinting intensity. 'And how are you keeping, madam?' Mrs Lockit asks. She never calls people sir or madam except at these parties.

'Oh, fine, thank you, fine.' Sybil sips at her glass. Mrs Lockit remains there, almost as though she expected Sybil to drain her glass and then replace it on the tray. 'And you?'

'Mustn't complain,' Mrs Lockit says and at last moves on.

'Strange woman,' Mrs Hanrahan murmurs.

Eventually Major Hanrahan arrives, to remind his wife that they will have to get going if they're not to be late for the theatre. 'Pinter,' he says. 'God knows what I'll make of

126

IS

it. My stomach always chooses to rumble in one of those pauses.' His wife tells him, 'That's because you're thinking of your dinner, instead of the play.'

Sybil is now alone. Dreadful people, she thinks, as she always tends to do when not with her cronies. She drains what is left of the sherry, places the glass on top of a pile of ancient copies of *Blackwood's Magazine,* and wanders out of the room, down the corridor and out into the garden. Mrs Lockit, shaking some potato crisps out of a packet into a bowl in the kitchen, watches her pass and, for a brief moment, seeing something of Hugo in those fine, aristocratic features, that tilt of the head and that upright carriage, she feels a sudden pang of remorse. But that soon passes. After all, he got what was coming to him, he had only himself to blame.

Though Henry, panama hat on head, often potters around in it, the garden is dishevelled. The grass between the beds is speckled white with daisies and the beds themselves are thick with weeds between the lanky stems of roses seldom pruned. At the far end, grass forcing itself up between the flagstones, there is a paved area, under a tattered weeping willow. The table and four chairs set out on it look as if they were made of wrought-iron painted white; but in fact they are made of plastic. An elegant woman of about forty, her hair prematurely grey, is seated alone on one of the chairs, hands folded in her lap, while she gazes out before her. She does not seem either to hear or to see Sybil approaching.

'May I join you? It's so hot and crowded in there.'

'Please.'

Sybil is sure that she has met this woman somewhere before. A former colleague? A former pupil? Or can she have been at one of Henry's parties in the past? Except that her nose is too wide and short, almost coarse in its modelling, she is extraordinarily beautiful. She is also dressed with an elegance which, of all the women guests, only Sybil herself can rival.

Sybil sits facing the woman. The woman looks, not at

127

her, but out at the garden, as she was doing when Sybil approached. But there is no constraint between them.

Eventually Sybil says, 'Have you known Henry long?'

'Henry? I hardly know him at all. But I've lived in the other half of this house in Codrington Villas, for, oh, five or six years. . . . Semi-detached acquaintances, that would describe us. We call this the Village, you know.' Sybil knew this and had always thought it a silly affectation. 'We each give a Village party, at least once a year. This is Henry's.'

'I expect that at the other Village parties one can get something other than cheap sherry to drink,' Sybil says maliciously.

'Usually. Yes.'

'I feel sure we've met each other somewhere.'

'Have we? People often think they've met actors some-where. What that means is that they've met them on the stage or in cinemas or on their television screens.'

'You're an actress?'

The woman nods. 'Was. That's more accurate. And you?'

'I teach. I'm headmistress of a school.'

'You don't look like a headmistress.'

'Don't I?'

The woman laughs. 'Far too elegant.'

'Anyway you look like an actress. I should have guessed. You're much the most elegant woman here.'

'Thank you.' The woman inclines her head, with the dismissive easiness of someone used to being complimented.

Sybil looks closely at her. Then she says 'You're Lavinia Trent, of course.'

'Why of course?'

'Well, you're so famous.' The woman is silent, as though musing on that. 'My brother reviewed your Hedda Gabler in the *TLS*. He said it was the finest he had ever seen. You may remember.'

The woman shakes her head. 'It's strange. I seem to remember only my bad reviews. Anyway, it was kind of your brother. Is he here today?'

'No. He's dead.'

The woman looks down at the ring, a diamond set in sapphires, on her wedding finger, above a band of platinum. She turns it one way, then the other.

Sybil says, 'He died here in Brighton. An accident. Seven months ago.'

'How strange. My son died here in Brighton seven months ago. Exactly seven months.' She looks up into the willow tree, its branches trembling around them. In a low voice ('I'm burning your child,' Sybil can hear her say on the stage of the Old Vic), she murmurs, 'Oh that we could have some two hours converse with the dead.'

Sybil feels first a shock of amazement and then one of pleasure. She has repeatedly said that line to herself since Hugo's going. 'Yes, if only.'

'I've tried', Lavinia says. 'How I've tried. But . . .' She shrugs.

'I've tried too. I go on trying.'

The woman turns the ring, one way, then the other, as though it held some magic. 'How do you try?' she asks. 'Tell me.'

'Oh, you'll only laugh. People always do. But I – I do this automatic writing. Sometimes I think – sometimes I believe . . . But there's nothing, oh, nothing conclusive.'

The woman nods.

'And you?' Sybil asks.

The woman laughs. 'Well, last week, a friend, a young actor, took me to this man, a friend of his, who does this – this psychometry.' The woman looks at Sybil, as though she expects her not to know what psychometry means. Sybil nods. The woman goes on; she tells the story.

The young actor, who played Tesman to her Hedda, told her about this man, a perfectly ordinary little man, who worked behind a counter at Barker's during the day and who, in the evenings, would give sittings to people. He lived with his wife, whom Lavinia never saw, and three children, whom she did not see either but whom she heard, rampaging

in a room above them, in a semi-detached house in Putney.
He had a little, wispy beard, which looked as if it had been
stuck on to his chin, large hands and feet, and narrow,
sloping shoulders. He spoke with such softness, in a monoto-
nous, nasal voice, that it was often difficult, what with the
noise overhead, to catch everything that he was saying. She
gave him a scarf which had been her last present to her son
and he had placed it over his bony knees and had then run
his hands over it, with a slow, smoothing gesture. 'I see a
theatre,' he said after a while, in a hesitant, puzzled voice,
and she had not replied, 'Well, yes, I'm an actress' or even
nodded, because she and the young actor had agreed that
in no way would either of them betray anything. But she
was not greatly impressed. No doubt, like Sybil now, he had
recognized her and therefore had not been taken in by her
assumed name. 'A theatre. The curtain is rising. An actress.
And a famous writer.' That had given her a jolt, because in
the past, well, there had been this famous writer and eventually she had married him, though the marriage had not
lasted. 'Lovers.' The hands continued to stroke the scarf,
with those long, slow, smoothing gestures and she found
herself now looking not at him but at them. He began to
speak of constant quarrels between the actress and the writer
– and that too had amazed her, because she and that man,
whom eventually she had married, had quarrelled incessantly. The actress was ill, dangerously ill, and while she
was in – what? a hospital? a sanatorium? – the writer, who
had written a play for her, gave the leading role in it to
another, younger actress and that actress became his
mistress. Now Lavinia was bewildered, because she was as
strong as a horse, she had never really been ill in her life,
certainly not dangerously ill, and though her former
husband had written some plays, some pretty dreadful plays
for her, he had never, during their life together, given the
leading role in any of them to a rival. The man began to
falter, as though he sensed that, having at first won her over
to belief, he had now lost her. He began to fold the scarf,

130

picking up either tasselled end in the palms of his hands and flipping them over and then making another, similar fold and another. He held it out to her. 'I'm afraid I can't do any more. I'm tired.' He looked at his watch and gave a smile, 'And my wife and kids will be wanting their supper.' The young actor who had brought her had already told her that the charge was ten pounds and she had the money ready, not in her bag, but in an envelope in the pocket of her jacket. She drew it out and leaned forward. The man took it from her, with no word of thanks and placed it on an occasional table beside him. Then he gave her a wan smile. 'I don't know if that was any good,' he said and, not wanting to disappoint him, though she herself, having hoped to hear something of her son, was disappointed, she replied, 'Well, part of it was right. A major part of it,' she added, though that was not strictly true.

'Oh, I'm glad' – and clearly he was.

She and the young actor walked in silence down the path to the gate and the young actor opened the gate for her, with a mock bow, and they emerged on to the dim, suburban street. 'Strange,' the actor said, taking her by the arm in that casual intimacy which, among stage people, has so little meaning. 'Strange?' she echoed. 'That scarf might have been mine,' he said. She asked him what he meant. Then he explained that, at that moment, he was writing his first play and the play was about d'Annunzio and Duse. 'Everything he said was not about you and Keith – ' Keith was her former husband ' – but about d'Annunzio and Duse. They were lovers, she had tuberculosis, he wrote a part for her in *Jorio's Daughter* – the part of a lifetime, and then he gave it to someone else, someone younger, whom he seduced.'

The women now look at each other. 'Then he got something,' Sybil says.

'Yes, he got something. But that's what is so infuriating. People get something, all the time they keep getting something. But the something is not what one wants. It's all so incalculable and uncontrollable.'

131

'ESP,' Sybil says. 'He got it out of the mind of your friend, not from the scarf.'

Lavinia nods. 'Precisely.'

Sybil says on an impulse, 'Shall I take you to Mrs Roberts?'

'Who is she?'

Sybil is amazed that someone should never have heard of this famous medium. She explains.

Lavinia says, 'Why not? It's worth a try. I'm prepared to try anything – in the state in which I find myself. Shall I give you my address?'

Sybil gets an address book out of her bag and Lavinia opens her own bag and takes out of it what looks like a miniature book of tickets.

She tears out one of the tickets and sticks it into the address book which Sybil has opened for her. That done, she smiles at Sybil. 'I'm glad I met you. Otherwise, it would have been an even more boring party than usual.' Sybil nods. 'I'm glad I met you. My brother was a great friend of Henry's. I could never understand it.'

'Perhaps Henry has qualities invisible to us.'

'Perhaps. Or my brother may have liked him for his absence of qualities. He sometimes did that with people.'

'So did my son.' Lavinia looks at the Cartier watch, beautiful but impractical with its absence of numerals, which she wears on a gold filigree bracelet. 'Gracious! Henry hates one to overstay one's welcome. He always puts six to seven-thirty on his invitations and after seven-thirty Lucy begins to collect the glasses.'

'Lucy?'

'Mrs Lockit. It's a little Village joke. I think I started it.' She gets to her feet. 'Then you'll be in touch?'

'Yes. As soon as I've got on to Mrs Roberts. She's always busy.'

'And makes a lot of money.'

Sybil nods. 'But I don't think money is important to her.'

'I always envy people for whom money's not important. It must make life so much easier for them.'

They laugh. Then Lavinia wanders off, her bag under her arm. Sybil sits on, glad of their conversation and of the late evening sunlight filtering down through the willow tree on to the shoddy table before her.

Eventually, Henry comes out. 'Thank God,' he says. 'The last of them have gone. Those vulgar people next door – not Lavinia Trent, the ones on the other side – stuck it out to the last. It's always the moot guests who are the first to come and the last to go. Have you noticed that?' He takes the chair in which Lavinia has been sitting, stretching his legs out to show woollen socks rumpled about his thin, blue-veined ankles, and plunging his hands deep into his trouser pockets. 'The amount people drink! Each year they seem to get through more and more. I was afraid we'd run out. I was determined not to produce any of my Dos Palmas for a party. In fact, I had to restrain Mrs L from opening a bottle.'

Sybil says, 'I liked Lavinia Trent.'

'Yes. Poor woman.' Henry stoops, retrieves a cigarette-end from under the table and, at first at a loss how to dispose of it, eventually puts it in a pocket. 'Mind you, she never seemed to show any particular interest in that good-for-nothing son of hers until he was dead. Now, of course, she's gone into retirement. Which is sad. Fine actress.'

'Probably our best.'

'Oh, do you think so? I wouldn't have said that. Though I don't go to the theatre all that much nowadays. Kitchen sink.' Sybil restrains herself from telling him that the kitchen sink was dismantled years ago. He fiddles with the ravelled end of his old Wykehamist tie. 'All right for you if we have a bite at about eight? That'll give the invaluable Mrs Lockit time to clear up.'

'Oh, I'm not hungry,' Sybil lies. During the party she has eaten two potato crisps and a salted peanut. She opens her bag, 'There was something I wanted to show you.'

133

'Yes?' Henry sounds wary.

'You know I do this automatic writing. Have done for years.'

Henry nods. 'Hugo told me you had had some remarkable results. But then Hugo was always so . . .' He is about to say 'gullible' but restrains himself in time.

Sybil takes out a sheet of paper, covered in her writing.

On the Tuesday of the previous week, Audrey drove over to visit her, with one of the dogs beside her on the front seat of the battered stationwagon and the other dog and the two girls behind. The school is deserted, it now being the summer holidays, and so Sybil, equally indifferent to animals and small children, at once said to Audrey, 'I expect the girls would like to play out of doors with the dogs.' Audrey nodded reluctantly, feeling as she always did on these occasions, like a hospital visitor to a long-standing patient, whose whims must be gratified. Sybil's malady was her obsession with the memory of Hugo; and just as she wished to talk incessantly about his death, so Audrey kept trying to divert her to some subject less morbid and inward-turning. Physically, the children might be out in the garden; but as Audrey prattled on and on about them – Angela seemed to be developing a jealousy of Betsy, Betsy was showing remarkable promise as a rider – Sybil grew more and more irritated by their constant intrusion. Audrey was determined to forget Hugo. Sybil was no less determined to remember him.

They had a picnic luncheon out under a chestnut tree, with the dogs, a dachshund and the dishevelled collie, perpetually pawing at them and jumping up for scraps. Angela tore the fat off her cold beef in her fingers and dropped it to the ground. Betsy, having eaten two spoonfuls of the lemon mousse prepared by Sybil, complained 'Oh, it's sour' and put her plate between her legs, to be demolished by the dachshund. Sybil all but reproved them, as she would have reproved her pupils in similar circumstances; but she had learned by now that Audrey, so lethargically tolerant in every other respect, could become ferocious if she felt that either her brats or her beasts (as Sybil thought of them) were under attack.

'It was so kind of you to drive over on such a hot day,' Sybil said, as they all began to pile into the stationwagon.

'It was so kind of you to prepare us that lovely meal. You must remember to let me have the recipe for the mousse.' Audrey was already thinking of the milking. She had once again forgotten to ask one of the two boys from the neighbouring farm to come by to do it for her.

'How brave you are, Audrey!' What Sybil really meant was that she thought Audrey callous to have forgotten Hugo so quickly.

Audrey, who knew that she meant this, did not answer.

'Thank you, Aunt Sybil,' Angela called out from behind the collie. She had suddenly remembered that her mother had told her and her sister that they must be sure to thank their aunt. Betsy echoed, 'Thank you, Aunt Sybil.' Already more socially adroit, though younger, than her sister, she added, 'That was a super mousse.'

'Well, the dogs seemed to like it.'

The car had already begun to move forward. Sybil, remorseful, hoped that they had not heard her.

She walked back into the deserted school building and, instead of going upstairs to her flat, wandered from classroom to classroom. The windows were all shut, imprisoning not merely the oppressive heat of the day but a host of flies, buzzing in angry frustration against their panes. In one classroom, she found a turd deposited on the podium, just below the blackboard. The children must have come in here, bringing the dogs with them. Sybil stared at it, then decided to leave it to the caretaker.

She wandered on, like a patient unable to sit still because of a constantly gnawing, unappeasable ache. Oh, that it were possible to hold but two hours converse with the dead, oh, that it were . . . The words revolved within her, making her feel giddy and nauseated until, in another classroom, she sank on to a cramped seat before a desk too low for her. She stared out of the window beside her at the redbrick building, little more than a shed, that housed the science laboratory. Her head throbbed, her throat felt dry, from the effort of talking all day about things totally without any interest to her. On the desk there were some sheets of foolscap paper and a blunt pencil, its end gnawed. She picked up the pencil and drew a circle on the top piece of paper, a triangle within the circle, a circle within the triangle. The inner circle swelled as she looked at it, an iridescent bubble. She drew a deep breath. She began to write, her eyes half-closed.

It is what she wrote, in that sealed classroom, the light green enough and the air humid enough to make her feel imprisoned under water, that she now holds out to Henry.

Henry is reluctant to take the sheet, because he feels it to be as much an intimate part of this woman whom he does not like as some excretion from her body. But he overcomes his distaste. He looks down through his thick, gold-rimmed spectacles, he reads.

The travellers journey. The traveller's journey? In a land of sand and ruin. Infinity in the palm of your hand. Eternity in an hour. Join the great majority. Mogadon...

As that last word halts him, clanging down in the tranquil, evening garden (*'I suppose you couldn't spare me some sleeping pills?'*), Sybil, who has been leaning forward, her eyes watching his eyes moving back and forth across the page, says, 'That first bit obviously refers to Madge and her mother. Madge is one of my teachers, her mother has been desperately ill for weeks. Now she has taken her to North Africa for her convalescence. Hell at this time of year but that's where the old girl wished to go, because as a child she lived there – her father was a businessman in Casablanca. The old girl will die out there, that passage convinces me. "The traveller's journey is done." "Joined the great majority" – Petronius's *Abiit plures.* I expect it'll happen in Mogador. That's one of their stops.'

Mogador! In the hurried, erratic scrawl, so unlike her usual neat, well-formed writing, the word had appeared to him as 'Mogadon'. Strange. Disturbing. But in a world in which there are a finite number of happenings and a finite number of words, coincidences are inevitable – as he often told Hugo, excited by some such conjunction, in the past. He decides to say nothing, merely nodding his head before he goes on reading.

. . . Like Lucifer. Son of the mourning. Tired of his dark dominion. So shorten I the stature of my soul. Betrayed by what is false within. As fly to wanton. Tired of his dark. Dominion? But death hath no. Henry. Ask. Love casteth in.

The writing ends with a line serpenting away, ever fainter, from that last 'n'. Henry looks over at Sybil, who is still crouched forward in her chair, her eyes, relentlessly burning, fixed on his eyes.

'Well. . . .' he says on a long exhalation. He realizes that, while he was reading the final words, he must have been holding his breath.

Sybil begins to explain the text as though to some dim-witted pupil. She has forgotten that Henry, unlike Audrey, is highly educated. '"Like Lucifer". That, of course, is from Shakespeare's *King Henry VIII.* "And when he falls, he falls like Lucifer, Never to hope again." Which links up with the Biblical description of Lucifer as "The son of the morning" – except that here "morning" has become "mourning" with a U. "So shorten I the stature of my soul" – that, of course, is Meredith's "And if I drink oblivion of a day, So shorten I the stature of my soul." Again Meredith – "Betrayed by what is false within." Then a *Lear* reference, which comes out merely as "As fly to wanton." "Tired of his dark" – a return to the Lucifer image, again Meredith. Of course the full quotation is "Tired of his dark dominion", which is taken up by that "But death hath no", the Biblical "Death hath no more dominion over him". Then your name, followed by "Ask". And finally "Love Casteth in", which is a peculiar variant of "Love casteth out fear." '

Henry listens with growing impatience and annoyance. Because she teaches English in a snob Home Counties girls' school, this beautiful, self-contained, demanding woman thinks that she can patronize him. When she has finished, he tweaks at one of the socks wrinkled about his ankles, tilts his head to peer, eyes screwed up, into the branches of the trees above them, and then gives her a small smile. 'Thank you for that, er, exposition. Most enlightening. If this is a message from Hugo, then clearly the dear fellow must still retain his well-stocked mind – or else have access to some celestial dictionary of quotations.' He speaks so blandly, now leaning forward in his chair, his hands clasped together, that at first Sybil does not realize that he is mocking her. 'But I wonder, my dear, if all this isn't merely a case of your subconscious mind working, well, overtime. After all, if Hugo had a well-stocked mind, then so indeed have you. And the sort of scraps that he would have chosen from Meredith and so forth are precisely the sort of scraps that you might choose too. Right?'

Audrey is stupid and ill educated, Henry is clever and well educated; but Sybil realizes that both of them have reached the same conclusion. In their view, she is suffering from self-delusion. She is certain that she is not but how, how, how can she prove it? If the scripts contained something that could not possibly be known to her, or if other people's scripts contained something that could not possibly be known to them and yet was known to her, or if there were some kind of link, a cross correspondence, impregnable against any accusation of conscious or unconscious collusion, between one script and another . . . Suddenly, she looks as vulnerable and uncertain as one of her own pupils under her interrogation. She holds out her hands to him, in submissive appeal, 'Yes, I know, I know. I can prove nothing. All this–'

she has taken the sheet of paper from him '—may just be some kind of gaseous exhalation from that subconscious which, in each of us, bubbles away constantly, waking or sleeping. I know, I know. But I also have this feeling . . .' She folds the sheet of paper and puts it away in her bag. Then, in a voice so quiet that it is all but inaudible to Henry, who is getting hard of hearing, she says, 'Henry, Henry, tell me. Is there anything you know about Hugo's death which you've never revealed?'

Henry shakes his head. 'I don't think so, my dear.' (Mogador. Mogadon. *'I suppose you couldn't spare me some sleeping pills?'*) 'No, I don't think so. It was odd, certainly, that he left here, telling me that he was going back home, and then took that room at the Clarendon. But there could have been all kinds of reasons for that. He may suddenly have felt tired. Or ill. Illness – a bad turn – might explain that, er, unwonted and slightly alarming consumption of a variety of spirits. Or he may have had some business of which he did not wish me to know. Or he may have intended all along to stay that night in Brighton but have become bored with me. If it was that last eventuality, I'd not be surprised – I often become bored with myself. At all events, we'll now never know.'

'I think we might. You see, I do believe – yes, I do believe – in life after death. I believe that if we want it enough and if they want it enough, then the living and the dead can somehow have converse with each other.'

Henry shrugs and gives a faint smile. All at once he feels compassion for her, at once so invulnerably sophisticated and so vulnerably superstitious, 'Oh, Sybil,' he says, half in this new compassion and half in the old mockery.

Sybil does not care to be simultaneously pitied and mocked. 'Well, I can see you think me a self-deceiving idiot.'

'Not at all. I only wish I could share your faith.' He spreads his hands. 'ESP, yes. Or, rather, perhaps.' He makes that qualification because, suddenly, he has had a vision of Hugo, white-faced and implacable, holding out the dog whistle on the palm of a trembling hand. 'But the idea that the dead can speak to us . . .' He shakes his head sadly.

'Those boys,' Sybil says.

Henry feels panic. Surely she can have no inkling of all that sordid business. 'What about those boys?'

'Are you going on with the sittings?'

'Dear me, no. Without Hugo, I lost heart for all that. And in any case, they were getting more and more reluctant to continue. A scientific researcher has the motivation to reproduce the same experiment over and over. But what motivation . . . ?'

'Other than money,' Sybil puts in quietly.

'Well, yes, Hugo gave them pocket-money. And very useful too, I should guess. But still and all.' He sighs.

As though she had overheard this mention of her nephews, even though the tree under which Sybil and Henry are seated is too far from the house for her to have done so, Mrs Lockit suddenly appears at the garden door. 'I'll be ready for you in five minutes,' she calls. 'Tomato soup, baked beans on toast, peaches. All right for you?' She reels off this menu, every item from a tin, with the relish of a sadist prescribing a course of punishment.

'Lovely, Mrs L,' Henry calls back, without irony.

Mrs Roberts is staying in the Knightsbridge house of her most fervent and frequent client, Lady Telzer. All those who visit her there are at once struck by the contrast between the vastness of the American woman and the tininess of the sitting room, once two even tinier rooms, in which she receives them. It is as though some fleshy, exotic plant were about to burst the pot in which it has been confined for far too long.

In the thirties, there was a terrible scandal when Lady Telzer, married to an ageing politician, deserted both him and their three children, all under ten, to live in Rome with a woman poet of doubtful accomplishment and even more doubtful reputation. The politician, a pompous and tricky womanizer, had never been liked; and so, in an attempt to excuse conduct inexcusable by the standards of the period, people told each other that the reason for the desertion was that he had infected his wife with syphilis. The true reason was more simple and less squalid: Lady Telzer had become bored with domesticity and had fallen in love for the first time in her life.

Soon, the woman poet died; and Lady Telzer then devoted the next forty or so years to attempts to get in touch with her often recalcitrant spirit. To this end, Mrs Roberts and her French communicator, Estelle, allegedly an aristocratic seventeen-year-old girl guillotined during the Reign of Terror, had proved particularly helpful.

Lady Telzer, who is now so shrivelled that she seems to drift through her little house like a dead leaf, answers the bell. She is wearing an old-fashioned deaf-aid, with a wire which trails down to what looks like a small transistor radio worn on her right breast. She has met Sybil several times but she never recognizes her, even though Sybil is not someone whom people usually forget.

'Hello, Lady Telzer,' Sybil greets her, thinking how, despite all her money, much of it inherited from the poet, the old woman had let the house get into a dreadful state of disrepair and mess. 'You don't remember me,' she goes on, though she has difficulty in believing it. 'Sybil Crawfurd.'

'Oh, yes! The wife of Hugo Crawfurd. How sad that was!'

'No, not the wife, the sister.'

'The sister, the sister!' Lady Telzer repeats insistently, as though to someone invisible beside her.

'May I introduce my friend Lavinia Trent? Miss Trent has a sitting with Mrs Roberts.'

The old woman, who until now has looked so haggard and dispirited, brightens as she glances at Lavinia. 'Lavinia Trent! Oh, you've given me so much pleasure over the years!'

Lavinia laughs. 'Let's not calculate how many years!' Like

most actresses, she constantly jokes about her age, since otherwise it would frighten and depress her.

The old woman opens the door into the sitting room and says, 'Clare, Clare, your sitter.'

'Thank you.' The voice is deep and breathy. Then Mrs Roberts appears, her lips purple and her hands and ankles swollen from the heart condition which has made her doctor repeatedly tell her that she must both lose weight and cease to subject herself to the strain of seance after seance. But she cannot obey him in either of these matters. In a curious way the seances and the overeating are compulsions inextricably linked. After she has come out of a trance, she must at once devour a bar of chocolate, several sweet biscuits or a thick slice of toast soaked in melted butter and spread thick with jam. She talks of this phenomenon with the same nervous jocularity with which Lavinia talks of her age. 'It takes it out of one and one has to put it back,' is something she often says, in that unattractive Brooklyn accent of hers, followed by a deep chuckle, which causes her chins to wobble above a three-strand necklace of real pearls, the gift of Lady Telzer.

She is a simple, kindly, snobbish woman – probably Jewish, Sybil has always thought – who, when she says, with transparent self-satisfaction, 'Yes, I think on balance I have an interesting crowd of regulars,' means by 'interesting' that they are famous or well-born. She does not really care about money, though her husband, a dentist now dead, certainly did. She would not mind if someone as well-known as Lavinia never paid her. It is enough for her to be able to open *Time Magazine* or *Newsweek*, see a photograph and say, not even to someone else but merely to herself, 'Oh, I gave her a sitting when last in Britain.'

'I'll sit over here,' she says, when the introductions and the small-talk are over. 'I like the light behind me. You sit there, Sybil dear–' she points '–and you there, Miss Trent. I don't know how this is going to work out, I just don't know. Estelle has been a naughty girl lately – mischievous, impatient, sassy. From time to time she goes through a bad time and then she comes out of it.'

Lavinia suddenly feels depressed, as one does when one visits a doctor about some mysterious symptom and, as he hovers, clears his throat and pulls his prescription pad towards him, one suddenly realizes that he is totally at a loss for a diagnosis or cure and one's money has been wasted. The rotund medium, dressed all in black with her dark, greasy skin, suggests a huge, overripe olive. Many rings bite deep into her swollen fingers and she has a small tic at one corner of her purple lips.

'Now,' she says. 'Let's see. You want to get into touch with a loved one.'

Lavinia nods. A loved one? Of all Stephen's accusations the most hysterical and the most frequent was 'You don't love me! You've never loved me! You don't know what love means!' But to someone like Mrs Roberts all the dead must be loved ones.

'Her son,' Sybil puts in. Lavinia wishes she had not done so. It makes trickery so much easier.

Mrs Roberts nods. 'Might one know his name?'

'Stephen,' Lavinia answers, feeling a sudden, terrible anguish at having to say it.

'Stephen.' Mrs Roberts seems to ruminate on the name with a faint distaste. Then she turns her whole cumbrous body round in her chair towards Lavinia, 'You've been to a seance before, of course?' Lavinia shakes her head. 'Well, all I want you to do at present is merely to relax. Then, if Estelle can get through to Stephen, you can put your questions. I don't have to tell Sybil all this. She's had so many sittings with me, both alone and with her brother.' She smiles, 'It may be a good day, it may be a bad one.'

Lavinia knows precisely what she means. Ill, tired or distracted, she has often felt a mysterious charge surging through her as she has emerged on to the stage. Or the opposite: fit, buoyant and concentrated, she has found herself functioning on a wattage so low that her performance has constantly flickered on the verge of extinction. It comes to her that her profession and Mrs Roberts's have much in common.

Mrs Roberts gently taps with the fingertips of her swollen right hand on the pie-crust edge of the small, circular Victorian table beside her. The tapping becomes louder, drums. She closes her eyes, her head pressing into the back of the winged armchair with the disconcerting effect of making it seem as if all her features had been pushed forward and together. She begins to breathe fast, with shallow gulps. Hyperventilation, Lavinia remembers from something read somewhere. The hand on the table now moves with the frenzied agility of some maestro of the keyboard, thumb and little finger alternately punishing the table-top. The eyes open, with a baleful, squinting expression in them. The jaw falls, saliva dribbles over the lower purple lip and hangs in a string to the wobbling chin. Lavinia feels repelled. She has always had an irrational horror of epileptic fits and this seems to be so like one. Sybil looks across at her and her gaze is reassuring.

'Estelle. Are you there, dear?' In her breathy, contralto voice Mrs Roberts might be calling to some naughty grandchild of hers, who had hidden herself in the darkness of an attic or the depth of a shrubbery. 'Estelle!'

Then in a totally different voice, high-pitched and clear, as of a young American repertory actress playing a French maid in some college production, there comes the answer, 'Oui, tante Clare! Me voici! 'Ere I am!'

'Good, Estelle. That's fine.'

There follow two or three minutes in which Mrs Roberts and Estelle carry on a trivial conversation. Then Mrs Roberts asks Estelle if she can fetch Stephen. Estelle giggles and says that he bores her, she's tired, she can't be bothered. In a heavy, stubborn voice, Mrs Roberts tells her, 'Now, Estelle, I don't want any trouble. Do what I tell you.' Finally, after some argument, Estelle agrees.

It is all so preposterous that Lavinia wishes that she could get up, place on the Victorian side table the money she has brought with her in an envelope, and quit the house.

Estelle is piping on and on. Lavinia forces herself to listen.

'Stephen, 'e say that 'is mother must turn 'er face to ze future, not look back to ze past. 'E say, "Remember Lot's wife."' Estelle giggles and Mrs Roberts prompts her, 'Yes, Estelle. Yes, tell him to go on.' Estelle continues. "E say, *Il la faut être sensible* – She must be sensible. She must think of 'er career, must return to ze stage. Zat is what 'e wants for 'er. Most important.'

Mrs Roberts asks, not looking at Lavinia but staring with a squinting, baleful expression straight ahead of her, 'Are there any questions you want to put to him?'

Lavinia can think of nothing. It is all such a farce. Then she says, 'I want to be sure that it *is* really him. Can he – can he give me some sign?'

The trail of saliva suddenly extends from Mrs Roberts's chin to the crisp broderie anglaise around the neck of her blouse. She makes a curious shying movement of the head, like a mettlesome horse surprised by a sudden movement on the other side of a hedge. Her breathing quickens again.

Then Estelle is speaking, "E say, 'e say, does 'is mother remember ze scarf? Cashmere. Brown. She gave it 'im. Present. 'Er last present to 'im.'

Lavinia nods. 'Yes,' she says in a low, bewildered voice. 'Yes.'

Estelle gives a trilling, artificial laugh. 'Now I go! I go to play!'

'Wait a moment, Estelle. Estelle, wait! Sybil wants a word with you too. And I'm sure that Miss Trent has other things to ask Stephen. Estelle! Naughty girl!'

Estelle has gone.

Mrs Roberts shifts in her chair, takes a handkerchief from a pocket and wipes at her chin. She pulls at the hem of her skirt, as though afraid that it might have ridden up, clears her throat, then yawns prodigiously, four times in succession.

145

'How was it?' she asks.

Sybil looks at Lavinia. Lavinia says, 'Yes, something . . . something emerged.'

Mrs Roberts rises and stretches. Sweat stains darken the fabric of the blouse under the plump arms raised above her. Her feet are tiny in their court shoes under swollen ankles. 'I could do with a bite,' she says. She goes to the door and opens it.

'Finished, dear?', Lady Telzer calls down the narrow corridor from the kitchen. 'That was quick. I'll bring in your tray.'

The little old woman, with her curved back and her small, shuffling steps, arrives, carrying a tray on which she has set out a strawberry milk-shake and a slice of chocolate mille-feuille. 'What about you two?' she asks, 'Some coffee? A drink?'

Simultaneously the two women shake their heads. Each would like something to slake a thirst that has become insistent in the heat of this little room but each is reluctant to put this frail, hunchbacked woman to any trouble.

'No?' Lady Telzer goes over to a tarnished silver box and takes from it a cigarillo and a book of matches. She lights the cigarillo, sucking on it greedily, like a wrinkled baby on a teat, and then, agitating a knobbly hand in front of her hooded eyes, waves away the thick, blueish smoke.

'How did it go?' She seats herself on a pouffe, crossing one leg high over the other and leaning forward, the cigarillo held oddly between middle finger and ring finger.

Sybil is clearly not going to answer and so Lavinia, after a hesitation, repeats what she told Mrs Roberts, 'Yes, something . . . something emerged.' She is still bewildered.

'Clare has such a gift,' the old woman says, looking over with a hungry devotion at the vast American, who is now totally absorbed in alternately gobbling the cake and gulping from the milk-shake on the tray over her lap. 'But things don't come through at once. One has to be patient. Our successes were so few in the beginning, I became

146

discouraged. But now my friend talks to me as easily as I'm talking to you now. Advises me. I'd do nothing important without her. She was the one with all the brains, you see. She made all the decisions for us. She even dictated some poems. They've been published, you know. I must show them to you some time.'

Quietly persistent, Mrs Roberts is scraping chocolate filling off the plate. Then she raises the seemingly empty glass to her lips, tilts back her head and lets the last drops trickle down into her open mouth. It is the action not of an adult but of a child; and she is like a child ('Wipe your mouth, dear') when she pulls a handkerchief out of her pocket and runs it over her lips. She sighs gratefully to Lady Telzel. 'Oh, I *was* glad of that.'

'Another slice?'

'I'd love to say yes but I really must say no. My figure!'

'Some people are born to be thin and others are born to be –' Lady Telzel hesitates '– well covered. It's silly to try to go against nature.'

Suddenly Lavinia leans forward, 'Mrs Roberts – may I ask you a personal question?'

'Of course, dear.' She smiles. 'But I can't promise to give an answer.'

'Do you believe there's personal survival after death?'

Clearly Mrs Roberts has been often asked this question, since it does not embarrass or fluster her. She strokes her large knees, wide open under her voluminous skirt, and puts her head on one side. 'Honestly, I don't know what to say. I have this gift, the dead seem to talk through me. Those who seek my help–' she does not like to use the word 'clients' since that suggests a purely financial transaction '–often go away convinced, even if they have come to me as doubters.' She screws up her eyes, genuinely attempting yet again to reach some solution which has always eluded her. 'Am I possessed? Am I obsessed? What happens when Estelle or one of my other controls takes over? I don't know, dear, I just don't know.'

'But you get such amazing results!' Lady Telzer protests, ascribing this doubt, as she always does, not to the genuine bewilderment felt by the medium but to the modesty which she knows, from years of friendship, to be an essential part of her nature.

Mrs Roberts acknowledges that, with a nod. But she goes on, 'I'm such an ordinary woman, as you can see. My gift only revealed itself when I was over forty. My husband took me to a seance after the death of our second daughter and I went into a trance soon after the medium had done so. I've never *wanted* this gift and yet I must not ignore it – must not waste it.'

Her simplicity is moving. The three women stare down at the carpet, each with her separate thoughts of the person lost to her.

As they walk away from the house, Sybil links her arm in Lavinia's, a gesture of comradeship. Normally, she does not care for physical contacts, least of all with women. '*Was* there anything in all that or were you being polite?'

'Do you remember my telling you about the psychometrist to whom I took Stephen's scarf?'

'Yes.' Sybil at first is hazy. But then the recollection grows more vivid. 'Yes, yes, I do!'

'Well, the scarf *was* the last present that I gave to him. And it was cashmere and it was brown. I didn't tell you that detail, did I?'

'No.' Sybil is thinking, with a disturbing sense of displacement, of a brown cashmere scarf that she herself waved on top of the Downs on the day of Hugo's death.

'So that's – that's something.' Lavinia is all but persuaded that Estelle and Stephen must both still exist in some other dimension; but then she says, 'It's not very easy to believe in Estelle. Is it? I mean, if she's a French aristocrat, it's odd that she should make the howler of imagining that "*Il la faut être sensible*" is the French equivalent of "She must be sensible." If she'd said "*Il la faut être raisonnable*", even in

148

that appalling French accent of hers, it might have been more convincing.'

'Oh, I don't think for one moment that Estelle ever actually existed, any more than Stainton Moses's mawkish 'Little Dicky' or Mrs Leonard's Red Indian Feda. In each case, it's a secondary personality – the result of dissociation. You know, don't you, that Meredith claimed that Harry Richmond's father had achieved sufficient independence to carry on conversations with him?' Lavinia has not known; she has never read a word of Meredith, except his 'Modern Love'. 'And that Dickens claimed the same about Sairey Gamp? But even if Estelle is a subconscious dramatization – as I'm inclined to think her – that is not inconsistent with her being a vehicle for the transmission of paranormal knowledge, any more than the fact that Prince Myshkin or Alyosha is merely a fiction is inconsistent with his telling us something new about the nature of human goodness.'

Lavinia nods, preoccupied. She is not a woman who often reads; and when she does read, it is certainly not Meredith, Dickens or Dostoievsky. She is thinking of the scarf. She has not told Sybil the story of the scarf. She will never tell anyone its story.

FOUR

WAS

The two sisters, Lettice and Lavinia, were perched side by side, their legs bare and brown, on the stile that Frank was always saying that he must mend. Below them the Long Field fell away in the slanting sunlight of evening. At the bottom of it, the tractor, coughing blue smoke, droned back and forth and the heavy sheaves tumbled.

'What name will he have?' In the years to come, his name would be important.

Lavinia stared ahead of her, her eyes heavy with the stubbornness of her grief. 'Well, Stephen, of course. What else?'

Lettice nibbled on the succulent blade of grass that she had snatched from beside her. She felt a terrible compassion for her sister and a no less terrible joy. 'I didn't mean that. I meant – what surname?'

Lavinia turned, as though she were going to strike her. 'Trent. He could hardly be Stephen Mukerjee. Even if he had any right to that name – which he hasn't – it might be something of a burden.'

'I suppose so.' Lettice had hoped that Lavinia would say, 'Perhaps Frank would agree to his having yours.' Stephen Cobbold: it sounded both right and desirable. At boarding school, the girls had had Cash's nametapes sewn into their clothes. Each nametape gave the right of possession.

Lavinia slipped off the stile. 'I know you'll look after him as if he were your own.'

Lettice shielded her eyes, since the sun, slanting lower through a wavering haze of heat, now struck into them if she turned towards her sister. 'Yes,' she said. 'Of course. That goes without saying.' She would look after him as though he were her own because a child of her own was something which, through a surgeon's catastrophic error, she would never have.

As Lavinia, changed now into her city clothes, climbed into the taxi, Stephen, whom she had scooped up in her arms, to hold him tighter and tighter against her chest before once again laying him out on the strange, narrow bed, stumbled out, barefoot and in his nightshirt, between Lettice and Frank. Lavinia saw his hands raised, his mouth opening, preparatory to a scream. Then Frank stooped and lifted him high against his chest.

'The station, please.'

'Yes, madam, the station.'

Gaur Mukerjee had occupied the room next to hers while reading for the bar. He had been to an English public school, where there had been other boys from India; but he had been picked on, he told Lavinia, because, unlike them, he had been useless at games and brilliant at work. It was his use of that word 'brilliant' that had first interested her in him. It suggested an extraordinary degree of self-knowledge, of self-confidence or of vanity.

His family, who were rich landowners, exploited their peasants; but here, in this alien country, alternately snubbed and patronized, it was as one of the exploited that he thought of himself. When their landlady asked him not to leave his washing things in the bathroom he was convinced that it was because she thought that they would somehow contaminate those of the other lodgers; and when, entertaining some of her friends from RADA, Lavinia did not ask him to come in and join them, merely because she thought that he would be bored by their theatrical chatter, he accused her of being ashamed of him.

He would give her extravagant presents and then chide her for not wearing them or using them. He would cook her curries, himself pounding the spices in a mortar with a dogged, defiant expression on his narrow, pale face, and then, when she refused a second helping merely because she was careful about her figure, he would snatch away her plate with an angry, 'It was no good. You don't have to pretend.' He would sew on the button that he found dangling from her overcoat, take her temperature when she complained of a sore throat, and bring an umbrella to Earls Court tube station when it was raining and he knew that she had gone to RADA without one. But he also kicked her violently and publicly, on the leg, when she arrived so late at Covent Garden that they were not admitted until the first act of *Pelléas et Melisande* was over, borrowed money off her which he forgot to return, and told her brutally in the middle of their love-making that she should use a deodorant, she stank. When he made that unfair accusation, it seemed confirmation of her persistent fear that his violent, derisive love-making was merely a way of getting back at all those people who had caused him so much imagined and so much real humiliation in this country which he both admired and loathed.

Leaning on his elbow, naked beside her on the bed in her room – he fastidiously refused ever to use his own bed for their love-making – he lectured her on the hideous scars left on his country by the Raj. India, as he saw it, had been a prelapsarian paradise before the arrival of people who were second-rate, middle-class trash; and now that the trash had been swept away, the attitudes that they had inculcated still hung on. 'I know nothing of all this,' she protested. 'No, of course, you don't. You're just an ignoramus.'

She was uncertain if she loved him; but in the middle of a voice class or movement class, she would suddenly think of that pale, narrow face and that pale, thin body and she would want only to get back to her room, strip off her clothes and draw him down on top of her. But often he would say 'No, no, I'm not in the mood,' or 'Aren't you ashamed of yourself?' or 'Do you never think of anything else?' She had only first given herself to him because, when she had withdrawn, dishevelled and flushed from his embrace on her sofa, he had rasped at her bitterly, 'Well, of course, you don't want a wog to touch you anywhere intimate.' Wog? She had never used the word in the whole of her life. He was an expert in making others guilty; he was also an expert in giving pain. Guilt, pain: she despised herself, as he despised her, for needing them.

His father died; but, though by then he had passed his Bar Finals, he was strangely reluctant to go back to India and so to become one of the exploiters, instead of one of the exploited. If she needed to be hurt and to be made to feel guilt, then he needed to be humiliated and to inflict guilt on others. There were also his political activities, shadowy and sinister to her, of which he would never talk. He would go out to 'attend a meeting' or just 'to see someone', or else he would be visited by people so various that the only thing which they seemed to have in common was their resentment of Lavinia's presence.

'You're just a silly little actress. You'd better keep out of it,' he warned, when once she asked him, 'But, Gaur, what's it all *about*?' She persisted, 'If it concerns you, then of course it concerns me.' But at that he shook his head. 'A false corollary. No.'

He refused ever to wear a sheath and, in those days before the pill, she herself was often careless. When she became pregnant, it was more with amazement than horror. 'Oh, Christ, you would, you *would*!' he shouted at her. 'But what are we going to do?' '*We*? You mean – what are *you* going to do?' But later he was remorseful. He took her out to an expensive restaurant, at which he took pleasure in chiding the waiters for the defects both of their service and of the food, and then to a nightclub, where he insisted on dancing on and on with her, into the early hours, even though she was dropping with fatigue and the strain of wondering about her pregnancy.

Soon after that, he vanished, leaving no word behind him. She had been on a weekend visit to Lettice and Frank in the country, throughout which she had thought of nothing but Gaur. Coming home, she had turned the key in the door of her room and had seen first the duplicate key, which she had given to him, lying out on the carpet, and then the envelope propped up on the toast-rack on the table. She had opened the envelope and inside had found the twenty five-pound notes. Nothing else. The landlady said that he had paid up, packed and left on Saturday evening. He had behaved like a gentleman, she went on, insisting on paying for the week of notice that he had failed to give. No, she had no idea where he had gone. He had said that he would write and give her a forwarding address as soon as he had one.

Some men came to interrogate the landlady and, no doubt tipped off by her or one of the other tenants, they also knocked on Lavinia's door. If they knew that he had been her lover and that she was carrying his child, they did not reveal it. Had she any idea of where he might have gone? Had he ever behaved suspiciously in any manner? Could she tell them anything about his visitors? No, no, no, to each of these questions in turn. 'He was always – kind. Quiet. No trouble.' The two men left.

There were many students at the drama school as gifted as Lavinia, some even more so, but not one of them had her quiet, stubborn persistence. She had little knowledge of what went on within her, but of her exterior – the texture of her skin and hair, the coarseness of her nose in her otherwise delicate face, the effect of this or that gesture or expression – she knew everything. Long before she had thought of the stage as her career, she had scrupulously monitored herself, as though attending to the demands and needs of some delicate, exotic plant. She was soon aware, for example, that her walk, which was similar to Lettice's, suggested, with its roll and energetic swing of arms and shoulders, some countrywoman striding out over ploughed fields, and, a girl of only fourteen, she had then set herself the task of patiently remaking it. In that process of remaking, there was an invisible other self who, as choreographer, stood outside her, watched with narrowed eyes and corrected now the tilt of the head, now the angle of an elbow and now the raising of a heel.

Later, at drama school, she also became aware that her taste in clothes was fallible; and so it was that, with no conscious intention, she set about making friends with the Greek boyfriend of one of the male students. Panos, having won as many prizes at art college as she was eventually to win at drama school, was already, at the age of twenty-three, designing sets and costumes for provincial theatres and even for an opera company. Delicate-boned, quiet and touchy, he immediately recognized in Lavinia an intensity of purpose as ruthless as his own. It suited him to have this beautiful girl, with her triangular face, the thick, yellow hair coming down in a widow's peak to a wide, serene forehead, as his companion to art galleries, parties and shows. He even referred to her, to her face, as his 'cover girl'. He was using her and she in turn was using him to tell her things like 'No, darling, frankly that blouse does nothing for you,' or 'You can't wear shoes like that, they make you look like a tart literally down on her uppers.' There was little affection between them; but their relationship, built on self-interest, was as durable as that between two dancers who, however much distrust or even dislike may exist between them, know that each needs the other to achieve complete success.

At the drama school there was a once famous actor who, ruined by a lack of self-discipline – he disappeared on alcoholic fugues, was late for rehearsals and even for performances, threw tantrums, changed his lines, dried – now, with the dazed moroseness of the reformed alcoholic, took a few classes each week, not because he was a good teacher but because the Principal felt sorry for him. He would become aware of Lavinia staring at him with a disconcerting fixity and, being vain, would wonder if, like some of the other girls, she had a crush on him. Once, meeting her by chance in the street, he even suggested that she should have a drink with him and was then affronted by the casual way in which she said, 'Oh, I couldn't now, thank you,' with no excuse offered, before she moved on. He did not realize that what fascinated Lavinia was not his past success but his present failure. She would never end up like that, she would tell herself.

Long after she had left the school and had made a name for herself, she met this actor in a television studio, when she was playing the lead and he merely a walk-on two. He had come up to her, truculently drunk and had said, 'My, you have got on since those days when you used to gaze at me with those beautiful sheep's eyes of yours!' He had disturbed her; but she was by now adept at concealing disturbance and so she smiled at him and said, 'How nice to see you again.' 'Is it?' Then a terrible thing happened. He sank into the chair opposite to her, put a hand, its palm strangely flushed, to his forehead, and began to emit one gulping, gasping sob after another. Fortunately no one was near enough to notice.

'What is it?' she asked.

For a long time he did not answer, his shoulders heaving and those gulping, gasping sobs going on and on, while she took in the shabbiness of his suit, the crack over the instep of the shoe on his left foot and the unshaven area around the curve of his jaw. Then he said, in a voice thick with hatred, 'You have everything, I have nothing.'

She stared at him with a cold detachment, wondering, Why doesn't this upset me, why doesn't it move me?

He took his hand away from his eyes and she saw, with disgust, that some greenish snot was caking one of his nostrils. 'I've lost it all,' he said. 'My memory, my job at the school, my marriage, my house, my nerve.' My nerve. She remembered that. That was the all-important thing.

She got to her feet. 'I'm sorry,' she said. 'I really am sorry.'

As she walked away, he shouted after her, 'Bitch! Bitch! Bitch!'

Whenever it was physically possible on a Sunday, she would make the journey, however long, tedious and expensive, down to Devon to see her son. He would always be waiting for her, standing at the attic window, high up in the steeply sloping roof of the farmhouse, of the little room which was his. As she walked or was driven up the drive, Lavinia got into the habit of looking up there. She would wave, as soon as she could make out his face, and he would wave back. Then he would rush down the narrow stairs, so that, at the sound, Lettice would look up from her pastry or her potato-scraping or her bean-stringing and shake her head in mingled sorrow and annoyance. Arms extended, he would rush out crying 'Mummy, Mummy, Mummy!'

While he was still a small child, Lavinia would then sweep him up into her arms and he would hang round her neck, his cheek pressed to hers, as he breathed in that smell, exotic and potent, which he associated only with her. Once, when he was four, he found an empty bottle of that scent in the waste-paper basket of the room that she used. He removed it, carried it up to his room, which was next to the room of the Danish au pair who helped both in the house and with looking after him, and hid it among his toys. From time to time, when he was alone, he would take it out, unscrew its stopper and hold it to his nostrils. Then, slowly the scent thinned, faded, became a mere ghost. He buried the bottle in the garden, under a lanky lilac tree which never produced more than a few weak blooms.

Often, in those early years, he would say to her, 'Why do you have to go away again? Why? Why?'

'Because I must earn money for us both.'

'Let me come with you,' he would also say; and she would
then have to explain that she was living in lodgings, going
on a British Council tour to the Middle East, was out all
day and late into the evening and so could not possibly look
after him. She would also often tell him that a city or a town
was no place for a child. He was much better off here, in
the countryside with his Aunt Lettice and his Uncle Frank
and Inge.

There were holidays, of course, between one job and
another; and then she would come down to fetch him or
Lettice would bring him to London. His hair cut and
brushed, in the grey flannel suit that Lavinia had bought
for him at Harrod's, he would look touchingly solemn and
adult. She would drive him, in the MG sports car acquired
after a part in an American film, up north to Scotland or
west into Cornwall or even across the Channel. He was
always taciturn – 'rather a boring little boy', one of Lavinia's
friends commented to another, not knowing that Lavinia
could hear her. He would sit in the car, glancing now at the
road ahead and now up at the face of the woman beside
him. When Lavinia asked him what he wanted to do, he
never seemed to know. 'Oh, what you want,' he would
answer. Then patiently he would follow her round country
houses, picture galleries and churches; would laugh, when
she laughed, in cinemas and theatres, and look tense or
sorrowful when she looked tense or sorrowful; would eat the
same meals that she ate and even sip some of the same
wine.

When he was a little over eight, a strange and disconcerting thing happened. They had been up to Edinburgh for
the Festival and though Lavinia had taken the boy along to
what an aunt of hers, resident in the suburbs of the city,
regarded as the most unsuitable places for a child – the
Festival Club, the Traverse Theatre, the Howtowdie – he
had, in his still, silent way, clearly been happy. Then, as
they approached the village outside which Lettice and Frank

had their farmhouse, Lavinia had noticed that he was looking less and less at the road ahead of them and more and more up at her face. She began to feel troubled by his scrutiny and eventually she asked, 'What is it, darling? Have I a smut on my nose?' He did not answer. 'Stephen!'

Then he said, in a constricted, grieving voice, which she would always remember, 'Please, Mummy, don't take me away again. Ever.'

'What do you mean? Haven't you enjoyed yourself? Oh, darling!'

He now stared straight ahead of him; and that narrow, pale face, so like his father's, under the blackest of hair, was immobile.

'Haven't you, darling?' she repeated.

'Yes,' he said. 'Yes, of course I have. That's it, you see, Mummy. It's coming back.'

'But aren't you happy with Aunt Lettice and Uncle Frank?' Lavinia was amazed. They were so patient and kind with the boy, even though he was so unresponsive to Lettice's love and so unlike the son, extrovert and athletic, whom Frank would have wanted.

He did not answer, merely twisting his long, delicate fingers over the model train that he had been holding in his lap.

'Aren't you?'

'Oh, yes, Mummy. Yes. But it's . . . coming back.'

However, when Lavinia had next said, half-expecting him to refuse, 'Darling, I've a week between plays in June, would you like to come to Athens with me?' he nodded and exclaimed 'Oh, yes, Mummy!' as though he had totally forgotten that plea of his. But Lavinia had not forgotten it; she was never to do so.

From time to time she would agonize to friends of hers – Did they think that she should try to make a home for him? Should she abandon her acting? Was she behaving badly, irresponsibly? – and they would then always give her the reassurance that, however unconsciously, she was seeking

162

from them. It was far better that he should grow up in the country, with a man to act as father to him. No, of course she must not give up her career, that would be criminal – particularly as the money that she earned provided his support. Badly, irresponsibly – why, she'd devoted her whole life, endlessly sacrificed herself, to give him everything any child could possibly want or need.

When he was nine, Lavinia paid for him to go to a boarding school, even though Lettice and she had repeated acrimonious and even tearful arguments about that. Lettice, fearing that his departure for the boarding school would be the beginning of a departure for ever, reminded Lavinia how much they two had hated boarding school. 'It's so old fashioned to inflict that kind of separation on a child. Particularly one so sensitive.' She went on to speak of the excellence of the local day school, concluding, 'Why waste money? You work endlessly to give him everything he needs. But this is something he doesn't need, it's only something which you want for him. God knows why!'

There was far more unspoken than spoken in the tussle between the two women, as there had been in that previous tussle over Stephen's surname.

The boy mentioned the surname to Lavinia as she drove him over to the school for his first term. 'What will they call me?' he suddenly asked.

'What do you mean? Christian name or surname? I imagine that nowadays both boys and teachers use Christian names. But when your aunt and I went to school, even we, girls, called each other by our surnames.'

'I meant – am I to be Stephen Trent?'

'Well, of course!' She laughed uneasily. 'What else?'

'But it'll seem odd. Because people will know – since you're so famous – that I haven't got a father.'

'Oh, I don't think they'll give the matter a moment's thought. Would you prefer to have Aunt Lettice's and Uncle Frank's name and be Stephen Cobbold?'

'No.' He did not seem to be sure.

163

'You could, if you wanted.'

Her acquiescence caused him a terrible anguish. 'Oh, no!' he cried out. 'No!' Then he asked a question that he had never before put either to her or to anyone else, 'Why did my father go away?'

'Well, as I've told you, he was from India. And I suppose he wanted to go back there.'

'Don't you ever hear from him?'

'No.' The truth.

'Don't you want to hear from him?'

'No.' A lie.

The headmaster, who might himself have still been at school, so young did he look in his neatly pressed grey flannels and blazer with the crest of a minor Oxford college on its breast pocket, looked away self-consciously, as he always did, when tearful mothers said goodbye to their embarrassed children.

But Lavinia was not tearful as she stooped to kiss Stephen, 'Goodbye, darling. Be good, be happy.'

He fulfilled the first of these two prescriptions, causing no one any trouble, as he moved, self-possessed and taciturn, between classroom, playing fields, chapel, study, dormitory. But whether he was happy, no one, least of all Lavinia – who made a point of visiting him on every parents' day, even though Lettice insisted that, if her sister was too busy, she and Frank could run over – could ever be certain. 'Rather a boring little boy.' Other people said it. 'So withdrawn.' They said that too.

'Darling, you *are* happy here?'

'Oh, yes.' He spoke it listlessly, on his face an expression of vague irritation.

'Sure?'

'Yes, Mummy. Yes.'

He would spend part of his holidays with her, accompanying her to adult parties at which he would solemnly hand round the canapés or stroke the family cat or dog; reading comics for long hours by himself; and in a small, unused room which she set aside for him in her flat, working at the carpentry for which she had bought him some expensive tools. He made her a rickety bookcase one holiday and a square box, unpainted and unvarnished, for which she could find no possible use, the next.

On the farm, he never made any attempt to help Frank, however hard-pressed he and his two workers might find themselves; but he would often sit in the kitchen watching Lettice and the au pair girl – a Japanese had now replaced the Dane – going about their tasks. That silent, intense scrutiny would worry both the women. They found that, under it, they tended to drop things, to fail at the simple task of separating the yolk from the white of an egg, and to let pans overboil or burn. 'Haven't you anything to do?' Lettice would ask him, in mounting irritation, and he would reply, 'Not really.' Once she said, 'Isn't there any school friend whom you'd like to ask to stay?' and again he replied, 'Not really.' He had no close friends at school.

His reports were lukewarm – he was 'diligent', he 'made progress', he was 'learning to express himself clearly on paper' – but never unfavourable, except for games ('could show more enthusiasm'). There was no doubt that he would pass into the famous public school for which Lavinia had long since put him down.

Then, when he was twelve, Lavinia received a telephone call just as she was about to set off for an important rehearsal at the Old Vic. It was the headmaster and he told her, in a grave voice, totally unlike his usual jolly, hectoring one, that he thought it would be a good idea if she could get over to the school as soon as possible. 'It's your son,' he explained. 'Something – er – rather unfortunate has happened.'

'You mean he's ill?'

'No.' He seemed uncertain. 'He's injured himself, injured himself slightly, while playing a silly game. We've put him in the sick bay, where he can be under matron's eye. But, no, he's not ill. No.'

'But you'd like me to . . . ?'

'Well, yes, it might be a good idea if you came down – someone came down – so that we could talk it all over.'

When she heard that Stephen was neither ill nor, as she had assumed for a brief, terrible moment, dead, Lavinia felt the sort of relief that is the nearest that many people ever come to joy. She explained that she had a rehearsal, a very important rehearsal, that morning, which she could not possibly miss. She even made a little joke, 'You see, Mr Harrison, it's not only the show, but the rehearsal, that must go on in the theatre.' She would snatch the first train, just as soon as she could.

At the end of the rehearsal the director wanted to take her out to luncheon to discuss with her the 'attitude' – otherwise, the insolence – of the up-and-coming young actor playing opposite to her. But she kissed him on the forehead, stooping over the bentwood chair on which he was sitting back to front, and explained that her boy had been taken ill and she must go down to his school to see how he was. 'Nothing serious, I hope?' he said, thinking of his production, not of Stephen, and she answered, 'Oh, no, darling! Back tomorrow!'

Saying, 'I think you'd better see for yourself,' the headmaster took her to the sick bay, a bare, rectangular room, painted sunshine yellow, with a washbasin in one corner and a high iron bedstead, a chamber-pot visible beneath it, against its further wall. 'Stephen has been rather silly,' the headmaster said benignly, smiling down at the pale, narrow-shouldered boy who gazed up at them with moistly shiny eyes surrounded by dark rings. Only then did Lavinia realize with a shock that Stephen was wearing a bandage round his neck.

'What is it?' she asked.

'He was playing a game – a silly game – weren't you, Stephen?' The headmaster continued to smile benignly, in a way – though he would have been taken aback to have been told it – which made him look quite as silly as he had accused Stephen of being.

The head on the pillow nodded. 'It was only a game, Mummy. But then I couldn't get myself free.'

'What was he doing?' Lavinia turned to the headmaster.

'He was playing around with a rope. As he's just said – as I told you on the phone – it was only a game.' Playing around with a rope? *Trying to hang himself?* Then she told herself sternly, It was only a game, they both say it was only a game. But that seemed to make it no better.

'The trouble is they see that kind of thing on the box and then they begin to experiment. Luckily one of the other boys went into the carpentry shed at that moment and managed to cut him down. If he'd been a few seconds later, well . . . You'd have been a goner, old chap, wouldn't you?'

The narrow head on the pillow nodded again.

'Well, I'll leave you both together,' the headmaster said. 'I expect you'd like to have a chat. There'll be tea downstairs when you want it, Mrs – Miss Trent.' Damn! He always made that slip. 'I'll be taking a class but my good wife will look after you. You know the way, don't you?'

'Thank you. Yes.'

After the door had closed behind the lean, boyish figure, smelling of pipe smoke, Lavinia dropped to her knees beside the child's bed, 'Oh, Stephen, Stephen, Stephen! Why did you do such a thing?'

She put her arms around him, lifting him up off the pillow and cradling him in her arms; but, though he suffered her, she could feel no response. He repeated, with the same mechanical languour with which he had said the words before, 'It was only a game, mother.'

A game! What a terrible game to play, by oneself, in that shed, smelling of sawdust like an abattoir, that Stephen had once shown to her!

'Promise me never, ever to do such a thing again. Promise, promise, promise.'

He nodded, his cheek strangely damp and chill against the cheek that she pressed against it.

'Say it. Say "I promise".'

'I promise.'

It was then that Lavinia first sensed, as she used sometimes to sense at the dress rehearsal of a play, too late to do anything about it, that something had gone wrong. But what? Again her friends reassured: children got up to these things, the failure was not hers, schools should exercise a closer supervision. The director of the play in which she was about to appear, wishing that she would stop talking about that wretched son of hers and concentrate on what he was trying to tell her about the end of the second act, leant across the restaurant table and put his hand over hers. 'Poor darling. I don't know why you've never married. It's what you need. Not someone in the profession, God forbid!' He himself had been briefly married to a film actress whose fame, growing like some plant in a cranny between two concrete blocks, had gradually prised their egos away from each other. 'But it would be right for you and right for the boy.'

Lavinia had had lovers, some of whom had wanted to marry her. Now the thought of that bandage around the pale, stalklike throat made her wonder. Was the director, his eyes brimming with sympathy as he still kept his hand over hers, not perhaps right? The psychiatrist, an elderly, chain-smoking Viennese woman, to whom Stephen had been paying weekly visits at the insistence of the school doctor, certainly seemed to think so. He needed, she said, a stable familial structure. There was a confusion for him between the two women who acted as his mothers. He was strangely devoid of any affection for the man who acted as his father. Yes, yes, his attempt to hang himself might have been a game. (She lifted her shoulders and hands, as though to suggest a doubt.) But games could be dangerous. People could get themselves hurt or even killed playing games.

There was now no conscious effort on Lavinia's part to

find a father for Stephen, any more than there had been any conscious effort on her part to woo this or that producer, director or critic; but within a few weeks she had done so. As always, like some heat-seeking missile, she was drawn, by that infallible mechanism within her of which she was hardly aware, towards a target blazing, however transiently, with energy and power. This was the dramatist, Keith Bertram, in the most successful of whose plays she had recently been appearing. The play, sexually explicit and politically extreme for its time, with its dangerously close shadowing of two real-life scandals, one in the police and one in politics, seemed as unlikely to have emerged from this lanky, timorous Old Etonian, with his overelaborate good manners and his tendency to blush when anyone addressed him, as strychnine from a milk bottle. Clearly, he was one of those writers for whom a pen in the hand acts as a magic wand, totally transforming them from their everyday selves.

Lavinia, a perceptive judge, unlike most actresses, both of a play and a part, had at first been dubious about appearing in a work which simultaneously outraged her innate delicacy about sex and the moderation of such political views as she had acquired. But that unerring mechanism within her forced her towards it, however much she might struggle to resist its pull. The woman whom she had to play was the vulgar, avaricious, crude mistress of a senior officer in Scotland Yard. A suburban Lady Macbeth, she eggs him on to one enormity after another until, foreseeing the multiple pile-up of careers and reputations lying just ahead, she abandons him to tell everything to a canny investigative journalist. It was not the kind of character which Lavinia had before attempted but it was probably the finest of her performances in a modern drama and it won her a number of awards.

As Keith would solicitously draw out her chair for her at a restaurant, before himself sitting down, would hesitantly tell her that this or that emphasis at a rehearsal was 'not quite on course', or would take her arm, not, it seemed, so much to protect her as to protect his own tremulous self when, late at night, they walked up the deserted alley which led to her flat, Lavinia would find herself speculating on what hidden pressures and compulsions had driven him to produce a work so violent in its hatred and so self-confident in its depiction of a world of which, when one talked to him, he seemed to have had no experience.

They drove to the school in Lavinia's MG – typically, Keith could not drive – and took Stephen out to tea at a nearby hotel. The boy's staid good manners were almost a parody of the man's. Now the one passed sandwiches, now the other the cakes. When, overheated by the wood fire before which they were sitting, Lavinia began to take off her jacket, each of them jumped up to assist her. Stephen called Keith sir, until Keith, blushing, told him to call him Keith. Stephen dropped the sir but he never adopted the Christian name, either then or subsequently.

After tea was over, Lavinia carefully wiped the corners of her mouth with the small, lace-fringed napkin provided by the hotel. She then took a mirror and a lipstick out of her handbag. Stephen watched her closely as she touched up her lips with swift, expert movements. She put away mirror and lipstick and gave him a smile. 'Darling, I have something to tell you.'

He nodded. He had guessed.

'I've felt for some time that I'd like to have you living with me not just now and then but throughout your holidays. That flat isn't a real home, somehow. It's so poky, no garden. I also think you need – well – a father.' Garden, father: she realized that she seemed to be equating the two things. 'So – Keith and I thought we'd get married. Then the three of us would make up a family like any other family.'

The boy said nothing. He stared tranquilly at her, his eyes dark and moist in his pale, narrow face and his hands oddly nerveless as they lay, one on top of the other, in his lap.

'How does that seem to you?' Keith asked, embarrassed and disconcerted by the silence. 'I'm very fond of your mother and I'm sure I'm going to become very fond of you.' The heat from the fire seemed to him suddenly to be shrivelling the skin of his forehead and his cheekbones.

The boy gazed into the flames, his face still expressionless. Then he said, 'If you marry, what will be my name?'

'Your name? Why, Stephen, of course! What else?' Lavinia laughed, remembering how two sisters had once perched on a stile beside each other and one had asked the other, 'What name will he have?'

'I meant – what surname?'

'Well, you can continue to be Stephen Trent. Or – I'm sure Keith wouldn't mind – you can become Stephen Bertram. I'll be Mrs Bertram, of course, so that might be the easiest.'

The boy chewed on his lower lip. Then he stared to her, head tilted to one side, like some dark, sleek bird of prey. 'I want to be Stephen Trent. Always.'

Lavinia laughed uneasily and Keith joined in. 'Well, of course, darling. If that's the name you want, then no one's going to take it from you.'

In the car driving back to London, Keith said, 'I don't think he likes me.'

'Of course he does. Don't be silly. Or at any rate, he doesn't *dis*like you. He just doesn't know you. When he does, then things will be different.'

'Different? Better?'

'Of course, better. He's a strange child. Not very demonstrative. But you'll see.'

Lettice howled when Lavinia told her. There was no other word for it. She was like a small child, her stance pigeon-toed and her mouth pulled out of shape, the back of a hand pressed to it, as the tears gushed out of her screwed-up eyes.

'I knew you would do this! I knew you'd do this to us! After all these years!'

Lavinia tried to put an arm round Lettice's heaving shoulders but Lettice first pulled away with an angry, inarticulate cry and then actually slapped out at the hand which Lavinia had extended. 'But Lettice dear, I never made any promise to you that you would have him forever. Did I? You and Frank were wonderful to take him in, give him a home, be, well, parents to him. But he wasn't a gift, Lettice, not a gift. I couldn't have made him a gift to you or to anyone.'

Lettice suddenly stopped howling. Her usually clear, good-natured face was dark and turbulent as she crossed her arms, one over the other, and then, gazing at her sister, said, 'You've always done and had precisely what you wanted. And to hell with anyone else!'

'Lettice, that's not fair!'

'And do you think this is fair?' Lettice cried it out passionately, so that Frank, agonizing over the farm accounts in the next room, looked up and shook his head, a pencil gripped between his teeth. 'Oh, it was easy enough for you. You paid the bills and you came down here when it suited you and you took him up to London when it suited you. But who had to cope with him day in and day out? Who had to see that he changed his underclothes and brushed his teeth and was not wearing wet socks?'

'I'm sorry it was such a burden.'

'It *wasn't* a burden! I was glad of it, Frank was glad of it. But we came to think of him as–' she all but said 'as our own' '–as part of our lives here on the farm. Oh, Lavinia, it's cruel, cruel, cruel!' Again she began to sob.

Lavinia perched herself on the edge of the kitchen table, self-possessed and sad. 'You can have him here often,' she said. 'He'll want to come back to see you. This has been his home for so long.'

Lettice said, 'No. If he goes, he goes.' She spoke with a sudden, cruel obduracy. (In the car, driving back to the farm, the child said, 'Please, Mummy, don't take me away

172

again.') 'I'd be grateful if you'd clear all his things out of that room. Not at once, of course. But as soon as it's convenient for you.'

'Oh, Lettice.'

Lettice began to bang around the kitchen, pulling down the pans that she would need for the supper still ahead of them.

Keith, suddenly rich from the success of his play on Broadway, in Paris, in Düsseldorf, in Tokyo, bought a large house. To Lavinia's amazement he insisted that it must be in Richmond, he had always wanted to live there, one of his aunts had once had a house on the Green. 'I should think you'll be the first Trotskyite to own a house on the Green,' Lavinia commented and Keith, who never cared for people to laugh at him, first blushed and then raised a hand to gnaw at a knuckle in baffled, undirected rage.

'Keith wants you to have this room, darling. Isn't it lovely? The other people had it as a second sitting room – breakfast room they called it. You could have a ping-pong table in here. And there'll be space for miles and miles of railway track.'

Stephen looked bleakly around him. Then he went to one of the four windows, each with a window-seat, and stared down at the Green.

'Don't you like it? You must like it.'

'I liked my room in the flat.'

'But that was a boxroom. It was tiny. There was hardly any room for anything but your bed.'

He hung his head, was silent.

During those holidays, he seemed to get used to the room, spending most of his time alone up there, instead of downstairs with the two adults. 'Stephen!' Lavinia would call to him. 'Why don't you come and sit with us in the garden?' to receive the answer, 'It's all right, thank you, Mummy.' Or Keith would call up, 'I thought I'd go for a walk in Kew Gardens. Why don't you come with me?' to receive the answer, 'It's all right, thank you, I'm doing some work.'

The 'work' was his carpentry, to which he applied himself with a tense, frowning persistence. Keith had objected to his using a room so elegant for an activity so messy but Lavinia had answered, 'Oh, what does it matter? There are so many elegant rooms in this house.' Keith had then complained that with all that noise of hammering and sawing, he couldn't think clearly, only to be reminded that in another five days the holidays would end and the boy would be gone.

Even in the then silent house, Keith continued to complain that he could not think clearly; and it was a complaint with which the critics agreed when, with Lavinia in the title role, his *Emma Goldman* was at last put on at a theatre noted for its near-Communist orthodoxy. Keith suddenly felt 'threatened' (the word was his), not merely by these critics, once so adulatory, who now found his work 'confused', 'dogmatic', 'predictable', 'wearisome' but by the suddenness with which, like Antony, he felt the gods to be forsaking him. He had been unable to do anything wrong; now he found that he was unable to do anything right. He astonished and shocked Lavinia by writing vicious and even obscene postcards to his chief detractors – 'You stupid cunt!' she read on one as she was carrying it to the post, and he himself, gleefully proud, showed her another on which he had inscribed the name of the critic of one of the leading dailies as 'Maurice Shithouse Baker' instead of 'Maurice St John Baker'. The childish malevolence of it frightened her.

The play came off and doggedly he began to write another, while she moved on to a Hedda Gabler acclaimed, not only by Hugo, as the best since Peggy Ashcroft's. She would hear Keith ceaselessly typing, early in the morning and late into the night; but when she asked how things were going, he would only reply, 'Bloody. They're going to hate it.' 'They' were the critics. More than once he reminded her that Terence Rattigan had remarked that the average effective life of a playwright was ten years. 'I've almost had those.'

174

Stephen came back from school; and then all Keith's frustrated malevolence - at the contemptuous refusal of any foreign management to take his last play, at his inability to produce even one act of another which satisfied him, at the critics' sniggering delight at the violent, obscene postcards which he had intended should strike home like so many stabs to their vitals - was directed at the boy. At first, he was sarcastic. 'Do you think that dear child could possibly do his fretwork in the garage or the potting shed or somewhere? I know it's of greater artistic importance than my writing but it is, after all, my writing which helps to maintain this enormous mansion in which the three of us live.' Then he became more vicious. Stephen was late for lunch and 'Where's the little bastard?' he asked. Or Stephen dropped the coffee pot and 'You bloody little wog!' he shouted. ('Of course you don't want a wog to touch you anywhere intimate,' Gaur had told her. She had never once used that word in her life.)

Stephen never responded either to sarcasm or abuse. He would merely look at his stepfather with a patient curiosity, as though trying to fathom, without rancour, how anyone could be so brutal and crude.

Eventually Lavinia said, 'Look, Keith, I can't have you speak to the boy like that. I've told you before. If it goes on, I leave.'

'You leave? Or you both leave? If you leave, you're not going to dump him on me, as you dumped him on that wretched sister and brother-in-law of yours.'

During those holidays, Lavinia awoke early one morning, in the bedroom which she and Keith no longer shared, and was drawn, she did not know why, to the open window beyond which the dawn light was still no more than a faint, pearly shimmer. She looked out, she drew the coolness and freshness deep into her lungs. Suddenly, on the spine of the roof of the greenhouse running the length of the furthest garden wall, she saw something - a cat? - edging along. She

175

leant out, peered. Then she realized. It was Stephen on all fours.

She ran out of the room in nothing but her nightdress, her feet bare, hurried down the stairs, tugged at the latch of the drawing-room French windows, and then, breathlessly calling, 'Stephen! Stephen! Stephen!' raced across the lawn. Her bare feet left marks, as of tarnish, on the silver of the dew.

He had reached the end of the spine. He jumped down, clumsily landing on the side of a foot, so that he all but toppled over.

'Stephen!' They stared at each other, she in her nightdress, he in his pyjamas. For an absurd moment, the thought came to her that he must have been sleepwalking. Then she demanded, 'What the hell do you think you're doing?'

He did not answer, hanging his head.

'Stephen! Answer me!'

He mumbled, 'I wanted to see if I could do it.'

'Do what?'

'Walk the whole length of the greenhouse without falling in.'

'But you're crazy. That's a terribly dangerous thing.'

He all but answered, 'That's the point of it.' But he said nothing.

'Why did you do it at this hour, when you ought to be in bed?'

'Because otherwise you or Keith or someone might have seen me.'

'Go back to bed this instant. And never, ever do anything like this again. Do you hear me? I forbid you!'

The paperboy's bicycle made a figure of eight on the gravel of the drive as he adroitly hurled that Friday's copies of *The Times*, the *Guardian* and the *New Statesman* into the porch. He saw the woman in her nightdress gesticulating at the boy in his pyjamas, but, a stolid, sleepy youth, he thought little of it.

Lavinia, however, cried out, 'Now the paperboy has seen us! It'll be the gossip of the place!'

Keith slept on and heard nothing. Lavinia never told him.

The holidays came to an end. Lavinia went up to Manchester, to appear at the Royal Exchange; Keith stayed in Richmond, to work on his play. Physically distanced from each other, they at once grew emotionally closer. They telephoned each other every evening before Lavinia left her rented flat for the theatre. 'How's it going, darling?' 'Fine. I've done that second scene. Got it right at last.' 'Oh, lovely! I hope you've produced something really exciting for me to do.' 'Yes. You murder your child.' Was he making some diabolical joke? But he went on, 'It's a really tremendous scene. I got the idea for it when I was rereading *Medea*. It'll make those bloody critics sit up and take notice.'

Stephen's letters – he had now moved on to public school – were at once adult in tone and empty in content. He always wrote to the Richmond house, so that Keith had to forward them, even though Lavinia reminded him over and over again to use her address in Manchester.

Lavinia returned to London and, the next day, Stephen was back from school. His voice was breaking, so that at one moment he would be speaking hoarsely as though with a cold, and at the next he would be piping. There was a faint down above his upper lip. On one occasion, when Lavinia came on him unexpectedly, lying out on a deckchair in a corner of the garden invisible from either the house or its neighbours, he stuffed a handkerchief into his pocket, his face scarlet with panicky embarrassment. He had obviously been masturbating. Keith no longer mocked or shouted at him; the two barely spoke to each other or looked at each other.

It was half-way through those holidays that Lavinia first noticed the slashes. She was at the kitchen sink, Stephen wandered in, as he often did, in search of a biscuit. As he put up an arm to fetch down the biscuit tin from the shelf, his sleeve fell away and, at the same moment, she turned round to ask him something. There were three of the slashes, not deep, each of precisely the same length and distance from each other. If they had been nearer the wrist, they might have severed veins.

'What on earth are those?'

As she pointed, he tugged down his sleeve.

'I cut myself.'

'Cut yourself? How?' Keith's mockery of the down on his chin and upper lip had eventually made him buy a safety razor. Could he have used one of its blades?

'When I was doing some carpentry. The – the chisel slipped.' The idea of a chisel slipping and inflicting wounds so neatly symmetrical was preposterous; but, obscurely disturbed, she did not pursue the matter. She had a matinee that afternoon; she did not want to be upset before it, and she knew that the truth, if she could ever discover it, might be upsetting.

A few days later, making up the laundry, she found blood caked on the leg of his pyjamas, where it would have covered his thigh, not far below his crotch. She touched the place wonderingly with the tip of a forefinger, held it close to her eyes, even smelled it. Should she mention it to him? She did not do so. Again, she succumbed to that self-protective instinct so strong with her. She must not be upset.

At breakfast one morning, she noticed the curious little punctures, like burst blebs, on the backs of his narrow, brown hands. Keith was not there. She said, 'Stephen, what have you done to the back of your hands?'

'Some insects must have bitten me when I was sitting in the garden. I scratched the spots and they began to bleed a little.'

She stared at him; he stared back at her, as though daring her to question him further.

Soon after that, Stephen now back at school, she realized that her marriage was over. Keith had become a burned-out star and without that former blaze of power to hold it

178

on course, the missile, controlled by that subtle mechanism within it, began to veer away.

Lavinia went into his study, where he sat hunched over the typewriter which from time to time would chatter out a few lines of effortful dialogue and then fall silent, and put a hand on his shoulder, as though to steady him, before she broke her news. Not merely the gods but his wife was also forsaking him.

'But why? Why?'

'Because the show has had too long a run. It's going to pieces of its own accord. It's better to take it off.'

He looked at her with small, timorous eyes. 'You can't hate it more than I can.'

'Hate what?' She thought that he meant the 'show' but could not be certain.

'The stink of my failure.'

He, like Gaur so many years before, had a talent for making people feel guilty; but she had perseveringly learned how not to succumb to guilt, as she had perseveringly learned so many other things to become a successful actress.

Keith sold up the house, which he was no longer earning enough money to keep up, and soon after that left England to take up a post as writer-in-residence at some mid-Western university. One of the critics to whom he had sent a number of those violent, obscene postcards remarked, the sterile mocking the sterile, that it would have been more appropriate if his job had been that of non-writer-in-residence.

Lavinia moved to the house in the Village, found for her by a theatrical knight already living in Brighton. She set aside the basement for Stephen's bedroom and workroom.

'I'm afraid it's not like that room you had in Richmond.'

He looked around him. 'Oh, this is better.'

She laughed. 'Nonsense, darling!' But she was secretly pleased.

At preparatory school, the reports on his behaviour had always been good; but, now disturbingly, each report contained some such work as 'rebellious', 'disobedient', 'undisciplined', 'defiant'. Yet at home, as he sawed and hammered and planed in the basement, he caused not a moment's trouble. She could not understand it.

'You seem to be such a bad boy at school,' she said on one occasion. 'Your work is all right but . . . look at that.' She held out the report.

He did not look. He merely shrugged and gave a small, furtive smile.

Months later, she met a playwright whose son was not merely at the same school but in the same house as Stephen. The playwright remarked to her, with an envious admiration, 'By all accounts, your boy's a real tearaway.'

'Is he?'

'So I gather.' He laughed. 'They don't beat much at that school, as they did in my day – more's the pity. But I gather that boy of yours holds the record. And, apparently, he's got so much guts that he takes six of the best as though it was nothing.'

The playwright laughed again and Lavinia laughed with him; but really she was shaken.

When Stephen was seventeen, the headmaster suggested that he might be happier – it was a form of words which he generally used in embarrassing circumstances like this – if Lavinia took him away. No, there had been no major problems – he was basically a thoroughly nice and decent chap – but there had been some minor ones and, since there seemed little likelihood that he would procure a place at a university, the way that he was going, it might be better if she were to have him stay at home and send him to one of the excellent crammer's, either in Brighton or in London, of which he was forwarding a list.

But Stephen had no intention of going to a crammer's; and he had no intention of getting a regular job.

'Surely you can afford to keep me,' he aggressively told Lavinia, when she suggested the job, after he had refused to consider the crammer's.

'Yes, I can afford to keep you. But the real question is whether you can afford to be kept.'

'What do you mean?'

'It's bad for you. At your age. Demoralizing.'

'I don't mind being demoralized.'

'Perhaps not. But I mind.'

'If you don't want to keep me, I can go on the dole.'

She shrugged. 'Then do so.' But from then on, she gave him an allowance.

Gradually, she became less and less aware of his presence in the house. He would come up to meals from the basement and sit opposite her, pale and silent, while he doggedly ate. Then he would slip away again.

'Stay with me. Why do you always disappear as soon as a meal is finished?'

Remorselessly he answered, 'Oh, you don't really want me with you.'

'But I do, I do!'

He shook his head, he gave that small, furtive smile. 'The trouble is, you've never loved me, Mother. Never, ever.'

'What a cruel thing to tell me!'

He shrugged and walked out. Later, she heard him sawing away at a piece of wood. He would be making another of the cupboards, bookcases or chest-of-drawers which he would then sell to some contact with a shop in the warren of squalid, small streets below the station. Each object took him so long to complete that his profits were tiny. He rarely went out.

Lavinia went for three months to the States, to appear in a film. 'Lots of lovely money, darling! Why don't you come with me?'

'Oh, you don't want me along. I might go and stay with Aunt Lettice and Uncle Frank.' She wondered if he had said that in order to hurt her. He never said it again, he never went to them. She left him some money and sent him more from abroad. She wrote him long, newsy letters, full of the people she had met, the places she had visited, and the

181

fortune she was making. He rarely answered and, when he did, the stilted phrases, written in a wholly impersonal calligraphy, with a broad-nibbed pen, told her nothing, absolutely nothing.

'It's lovely to be together after all those months.' She had opened a bottle of champagne and had bought smoked salmon, his favourite food. She had also roasted a pheasant.

'Is it?' He looked shabbier, thinner, older than when she had left him. She leant forward to put a hand over his, clutching the long, thin fingers between hers. But he extricated them, gently but decisively.

'For me it is, yes. Isn't it for you?' She had thrown down a challenge.

'Oh, don't give me all that crap, Mother! You get no pleasure out of being with me, you never have. And I no longer get any pleasure out of being with you.'

'How can you say that!'

'True.'

Suddenly, for the first time in years, she gave vent to the fury within her. 'Don't speak like that to me! You don't know the things I've done for you. Ever since you were a baby. Worked. Plotted. Denied myself. Never had a holiday, never for years and years, except when there was no work for me. Took terrible parts, toured, lived in digs. Put up with anything, everything. Slept with men who disgusted me for the sake of a job. And all for you, for you! So that I could pay Lettice and Frank and send you to the best of prep schools and the best of public schools and now keep you, year after year, in idleness, while I go on killing myself.'

He looked at her. He began to laugh. 'You really do have the most amazing powers of self-deception. You did none of those things for me, I was merely the pretext for doing them. You did them for yourself, of course you did.' She was about to interrupt him. 'The nobility of your sacrifices is just a load of crap. Even poor old Keith would not have used it in one of his shitty plays. But it served its purpose. If you were so demanding and ruthless and selfish, well, people told each other, "You can hardly blame her, she's got that bastard son of hers to support".'

This revelation of his view of her was shattering. It was as though he had picked up the hammer, lying out on the tool bench of the bare, orderly room in which he worked at his carpentry and with a single blow had struck at the clear glass through which she had always looked out on her world. The glass became an opaque cobweb; when she peered through it, everything appeared horribly distorted. Or was it – the doubt gripped her like an abdominal spasm – that the glass through which she had been so serenely gazing had never in fact been clear and that the blow of the hammer, demolishing it, had at last enabled her to see things as they really were?

'I don't think we've anything more to say to each other.' She did not know whether she meant on that particular day or for the whole future ahead of them.

'You've never had anything to say to me.'

She left him in the kitchen, shutting the door quietly behind her, and ran up the stairs to her bedroom. There she sat motionless for a long time in an armchair by the window, the light off and the blinds open on to the street. She found herself panting as though that ascent to get away from him and his abominable lies – they were lies, they were, they were! – had been one not of some dozen stairs but of miles.

Suddenly, she did not know why, she thought of Keith; and the remorse that Stephen had clearly wanted her to feel for her behaviour towards him, she now felt for the sad, frustrated, choleric man who had, so briefly and so disastrously, been her husband. There had been something pathetically clumsy and childish about Keith's love-making. He might have been another son, another Stephen, seeking comfort and consolation in her arms before procuring his jerking, panting onanistic pleasure. Eventually, she had shown him, beyond all doubt, how little satisfaction he was able to give her; and that contemptuous dissatisfaction of hers had merely paralleled, in all its cruelty, the contemptuous dissatisfaction of the critics who had shrugged him off. He had written to her recently to tell her of his desire for a divorce. He did not mention, though she had heard it from others, that he wished to marry one of his former students.

Poor Keith! Poor Stephen! As she stared down into the deserted street, she thought, Yes, I've behaved badly to them both. I've always been generous, yes, but I've always given them what I wanted to give them, not what they wanted from me. She wondered whether to go down to the basement and say to the boy, 'Forgive me, you're right, let me try to do better.' She even got as far as the hall with that intention in mind. But then she heard the rasp of his saw, back and forth, back and forth. She could see him, sullenly aggressive, bending over some length of pine and driving the saw with repeated thrusts and tugs of his narrow, sinewy arms. He no more liked her to interrupt him when he was at work at his carpentry than Keith had done when he was at work at a play. Another time. Better another time.

But she was always so busy and Stephen was always so elusive. There were snatched breakfasts, before a television rehearsal, or late suppers, after a performance, when she might have spoken; but at the breakfasts she was too distracted, at the suppers too exhausted. They would sit facing each other and barely a word would pass between them.

'Some more toast, darling?'

A shake of the head; a crackle as he turned a page of the *Guardian;* a brief laugh.

'What is it?'

'Oh, another silly misprint.' He did not tell her what it was.

Or, 'How did the show go tonight?' He had never bothered to go along to see it, though she had repeatedly offered him tickets.

'We're all getting rather tired, I think. And in those

circumstances, one overcompensates by artificial high spirits and energy. I'll be glad when the run ends.'

No answer. It was like a tennis match in which one's opponent has not grasped that it is not enough to stop the ball, one must also return it.

Lavinia noticed that, from time to time, Stephen would now return to the flat in the company of a stocky woman, with a round, shiny face, clearly much older than himself. Sometimes the woman would visit the basement on her own, letting herself in with a key. One could imagine such a woman dealing effectively with rowdy youths on the bus on which she was conductor or acting as a cool, stern wardress in a prison. From her sitting-room window, Lavinia would look down on her head as she descended or ascended the basement stairs, always at the run. The hair was thin at the centre parting, she had a way of hunching her shoulders, almost as though she had a curvature of the spine.

'Who is that friend of yours?' Lavinia dared to ask one day.

'What friend? I have no friends.' For a moment, Lavinia thought that perhaps the woman came to clean; Stephen had always refused to have her own Mrs Lambert clean for him, preferring to do it himself.

'Of course you have friends! I saw you with a group of them at the Temple Bar only the other night.'

'Those were acquaintances, Mother. I expect the woman you mean is Lydia. She's also an acquaintance.'

'What does Lydia do?'

'I've no idea.' He hit his breakfast egg sideways with his spoon, neatly decapitating it. 'I've never asked her.'

Perhaps this was the truth, perhaps he hadn't. All his life, he had been strangely incurious.

When the play in which she had been appearing at last ended its run, there were two weeks in which she had nothing to do, before beginning a film; and it was then that she became both depressed and obsessed by the distance between them. She would ring down – 'Are you ready for

f6

breakfast, darling?' – or she would descend into the area, having returned from a party, ring the bell and say, when he opened to her, 'I'm just back. I'll have some supper prepared in about half an hour.' He would eat the meals. Sometimes, he would have helped her with the laying of the table; always he would join her in stacking the dishes in the dishwasher. But there was no communication between them; they might have been two strangers obliged to share a table in a boarding house or on a ship and trying to make the best of it, with 'Shall I cut you another piece of bread?' or 'This Blue Cheshire is really rather good.'

One day, as he was about to leave the kitchen, she said, suddenly angry, 'How deadly you've become.'

He looked back at her, his hand, the nails discoloured from the varnish that he had been applying to a table recently made, curled around the doorknob. He smiled. 'I thought I was always deadly. "A rather boring little boy".' So he, too, like herself, had overheard that friend of hers, so many years ago.

'You must talk to me sometimes.'

'Don't I talk? Then what are the noises that the two of us make twice or three times a day at each other?'

'Just noises. That's the trouble.'

'Sorry,' he said abruptly. He went.

A few days later, it was his birthday. She wrote him out a cheque for fifty pounds and then tore that up and wrote him out another for a hundred. She placed the cheque in the birthday card that she had spent a long time choosing at a shop on the corner of the street. Would he like a jokey one? But each joke – whether about sex, work, looks, money, age – seemed to contain some innuendo to which he might take exception. In the end she opted for Manet's *Au Bar des Folies Bergères*. Safe, if hackneyed, she thought, until, on the walk home, she began to wonder morbidly whether he might not decide that she was making some subtle, malicious allusion to his visitor. She might, indeed, be a barmaid if she were not a bus conductor or a prison wardress.

186

As Lavinia went out of her front door, the envelope containing cheque and card held in a hand, she suddenly thought of the cashmere scarf, presented to her as a farewell gift by the actor, notorious for his stinginess, who had been playing opposite to her in the play just ended. Of a beautiful quality, it carried a Sulka label; but it was so clearly intended for a man, not a woman, that another member of the cast had at once suggested that 'the mean old brute' had no doubt himself received it as a gift from one of his boyfriends and had then decided to pass it on, brown not being a colour to go with the black overcoat with a mink collar which, in the manner of an actor-manager of the past, he always wore when in London in the winter. She went back into the house, fetched the scarf and the wrapping paper in which the actor had presented it to her, and made a neat parcel.

Stephen looked feverish when he opened his door to her. There were red spots on each of his high, usually sallow cheekbones and his eyes glittered. His lips, she noticed, were dry and cracked.

'Are you all right?' she asked involuntarily.

'Fine. Why?'

Earlier that morning, when she had telephoned down to tell him that breakfast would be ready in a quarter of an hour, he had replied, 'Oh, I've made myself a cup of Nescafé down here already. I don't feel like eating anything.'

She refrained from telling him that he looked ill, since his answer to that would always be a fretful, 'You make people ill by telling them that they look it.' Instead, 'You didn't come up to breakfast.'

'I felt I couldn't face breakfast. And, frankly, I felt I couldn't face you.'

She did not reply to that. 'Anyway, many happy returns.'

'Oh, God! Is it my birthday? That explains the letter from Aunt Lettice. I put it on one side, unopened. It must be a card from her and Uncle Frank.'

'Am I allowed to come in? I have a card for you and a present. Or, rather, two presents.'

'Two presents! How generous!'

He stood aside, with a small, ironic bow, and she went into the front room, with the dusty work bench, its cheap transistor radio on the sill of a window which badly needed cleaning, and its sawdust thick on its linoleum-covered floor. There was a mug of half-drunk coffee, a white film, speckled with sawdust, on its surface, resting, at an angle, against a pile of motoring magazines on an unvarnished table made by himself. Since he had no car and did not even drive, she was always puzzled as to why such magazines should interest him.

She held out the envelope and the package.

He took them from her and placed both beside the mug, on top of the unopened envelope addressed to him in Lettice's large, childishly unformed handwriting.

'Aren't you going to open them?'

'Would it give you pleasure, if I did?'

'I think it would be courteous.'

He laughed. 'All right.' He inserted a forefinger under the flap of the envelope and tore it open untidily, drew out the card and the cheque within it, and dropped the envelope to the floor. He looked for a long time at the Manet, as though he had never before seen it either in reproduction or at the National Gallery. 'Nice.'

'There's a cheque there.'

He examined it. 'Even nicer.'

She felt a choking fury rising up within her as she waited for a word of thanks.

'You'd better open the package too. I hope you'll like what's in it.'

He put down card and cheque on the table and then took the package from under his arm. He unwrapped it, shook out the scarf; dangled it back and forth, his thin arm extended, so that its end swept the floor, gathering sawdust on its silky fabric. Both of them stared down at the scarf, as

188

though it were a snake, at once beautiful and terrible, wavering between them, before it lashed out and struck. He looked up at her and there was now a cruel mockery in those black eyes glittering with what seemed to be a fever. 'Must have cost you a bomb.'

Had he guessed that the scarf had been a present to her? She could not remember ever having shown it or even mentioning it to him. She shrugged.

He leant forward and threw the scarf round her neck, drawing its ends tight, so that she felt a soft but insistent constriction round the throat. 'I think it really suits you better than it'll ever suit me.'

She put both hands to the scarf to ease its pressure. 'Nonsense. It'll go with your overcoat.' She felt suddenly wary, even frightened. Though he spoke so gently and smiled so constantly, beneath all that a concealed menace hissed.

'Don't do that,' she said. 'Don't!' With a violent gesture of both hands, she pulled the ends of the scarf from her throat.

He laughed, walked a pace away from her, the glittering eyes on her whitening face, and then chucked the scarf across the work bench. 'Thank you kindly, mother dear.' He went back to the table and picked up the cheque and examined it with the same long, intense scrutiny with which he had examined the hackneyed birthday card. Suddenly, he ripped the cheque across, ripped and ripped again, to scatter the fragments over her head as though they were confetti. She cringed as she felt them in her hair. They might have been steeped in some corrosive.

'What's the point of that?' She was even more frightened than when the scarf had been round her throat; but her tone was calm, amused.

'I don't want your money, mother dear. I want nothing from you. Nothing at all. Today or tomorrow or the day after tomorrow. I'm going to move out.'

'What!'

He nodded, taking in the effect of this statement on her,

189

as a terrorist, mouth parched and heart lurching painfully, might take in the effect of the bomb that he has just lobbed into a crowd.

'But why?'

He shrugged.

'And where will you go?'

'No idea. Yet.' He turned away from her, again picked up the card, again scrutinized it. 'Pretty. Pretty picture.'

'Well . . . If that's what you want . . .'

'I think you want it too.'

She was thinking of the departure of his father; that had been even more abrupt and even more cruel. How like Gaur he looked, with strands of the same black hair, as coarse and shiny as the mane of a horse, falling across the same wide, sallow forehead, the same beautiful, slightly depraved face, with heavy shadows beneath the cheekbones, and the same delicate, tensile physique.

'Of course I don't want it.'

He stared at her. Liar.

'Well, I'll go on paying you your allowance.'

'No, I don't want that.'

'I must.'

Still he stared.

She walked slowly out of the room and towards the front door. 'You may change your mind. Anyway – I'll see you before you leave.' She was speaking to no one. He had not followed her. 'I'll see you before you leave,' she repeated, raising her voice. No answer.

She went up the crumbling steps, gripping the rail, as though she were hauling herself, hand over hand, up a cliff face. At the top, she felt breathless and giddy. She fumbled for her key in the pocket of her jacket, had difficulty in inserting it. The telephone was ringing.

She all but left it. Then she crossed over to the sitting room from the hall and raised the receiver. It was her agent, in a state of excitement. She had been nominated as Best Supporting Actress for the forthcoming Academy Awards.

190

'How nice,' was all she could find to say.

'*Nice!* It's terrific!'

'Yes, it's terrific.'

'Are you all right?'

'Of course I am.'

When she eventually put down the receiver on the excitedly gabbling voice, she could hear the rasp, back and forth, back and forth, of the saw in the room below.

Lavinia rang down that evening to ask Stephen if he wanted any supper and again the next morning to tell him that she was about to get the breakfast. She could hear his telephone ringing on and on, both in the receiver held to her ear and beneath her in a room which, she told herself with mounting desolation and anger, could only be empty. But when could he have left? She had heard nothing. Was it possible that, like some tenant unable to pay arrears of rent long overdue, he had furtively slipped out of the house in the early hours? She sat on and on in the sitting room, her hands in her lap and her feet resting on a footstool before her, and listened, for some sound from below: footsteps, a door, a cough, that saw. Eventually she telephoned yet again. Silence. She was meant to meet a friend, another actress, for lunch at the Connaught. She did not go, she did not get in touch with her. When the telephone rang at twenty minutes past one and again at half-past one, she did not answer. The friend would be anxious: it was so unlike Lavinia to be late, even more unlike her to forget.

In the late afternoon, Lavinia took her duplicate key to the flat out of the silver box in which she kept it on the chimneypiece of the sitting room and, once again as unaccountably breathless as when she had climbed the steps out of the area the day before, she descended into the area as into an icy pool. She rang the bell, rang again, kept her finger pressed on the button for seconds on end. Then she inserted the key, turned it, gave the door a little push. Pushed harder. 'Stephen!' she called. No answer. If he had gone, he had left everything behind him. His dufflecoat and his brown tweed overcoat hung in the hall, with his greasy cap above them. A pair of sneakers lay in front of her, asymmetrically placed, one on its side, as though he had hurriedly kicked them off. There was some mail: three letters in buff envelopes and a circular. 'Stephen!' she called again, her voice rising. 'Where are you?'

The curtains of the workroom were closed. She could feel the sawdust softly yielding like sand beneath her feet; she could smell it, pungently resinous. She screwed up her eyes. There was no sign of him.

In mounting dread, she walked into the tiny, musty kitchen, its refrigerator humming in one corner. There was a magazine open on the table, with a cup and plate, containing a half-eaten piece of buttered wholemeal bread and a single sardine resting in a pool of thick, yellow oil. She assumed the magazine to be one of his motoring ones. She did not look at it. The bedroom, off the other side of the hall, was also empty, with an unmade bed, pyjama trousers flung across it, the figures of a digital alarm clock burning hot, on a flimsy, unpainted table made by himself, and the door of the built-in cupboard hanging ajar, so that she could see herself, pale-faced and anxious, reflected in its tarnished glass.

She went through the bedroom to the combined bathroom and lavatory beyond it. She looked up, she gave a gasp, fingertips pressed to lips. The first thing she saw was that narrow, long, grey penis, so like his father's (all through the day at the drama school it would be constantly in her mind). Then the narrow, hairless chest, with its small, prominent nipples, revealed by the unbuttoned red pyjama-jacket. Then the purple face, the tongue protruding. Then the scarf.

'It was only a game,' she told one of the two young, fresh-faced, visibly appalled policemen who arrived. 'I know it was only a game, only a game.'

The coroner confirmed that. In the flat of the deceased,

there had been found magazines and implements which suggested that he had been indulging in sado-masochistic fantasies and, it seemed probable, practices as well. It would be an act of unnecessary cruelty to his mother and the other members of his family to be more specific about their nature. But it was clear that, like many people who suffered from the same abnormal condition, the deceased indulged in games of a kind which could only too easily prove either dangerous or, as in this case, fatal. No doubt, he had intended to release himself from the noose of the scarf before he became unconscious, but, sadly, he had been unable to do so.

On the day after Stephen's death, Lavinia received a packet by the first post. She saw that it was addressed in Stephen's hand and so, as Lettice and Frank had both arrived to be with her, she at once carried it upstairs to her bedroom. She stretched herself out on the unmade bed, from which she had so recently arisen, as though in preparation for some operation to be performed without an anaesthetic and then, raising her hands, the envelope between them, high above her head, she tore it open. Photographs and cuttings from newspapers showered down on to her face and body, as the fragments of her cheque had showered over her the day before. She raised herself on an elbow. Something remained within the envelope. She extracted it. It was the birthday card; but now, where she had written 'From your loving mother', there was scrawled a thick palimpsest of obscene words of a kind which she had never once, in his whole life, heard from his own lips.

She dropped the card, so that it fluttered to the floor beside her bed. Then she picked up one of the photographs, stared at it, laid it down. Picked up another. Picked up a cutting . . .

Cars were piled up on top of each other with, in the foreground, a single blood-stained boot. A child lay back, its mouth wide open in a rictus of agony, while its abdomen gaped. A woman, a mask obscuring her face, dangled, trussed up like some chicken, her pudgy flesh blue, from a meathook embedded in a cracked, white ceiling. A muscular oriental, his head shaved, slumped stiffly in a corner, with his inert body covered with innumerable lacerations oozing blood. A breast, no more, part of some photograph hugely enlarged . . .

She leapt off the bed, rushed to the washbasin and began to vomit, repeatedly, with a force so violent that each spasm was like a blow to her solar plexus.

Lettice must have heard her. 'Lavinia, are you all right? Are you all right?' she called anxiously as she approached down the corridor.

Lavinia hurried to the door and turned the key.

'Lavinia!' The handle rattled from side to side. 'What's the matter?'

'Nothing. Something I ate. I'm all right. I'll just lie down for a moment.'

'Well, let me in. Why's this door locked?'

'It's all right. Go away. Go away.'

'Well, if you really . . .'

Lavinia could hear her sister's footsteps. She imagined her standing there, a small, dowdy matron, with a look of perpetual disappointment on that face which had once been so ardent. Then, at long last, she heard her moving off, the floorboards creaking under her slow, dragging tread.

Lavinia began to amass all the photographs and cuttings. She could not bear to look at any more.

A note, a note: was there no note?

Again she read those mindless obscenities scrawled over the card.

That afternoon, when Lettice and Frank went out to do some shopping ('Are you sure that you'll be all right on your own just for half an hour?') Lavinia carried the envelope, refilled with its contents, down into the sitting room. She took a box of matches off an occasional table, knelt by the hearth and then drew out from the envelope one of the photographs and laid it across the empty bars. She lit a match, applied it. A thick, grey, acrid smoke curled up, to be followed by a licking tongue of flame. She put out a hand, inserted fingers in the envelope beside her, drew out between forefinger and middle finger two of the newspaper cuttings. Then, as though an invisible hand had gripped her arm above the elbow, she found she could not continue. She stared into the grate, where the photograph was now no more than a silvery, friable coil, lying across the bars.

She got to her feet, the envelope in her hands, once again stared down at the grate and then began to mount, slow step by step, the stairs to her bedroom. She went over to her desk, pulled down its flap, eased open a drawer and thrust the envelope far into the back of it.

When Frank and Lettice returned, Frank, grizzled, close-cropped head on one side, sniffed the air like some ancient bull terrier. 'Is something burning?' he asked.

'There was,' Lavinia answered calmly. 'Over now. Only a letter.'

They did not ask what this 'letter' might be and she did not tell either them then or anyone else in the future.

FIVE

IS

There is a large, defective television set in one corner of the sitting room. Phantoms flicker across it, playing tennis in what appears to be a snowstorm under a brilliant sun. 'We've interrupted you!' Sybil exclaimed, as Mrs O'Connor, Sean clinging about her waist, opened the door for her and Bridget Nagel.

'Interrupted me?' Mrs O'Connor was puzzled.

'Wimbledon,' Sybil pointed.

'Oh, that!' Mrs O'Connor crossed over and turned down the sound.

Now Mrs O'Connor stares morosely at the phantoms, her elbow on the table before her and her chin on her palm. An antiquated sewing machine rests on the table. She has been using it to lower the hem of one of Maureen's skirts. Maureen seems never to stop growing – unlike Sean who never seems to start.

Although the housing estate and this flat, giddily high above the wastes of South London, are depressing to others, Bridget Nagel, who finds herself sinking into a morass of inertia and depression whenever she is at home, finds that they invigorate her. She cannot explain this, either to herself or to her friends. It may be, she sometimes thinks, that all that erratic psychic energy, which hurls pots and pans around the kitchen, overturns a wardrobe and pushes people from their chairs, revitalizes her.

'How's it going?' Bridget asks. She knows that she ought

to hope for the answer that 'It' has gone; but, if she were to learn that, she would suffer a secret disappointment.

Mrs O'Connor shrugs, as she puts out a hand and twirls one of the reels on the machine. 'Better, worse. You never know. We had this reverent in, not a priest, from the Church of England, and he did this, this exorcism lark. For a while – for, oh, five, six days – everything seemed to stop. And then, suddenly, last night, all hell broke loose. Chairs falling over, a cup breaking, the doors slamming. You name it, we had it.'

Sybil looks up from her contemplation of a peculiar, jagged stain on the carpet between her feet. 'Was Maureen here during that period?'

Mrs O'Connor does not appreciate the drift of the question, though she has been vaguely aware that all the experts – social workers, policemen, the health officer, investigators from the Society for Psychical Research and the Institute of Paranormal Studies, even the 'reverent' (as she calls the epicene High Church clergyman) – suspect that Maureen has been having everyone on. To Mrs O'Connor that idea is preposterous. Only last week, the girl was tumbled out of her bed, with the bed on top of her, and there was that time when she, Mrs O'Connor, hunted high and low for her brassière, for minutes on end, before Sean spotted it, inaccessible except with a ladder, inside the unlit light-globe in the kitchen. Mrs O'Connor nods, 'Yes, she was here. I wish she hadn't been. Sean takes it all so calmly but you can see that it's getting on Maureen's wick. She spends a lot of her time away from home now, mixing with undesirables. I tell her to be home by ten but often she's later. What can one do?'

There is a terrible helplessness about this woman, at the mercy not only of her poverty and her recalcitrant daughter but of the demons who smash her crockery, rip the clothes off her and her children, and interrupt her sleep. Bridget has succumbed to that pathos, slipping money to Mrs O'Connor, buying Maureen a tennis racket, and always remembering to bring sweets for Sean. She can understand the erratic, malevolent demons; such demons have wrecked her life, just as they are now wrecking this cramped and dingy flat high up on the nineteenth floor of a tower block already due for demolition less than a dozen years after its erection.

'That sounds like Maureen.' The lock of the front door has clicked. Mrs O'Connor hurriedly pushes the wizened boy to one side and calls out, 'Is that you, Maureen? The ladies are here.'

'Which ladies?' There have been so many visitors in the past weeks, some sympathetically credulous and others aggressively sceptical; many of them have been women.

'Miss Crawfurd and Mrs Nagel.'

Maureen does not care for Sybil, who treats her as though she were one of her pupils; but she likes Bridget, who is soft, hesitant and, above all, generous. Maureen now sidles reluctantly into the room, in white tennis shorts, which reveal her thin, wiry legs, a white aertex blouse, the points of the nipples of her small breasts visible beneath it, and once-white shoes scuffed with an orange dust. Her hair has recently been cropped as short as a boy's and she has used peroxide to bleach one strand, springing up from her low, slightly bulging forehead, a brilliant, unreal ochre.

'Hello, Maureen dear,' Bridget greets her. 'I'm glad you're using the racket. How's the tennis going?'

'I beat 'im,' Maureen states, in a flat, staccato, nasal Cockney, unlike her mother's sing-song brogue. She does not specify who her opponent was. 'And 'e's been playing for more'n two years,' she adds.

'Wonderful!'

'You won't be wanting your tea yet awhile,' Mrs O'Connor says.

Maureen shakes her head, stooping to pick negligently a scab on her shin. 'I've some 'omework to do.' She looks boldly at Sybil, 'Perhaps Miss Crawfurd would like to 'elp me?' Sybil does not respond. She notices that the girl's elbows, knees and ankles are grey. What she clearly needs is a bath.

Maureen goes out, whistling 'Don't Cry for Me, Argentina' with all the perky shrillness of a boy. When Bridget realizes what it is that she is whistling, a grey film seems suddenly to have appeared between her and the three other people in this damp, dingy flat. It was on the Falklands, only seven weeks ago, that her husband was killed. Surely Maureen, who has been so persistently inquisitive about his death – Was he shot or blown up or burned? Did he die instantly? Where have they buried him? – could not have chosen that tune on purpose.

Mrs O'Connor says, 'I'd expect you'd like a cup of tea.'

'Well, that would be very nice,' Sybil says briskly. 'Very nice indeed.' She would rather have a drink, since she feels tired after wandering around London in this heat, but she will have to wait for that.

Mrs O'Connor gets to her feet with a sigh. A hand is pressed to the small of her back, where she has had a constant pain for some days. She does not want to go through all the bother of making the tea but she feels that she owes it to these two ladies who have given her both time and money. Sybil rises with her and follows her into the kitchen.

Alone, Bridget puts her hands to her cheeks. She is a small, pretty woman of forty-eight, her crisp, short-cut hair arranged in small curls around her trianglar face. Her three children, one of whom is married to an American and living in New York, one at an ashram near Delhi and one spending part of the summer holidays with a cousin in France, all mock at her for her belief in 'spooks'. But they cannot shake it. She has no doubt that somehow, somewhere – she cannot be specific – she and Roy will be reunited, just as she and her father will be reunited. Love conquers death and love casts out fear.

This room is so gloomy. The light is oddly opaque as it filters through the thick, grimy net curtains beside her, there is a crack across the ceiling, and everything has about it a sour odour, as though someone a long time ago had vomited in it and no one had bothered to clear up the mess. Yet she feels at peace. What, she wonders, lies behind the net curtains? Is there a balcony or merely a sheer drop? She puts out a hand and, as she does so, an extraordinary thing happens. One of the net curtains, as stiff as a flap of wood on a hinge, rises up, so that all at once the sunlight previously diffused behind it floods into the room. Beautiful! She feels such joy at this unexpected illumination that, for a moment, she does not question the manner in which it has happened. The sun is on her face, on her bare arms, on one of her legs. Then the flap crumbles, disintegrates, subsides into the dirt-engrained fabric of net. She stares at it.

Mrs O'Connor comes crablike into the room, the plastic tray with the tea things on it held in her hands. First Sean and then Sybil follow her. 'Sorry to have kept you waiting, dear. That kettle's all furred up, it takes an age to boil.'

Bridget is staring straight ahead, her eyes glazed and a smile on the corners of her lips, her cheeks puckered slightly.

'Are you all right, Bridget?' Sybil asks. There is something about the withdrawn expression and the rigid posture of her friend which alarms her.

Bridget gives a little shudder. 'Yes, oh, yes.' She can still feel, though the room is now dim, that sunlight on face, arms, leg. 'I – I had an odd experience while you were gone.'

'Odd? How?'

Bridget describes it. Sybil listens to her attentively, but Mrs O'Connor, as though it were the most ordinary thing in the world, goes on with her pouring out of the dark, stewed tea from the brown teapot which dribbles because of a chip in its spout.

When Bridget has finished, Sybil says, 'How extraordinary,' and simultaneously Sean, who has been sitting on the sofa, absolutely still, his eyes fixed on Bridget's, cries out, 'I see'd that too. I see'd it!'

Sybil turns to him, 'Do you mean that you've also seen the curtain rise up like that – stiff, of its own accord?'

There is something stern and inquisitorial in her voice and it may be this that prevents him from answering her. He jumps off the sofa, with a little squeak, runs to his mother and hugs her about a knee. She runs a hand, affectionate and protective, through his tousled hair.

'I felt so happy,' Bridget says. 'For a moment, I felt so happy. And some of that happiness remains.'

Suddenly, Maureen is there in the room. They have none of them heard her approaching or opening the door. Her far from clean feet, with their talonlike nails, are bare. She is wearing a dressing-gown over pyjamas. She stares at Sybil with a hungry intensity.

Mrs O'Connor puts a hand to her forehead and then lowers it over her eyes, as though to shut out a glare. 'Bless me if I'm not starting one of my heads again. Get me a Paracetamol from the kitchen, Maureen, there's a pet.'

Maureen goes out as silently as she entered.

Sybil, adept at organizing other people's lives for them, says, 'I do wish you'd let me take you to the Migraine Clinic. I'm sure they could do something there to help you.'

'I've tried everything,' Mrs O'Connor says. 'Every blessed thing. Nothing seems any good.'

'Diet is very important,' Sybil tells her. 'You probably don't eat the right things. Or eat the wrong ones. At the Migraine Clinic they'd tell you.'

Maureen returns with two tablets in the palm of one hand and a glass of misty water in the other.

'Bless you,' Mrs O'Connor says. She takes the tablets and glass from her, and then, having put one of the tablets on her tongue and having sipped at the water, she throws her head back abruptly a number of times, the muscles in her neck going into spasm. 'It's all I can do to swallow the blessed things,' she says, having at last succeeded with the first. She then goes through the same process with the second.

Sybil tells her, 'I'm sure you'd find it just as easy or even easier if you didn't tilt back your head.' But Mrs O'Connor, as so often when people give her advice, does not seem to have heard.

Eventually, the two women get up to go. Not a moment too soon, Mrs O'Connor thinks. The kids want their tea. Bridget hands Maureen a five-pound note – 'Use that for something for yourself and your brother.' In giving the money to the girl, instead of to her mother, it is as though she were acknowledging that that moment of literal illumination by the window had somehow, however obliquely, been Maureen's doing.

On the stairs, Sybil, who is walking ahead, turns round to ask, 'Are you sure about the curtain?'

Bridget nods. 'As sure as I'm sure of anything that has ever happened to me.'

'Interesting that Mrs O'C started one of her migraines immediately after. And that Maureen had just come home.'

When they have left the housing estate, with its broken or blackened trees, each within a circlet of wire, its low garages and coal bunkers daubed with graffiti and its group of children, boys and girls, noisily kicking a football about on a yellowed patch of grass, Sybil says, 'I could do with a drink.'

'So could I.'

'Let's try that pub over there.'

Bridget is surprised. She has never imagined Sybil entering a pub, certainly not one in a working-class district like Stepney. When Sybil asks her what she wants, she giggles and says, 'I suppose we ought really to settle for port and lemon.' But, in the event, each has a gin and tonic, which they carry over to a corner, where they can sit, inconspicuously behind a pinball machine.

'Did the police ever retrieve your car?' Sybil asks.

'Yes. The day before yesterday. In Streatham. It was in

an awful mess – the front bumper had been all but knocked off, one headlamp was smashed, there was a scrape and a huge dent along a door. He must have been in a smash. And the inside . . . !'Bridget pulls a face over her drink. She does not want to think about the car, much less about the circumstances leading up to its theft. Those demons, erratic and malevolent, will not leave her alone.

'What a brute!' Sybil says. 'One would like to see him flogged within an inch of his life.' Neither Bridget nor she herself is wholly certain that she is joking. 'And after all you've been through already.'

To Bridget it seems that she has not been through the events of the last months but that they, like some corrosive poison, have been through her.

Sybil begins to talk about her automatic writing. Before the Falklands crisis occurred and before she knew anything about the Islands, a sentence appeared in one of the scripts: 'The goose walks the green, the white flag is black.' She thinks now, with her knowledge of Goose Green and of what happened there to Bridget's husband, that it must have been prophetic. Bridget shares her belief.

'I've spent the last days combing through my scripts, reams and reams of them. And, since that letter of mine in the Journal last month, a number of people have begun to send me theirs. I'm deluged with them! Most of them are useless. But there *are* oddities, cross correspondences. For example, as you probably know, Hugo's chief scholarly interest, before he and I began to collaborate on our edition of the Meredith Letters, was in early drama and, in particular, in tropes and liturgical plays.' Bridget who is an unliterary woman, has no idea what is meant by tropes or liturgical plays but she nods, as though she did. 'I expect you've heard of the tenth-century *Quem Quaeritis* – some people have called it the first modern play, even though it consists of only four lines.' Something in Bridget's expression tells Sybil that, for all her pretence of eager comprehension, she is wholly at sea. Sybil adopts the tone which she uses to one of her dimmer pupils, 'The play was performed in churches at Easter. A priest would stand by the altar. He would be playing the role of the Angel who acted as guard at Christ's sepulchre. Three other priests in drag – impersonating the three Marys – would approach him and ask for the whereabouts of Christ. Now Hugo of course knew the four lines by heart; but of the three scripts between which I have found cross correspondences, one emanates from me – I, of course, know the lines – and two from housewives who are extremely unlikely ever to have heard them, much less to have memorized them. Embedded in my script is the sentence in Latin *Quem quaeritis in sepulchro, O Christicolae?* – "Who is it that you are seeking in the sepulchre, O Christian women." In a script, of almost the same date, from a farmer's wife in Yorkshire, I found the words, "Jesus of Nazareth" repeated four times – and *Jesum Nasarenum crucifixum* or "Jesus of Nazareth who was crucified" is the answer given by the Angel. In another script, also of approximately the same date, produced by a shop assistant in Bath – unknown both to the farmer's wife and to me until she got in touch with me – I found "He has arisen." And "He has arisen" or, in Latin, *Surrexit,* is what the Angel then goes on to assure the three women.'

As Bridget stares at Sybil with unnaturally wide-open eyes, the tips of the fingers of one hand pressed to her lower lip, Sybil wonders irritably if she has really seen the point. 'All this *may* be coincidence. Many people would say that it was. But I feel sure that Hugo has been the controlling communicator, making a definite statement through three entirely different people, all unknown to each other and only one known to him, about the certainty of resurrection. The ingenuity is typical of him. Clearly there was a prearranged plan in the three different communications; but none of us made that plan, since, at the time that the communications were received, I certainly did not know of the existence of the other two, even though, admittedly, they knew of my existence through my writings in the Journal.' Sybil sips her gin and tonic. 'It's exciting,' she says. 'Heartening.'

Bridget does her best to look excited and heartened; but what happened to her in that small, frowsty room on the housing estate was far more exciting and heartening, even if – as in the case of that terrible vision of her father's death in the Western Desert, which she had at the age of seven – people would merely ascribe it to hysteria.

Suddenly, Bridget wants to talk about that vision. 'I've never told you this,' she begins, irritating Sybil with her constant tendency to go off at a tangent (butterfly-brained, Sybil calls her). 'It was during the war, when I was seven.'

As she has repeatedly told the story over the years, she has found it harder and harder to distinguish between what actually happened and what she has added, grain by grain, in order to achieve a neater shape and stronger consistency. The father was in the Western Desert, the child had known that; but her mother and her grandparents never told her that he might be in danger, much less killed. One morning she awoke extraordinarily early – Bridget can still hear the birds chirping in the dim garden of the rectory in which her grandparents lived and feel the cool of that summer dawn on her bare arms and legs as she threw off her bedclothes – and she had then known, known with total certainty, that something had happened to her father, though she did not yet know what. She lay in mounting terror on her bed under the open window. Then she heard a strange sound from the washbasin in the corner: a kind of turbulent threshing, as of a fish in water. She got off the bed and went over to the basin and looked down, horrified and fascinated. Blood kept shooting up in spurts from the waste pipe, to splash the sides of the basin and then trickle back. She watched for a long time. Then she ran out of the room, crossed the landing and banged on the door of her grandparents, since that was nearer than her mother's. Her grandfather, the vicar, appeared in his nightshirt, his eyes bleary and his face unshaven and creased down one side. 'Come, come quickly!'

She grabbed him by the hand and dragged him towards the door of her room. 'Look in the washbasin, look in the washbasin, Grandpa! Look at the blood.'

The old man looked. There was nothing there.

'What blood?'

'Oh, it's gone!' She put a hand down, touched the pristine enamel. 'But it was all splashed, all splashed here, splashed with blood.'

'Now come on. Get back to bed. It's far too early for all this nonsense. It's not yet five o'clock. Come along! Back to bed!' He lifted her up with a grunt and carried her to the bed and threw her across it. 'Now, no more of this nonsense, young lady! I have to get my beauty sleep if I'm to give a good sermon.' The day was Sunday.

'But there was blood, there was! It was bubbling up. Making a noise. I saw it, heard it.'

The door closed behind him.

Her father had been killed by a sniper's bullet in his throat. He had bled to death before anyone could do anything for him. He had died at the hour of her vision.

'My family never wished to talk about it. Odd. You'd have thought that people so religious would have found some confirmation of all they believed. But, no, they did not wish to talk about it and they did not wish me to talk about it. I never did until I grew up and read that pamphlet of Hugo's – *Apparitions and Survival*.'

'You must meet Lavinia Trent,' Sybil says.

'The actress?'

Sybil nods. There has been something histrionic about the way in which this totally unhistrionic woman has told her story. That is why Sybil has been put in mind of Lavinia. 'I think you'd get on together. Though you're wholly unlike.' She does not specify the points of unlikeness; it would be too cruel. 'She, too, has had a recent – death.' Sybil, so straightforward and strong, hates such softening euphemisms as 'bereavement' or 'loss'. 'Her son.'

'How awful!'

209

'Yes.' Then Sybil adds drily, 'Though I rather doubt if she ever loved her son as you loved Roy. But she's taken his death very badly. Remorse perhaps?'

'Remorse?'

' "We have left undone those things which we ought to have done and done those things which we ought not to have done." When people die, that thought haunts one. I know I often think it about Hugo.'

Two youths in overalls, their hair piebald with splashes of white distemper, have come over to the pinball machine. They glance at the two well-dressed, middle-aged women, talking in quietly confidential voices to each other, with empty glasses before them, and then look away. Too old. Hags.

Sybil picks up her bag.

'Shall we be on our way?'

'I suppose so.' The terrible thing is that, whenever Bridget is now on her way, she has no idea where that way may be tending.

Sybil calls over her shoulder to the moustached, red-faced man in a blue blazer behind the bar, 'Goodbye' and he responds, 'Goodbye, ladies, thank you kindly for your custom,' in a parody of a military voice, which disturbs and startles Bridget.

Outside, Bridget says, 'Perhaps I'll give it a try.'

'Give what a try?' Bridget has this habit, maddening to Sybil, of assuming that others have been miraculously privy to some train of thought that has been going on within her.

'This automatic writing.'

'It takes up an awful lot of time.'

'Oh, I've got time. All the time in the world.'

SIX

WAS

Bridget's two sons, seventeen-year-old Eric and thirteen-year-old Oliver, moved viewers even more than she did when they appeared on television. All three of them looked and behaved as people would hope themselves to look and behave in such circumstances but, in many cases, would never succeed in doing. They were clearly grief-stricken but they showed none of the wildness, disorder and self-absorption of grief. Bridget was wearing a simple, brown dress, a shade darker than her hair. A puffiness about the eyes suggested that she had been weeping. The boys flanked her, each in grey flannels, tie and pullover, with grave, stoical faces. Friends later told her that she should have refused to be interviewed, it was an unforgivable intrusion; but she replied, 'No, I felt it to be my duty.' Then, at least, the friends countered, she should have refused to involve the boys. But the boys, at that brief time of solidarity, had wanted to be involved.

'This news must have come as a terrible shock to you, Mrs Nagel?'

For a hysterical moment, equally invisible to the interviewer and the camera, Bridget had had the impulse to answer, 'No, it came as a lovely surprise,' so idiotic was the question. But instead she nodded, putting a protective arm around Oliver's narrow shoulders.

'Do you find that you regret that the whole operation ever took place?'

'Well, of course, I'd have preferred it not to have taken place – and him not to have gone.' Oliver, small and beady-eyed, looked up at her, like some baby bird at its mother. He dreaded that she might cry. But her voice was steady, her eyes wholly tearless, as she continued, 'Of course, I'd have preferred it if my husband – and so many others, Argentines too – had not been killed. But, well, he was a journalist, a wonderful journalist, and he couldn't miss a story, not one like that. He survived Korea, Vietnam, Salvador . . .' She lowered her head, biting her lower lip, and then raised it again as though in a valiant, doomed effort to stare down the intrusive camera. 'I'm proud that he did what the job demanded, did it like that. Yes, I'm proud.'

'I'm sure your sons feel your pride.'

'I think so. I believe so.' Again Oliver turned his head upwards, like some famished bird waiting for its mother to feed it. Eric stared ahead of him. He hated the idea of the war and the idea of his father's death but a loyalty to his mother and to the memory of the father with whom he had never really got on made him dissimulate.

He swallowed. 'Yes, we do,' he said. 'We feel very proud of what Daddy – my father did. It was typical of him. He did not see why a journalist should be any safer – or have any more privileges – than the men who were fighting.'

When the interview was over, the three of them re-entered the Georgian-modern house on the outskirts of Chichester. Eric resolved, silently, to mow the lawn the next morning, as a kind of propitation of the shade of his father, who would so often exclaim, 'Oh, for God's sake Eric, you'd think that when I'm not here you'd see to the lawn.' His father had always preferred Oliver, who was docile, unintellectual and so good at games that, at his first term at Dartmouth, he had been chosen as fly-half for the Rugby football second eleven.

'We must try to go on with our lives in the ordinary way,' Bridget said, not for the first time. 'That's what Daddy would have wanted.' But it was difficult to go on with one's life in the ordinary way with reporters, cameramen, visitors, telephone calls and letters perpetually distracting one. 'You must both do what you want to do and not worry about me.'

But though the boys would have been far happier following this instruction, they felt, guiltily, that they must not abandon their mother. When, forgetting their bereavement, one of them would shout to the other, crack a joke or burst into laughter, a terrible shame would follow; and Bridget would make that shame worse by the bruised, stricken look that would pass across her face.

From New York, Bridget's daughter, Pamela, rang daily. 'I wish I could come over to be with you. But Mel has this conference in Detroit and I couldn't bring the children and I don't know who'd look after them for me. I feel real bad about it.' She was so impressionable that, after some half-dozen years of marriage, she had already acquired both an American accent and a repertoire of American idioms.

'Oh, don't do that, dear. I fully understand.'

'Everyone here is one hundred per cent behind the British,' Pamela assured her, as though she herself had never been British. 'Don't bother yourself about that hag at the United Nations.' Bridget could not think who this 'hag' might be. She did not ask.

One night Bridget found Oliver sobbing in bed, his face turned to the wall as the sound, an effortful hiccoughing, reverberated round and round his bedroom. When she tried to comfort him, he pulled away from her arm. 'Oh, go away!' he cried out fretfully. 'Go away!' He was ashamed that she had seen him do what he had been so careful not to do in front of those television cameras.

For a few days, Eric ate little, and when he did so, there would be an abstracted look on his face, as he chewed slowly, his eyes carefully avoiding having to look at his mother, his brother or, worst of all, the snapshot of his father in battle-dress in some jungle, in the silver frame on the reproduction Queen Anne walnut sideboard.

For the next few days, friends of the family – two of them women whose husbands were away on service in the Falklands and who, in their visit, kept asking themselves the unspoken question, 'Would I behave as well as she is doing?' – continually appeared up the drive, some in cars and some on foot, often accompanied by children and dogs.

'Are you sure there's nothing I can do for you?' 'Sure.' 'Oh, poor Bridget!' Bridget would shrug, her mouth twitching.

Or, 'Why don't you get away from the house? The change might help. Come and stay with us.' (Pamela had suggested the same thing, though she had added dubiously, 'I'm sure the two girls won't mind mucking in together so that you can have one of their rooms.') But Bridget would reply that she preferred to be where she was. She had never greatly cared either for travel or for staying with other people. Roy had laughed at her for that – 'You made the wrong choice in marrying a hobo like myself.' The wrong choice? Perhaps, after all, she had.

Then, inevitably, the visitors became less frequent, the letters and telephone calls fewer. There was a victory and people told her that they expected that that made her feel better, at least Roy's death and all those other deaths had not been for nothing, and she replied, wanly, that yes, she supposed that it did. Oliver spent more and more time away from home, either sailing with friends at Bosham or bicycling around to make brass rubbings in churches. Eric, shame-faced, asked if his girlfriend could come and stay and Bridget, who had never agreed with Roy's verdict that she was 'a common little tart', replied, 'Yes, of course'. But Eric then announced that, since she had a job in a boutique in the King's Road, it might be easier if he were to go up to London than if she were to come to Chichester. The truth was that Chichester bored her and was beginning to bore him.

'Yes, do go, darling.' Bridget did not ask where he would be staying, since she already knew that it would be in the flat which the girl shared with four other people, male and female, in Earls Court Square.

'But are you sure you'll be all right?'

'Quite sure.'

'I hate to leave you.'

'I'll have Oliver.'

'But he's never here.'

'And the Nicholsons up the road. I can always go over to them for a bit. They're always asking me.'

'It'll only be for tomorrow night and perhaps the night after.' But, in the event, it was for almost a week.

Then Oliver reminded his mother that the French cousins, tough boys, with hands greasy from the motorbikes that they were constantly cannibalizing, had asked him to go and stay with them during the summer holidays. In fact, it was their mother, Bridget's half-sister, married to a French garage-owner, who had asked him. Bridget said that yes, of course, she hadn't forgotten and he must get away. Oliver felt not so much drawn to the cousins, whom he both admired and dreaded, as driven by bereavement from Chichester. He would not forget his father but he did not want to be reminded of him.

Then it was Eric, who announced that Carrie wanted to throw up her job and go to stay at an ashram near Delhi and that he would like to accompany her. Otherwise, he explained, he might lose her, lose her forever. His father would probably have replied to that, 'And a good thing too!' but Bridget was more sympathetic. Again she said, as she had said to Oliver, that of course he must go, she would be perfectly all right, she might even go somewhere herself. That night, as she lay sleepless in the high double bed which now seemed so vast, she went over her finances in her mind, to decide how much money she could spare each of the boys for their trips. She had never been good at money; she had always left that kind of thing to Roy, even though he had hardly been better at it.

On the telephone from New York, Pamela was indignant, 'Well, I really do think that one of them should have stayed with you. I can't understand it. It seems to me most thoughtless, even callous.' But Bridget paid little attention, knowing that the indignation was merely a symptom of guilt.

Bridget began to spend more and more time at the Institute for Paranormal Studies. When, at the station or on the train, some friends would ask her what she would be doing in London, she would answer vaguely that there was this show she thought she might take in, she had to see a friend of hers in hospital, one of Roy's relatives had asked her up. She guessed rightly that most of these decent, sensible, down-to-earth people would think it odd and sad if she were to tell them, 'Actually I'm going to attend a seance.'

At the second of these regular visits to the Institute she had run into Hugo. Instead of treating her, as he usually did, with a vague, distant courtesy, he made an effort, since he had learnt of her bereavement, to be friendly to her, introducing Henry to her and telling her of these two boys, these two quite remarkable boys, who had this amazing ability to transmit information to each other by ESP. There was to be a demonstration at the Institute the following Wednesday – perhaps she had heard about it? Bridget nodded. Then she must be sure to come, Hugo said, and Henry added, 'I don't think you'll be disappointed.'

But, in the event, she was disappointed, as she had been disappointed in all her efforts to make some kind of contact with Roy. It had been an extremely hot day and the atmosphere in the Institute, with its skylights high up in its vaulted roof, was all but unbearable. The more fragile of the two boys – they were so unlike each other that it was hard to think of them as twins – had suddenly become hysterical, screaming that he could not go on, and had then had what looked like some kind of fit. The combination of the airlessness of the hall and the scene that had taken place in it left her feeling shaken and nauseated long after she had stepped out into the street.

On the train home, travelling before the rush hour, she found a first-class carriage to herself by skilfully avoiding the elderly man, a retired naval commander, who had ceaselessly talked to her about his garden throughout the journey up. As she looked out of the window at the parched countryside, she felt a similar parchedness within her. She might have been a husk. All flesh is grass. The dean had said these words at the funeral, plangently sonorous. And not only all flesh but also the bones within it. The lips approached the juddering flame of the candle, they blew. Darkness. 'I have a message here for a lady – I think the name begins with A but it could be B – a lady with a recent bereavement. It's her, yes, I think it's her brother but it could be her husband. Now does that apply to anyone here?' Nonsense. She wanted to believe that the 'lady' was herself, that the B was for Bridget and that the husband was her own. But she couldn't. She had even come to doubt whether, so many years ago, a seven-year-old girl with plaits dangling to her shoulders had really stood on tiptoe and looked down as, with a turbulent threshing, blood had spurted up from the waste pipe around the sides of a high, old-fashioned basin. Perhaps she had imagined it all. Hysteria. Coincidence. Perhaps. That was why Mrs O'Connor and Maureen and Sean and that disembodied spirit or spirits, mischievously or malevolently smashing milk bottles against the half-open door of the refrigerator, scattering clothes down the hall as though in a paper chase or tipping Mrs O'Connor out of her favourite chair in an ungainly bundle on the floor, so much fascinated her. If, between them, they could defy the physical rules decreeing that in certain circumstances all matter must behave in a certain way, then might it not be possible that that other rule of inevitable decay, death and extinction might not also be defied? She hoped it, she all but believed it.

As she began walking briskly up from the station, a small,

almost childlike figure, in a pale blue coat and skirt and a matching pale blue toque, the retired naval commander, avoided in the train, drew up in his Saab. 'May I offer you a lift, Mrs Nagel?'

'Oh, that's very kind of you.' She was flustered; and to the old widower, with his red, good-natured, slightly lascivious face, that was something flattering. 'But it's no distance at all. I could do with a walk.'

'Nonsense. Hop in. It's far too hot.'

Reluctantly, she obeyed him.

'Been to the theatre?' he asked.

She shook her head.

'Thought I might see that Shaw play. What's it called? *On the Rocks*. Well, we're even more on the rocks now than when he wrote it.' He chuckled as though the thought gave him satisfaction.

'Yes, I suppose we are.' She was thinking of that strange, pale boy, so unlike either Oliver or Eric, screaming out 'No, no!' and then writhing and twitching on the floor, with Hugo kneeling beside him.

The car grated up the drive. 'My word! Your lawn could do with some cutting.'

'Yes. I'm afraid so. My husband usually did it. And now my two boys are away. I suppose I must do it myself.'

'I'll come by. Glad to do it for you. Maybe tomorrow afternoon, if this weather continues. How about that?'

'Oh, really . . . I don't want you to take all that trouble . . .' She did not know what to say.

'Delighted. Have far too little to occupy me.'

She got out of the car, 'Thank you so much.' She knew that she ought to invite him in for a drink or at least a cup of tea; but she did not do so. 'Please don't worry about the lawn. Please!'

'Nonsense!'

When she went into the kitchen, to get herself a cup of tea, she saw that, in hurrying out that morning, she had left the light on. Leaving lights on was something she was always doing, and to forestall her doing so had been an obsession with Roy. Before they left the house, he would run up the stairs to look in bedroom, bathroom, lavatory, kitchen; and if, despite this vigilance, they returned to find a light none the less burning – in the linen cupboard, in the scullery now used for the washing machine and dishwasher, in one of the two empty guest rooms – he would shout at her, 'Oh, for Christ's sake! Our bills go up and up and you know we're not made of money.' There was no one now to shout at her and, as she stared up at the bulb, she felt a clammy desolation.

She went to bed early and, after lying awake for a long time, trying not to imagine the exact circumstances in which Roy had died and yet failing to do so, she plunged into sleep as though into a sea full of monsters. 'I don't think I've ever dreamed so much in my life,' she remarked once to Eric. But when he had asked her to describe her dreams, she had been unable to do so. She only knew that she always awoke with a sense of having endured something unspeakable, while drifting, half-conscious, under an anaesthetic. 'You must remember *something*,' Eric insisted. She shook her head, mute in despair. Now, once again, she plunged into that sea, to suffer that violation of which, on opening her eyes on the first glimmer of dawn, she could remember nothing other than the emotions of horror and pain which it aroused. But with those emotions of horror and pain there were gratitude and relief. For what? One strand of her dreams had been like a rainbow in a sky of otherwise baleful leadenness. But she could not now, her eyes on the ceiling above and her arms resting, above the bedclothes, straight along her sides, remember the details, hard though she tried. She got off the bed, as she always did nowadays, with an ache and stiffness of the bones such as might have followed some long, arduous climb of the kind which Roy, who punished others as well as himself in his pursuit of self-discipline, would inflict on her on their holidays in the Lake District or on the Welsh mountains. It was only just past five.

221

She had an impulse to go out into the cool garden and weed the herbaceous border in nothing but her nightdress and slippers; but the paperboy or the milkman, both always early, would see her and there would be talk, not malicious but pitying, among the neighbours, and she did not want that. So, instead, she went into the kitchen and began to cream the butter and sugar for a cake, until, suddenly, she remembered that she herself did not eat cake, the boys were away and Roy was dead. She ran hot water from the tap into the bowl and then tipped out the mixture, her hand to the switch of the waste-disposal unit. Grease still clung to the sides of the stainless-steel sink; she did not bother.

The daily, a young girl married to one of the electricians at the theatre, arrived with a packet of passiflora tea. She was a vegetarian, who enjoyed describing how she had had her only child at home, standing up, by the natural method. The tea, she said, was not dangerous like those tranquillizers and sleeping pills that Bridget was always swallowing. In fact, though Bridget's doctor had prescribed both tranquillizers and sleeping pills, Bridget rarely took them. But she did not argue with the girl, who treated her with the same slightly hectoring protectiveness with which she treated the child brought with her. Instead, she put the packet of tea on a shelf in the kitchen, among all the things bought, like so many of her clothes, on an extravagant impulse and then never used. 'How kind of you,' she said; and, yes, the girl was kind, genuinely kind.

Later, the two of them drank cups of the tea together and ate crumbling, wholemeal biscuits. The tea had a bitter, vaguely unpleasant taste but Bridget, not wishing to hurt the girl's feelings, persisted with it. The child lay, fat and contented, in its pram beside them. So calm was it that it might have sucked passiflora and not milk from its mother when, unselfconsciously, she had unbuttoned her blouse and pulled out one of her firm, white breasts. 'Any news of the boys?' the girl asked. Like everyone else, she thought that they should not have left their mother at such a time. 'I had a card from Oliver and a telephone call from Eric.' Bridget did not add that the postcard had nothing more informative on it than 'Having a super time, Love Oliver' or that Eric had reversed the charges – which must have been enormous from India – and had then said little except that he was getting over a go of dysentery and was running out of money.

Eventually, the girl left. Bridget stood at the window and watched her, as with that gracefully swaying walk of hers, her head held high, she pushed the pram down the drive and out into the lane. 'She's happy,' Bridget thought with a pang of envy. 'Absolutely happy.' On her feet, the girl was wearing a pair of raffia sandals, laced about the ankles, which, she had told Bridget proudly, her husband had made for her. She was now on her way to make him a leek-and-potato pie. She had promised that she would also make a small pie for Bridget, to bring with her the following morning, even though Bridget, careful about her figure, never touched either potatoes or pastry.

It was as Bridget was eating a solitary luncheon of cold chicken wing and a watercress salad that she heard the front door chime. The chimes had been there when she and Roy had bought the house and, though Roy had frequently said that they were as horribly twee and lower-middle-class as gnomes in the garden or flying ducks on the wall and that they really must have them removed and a bell installed, somehow, like so many other improvements, which they promised each other, the change was never made. Hell! It must be the naval commander come to mow the grass, she had forgotten about his promise. Running her tongue over her teeth to remove any traces of food, she went to the door and opened it.

It was not the commander but an extraordinarily handsome, extraordinarily pale young man, with one foot in plaster, the toes bare. He was in slacks and open-necked, short-sleeved shirt.

'Mrs Nagel?' he asked hesitantly.

She nodded.

'I hope you don't mind my ringing your bell like this – on an off-chance.'

She stared at him, waiting for an explanation, but, as he edged nearer the door, the iron under the plaster scraping on the paving, he seemed to be in no hurry to give her one. He screwed up his eyes, the muscles of his jaws tensing, as though the movement forward had caused him pain. Then he smiled. 'I was passing through here on my way home to the West Country. And I suddenly thought "That's where Roy had his home" and so I looked in my address book . . . Of course I should have rung first. Bad manners, I'm afraid.'

'So you knew my husband?'

He nodded. She stood aside for him and he limped in. In the hall, he looked around him, as unhurried as someone returning home, and then, turning to her, said, 'I'd better introduce myself. Michelmore, Tim Michelmore. I expect your husband mentioned me.'

She frowned.

'No?'

'I can't remember. I daresay he did.'

'Lieutenant. He was attached to our unit.'

'Oh, I see,' She began to walk down the hall towards the sitting room and he limped behind her. She could hear the clank, clank, clank of that iron on the stone floor, wherever there was no rug. 'Have you eaten or can I offer you something?'

'Well, to tell the truth, I haven't eaten. But if you've already done so, please don't bother.'

'No bother. None at all. I've just had some cold chicken and salad. There's a lot more left. Would that do for you?'

'Smashing.' There was something boyishly immature about the choice of word and the way in which he said it, just as there was something boyishly immature about his whole appearance.

'Do you mind eating in the kitchen? I do most of my eating there now.'

'Good God, no!'

'Roy hated kitchen meals. He said they were squalid.'

'Well, he was something of a stickler, wasn't he?'

She nodded ruefully, as she began to get down a plate for him.

'Of course, we admired him for that. The way he always kept up appearances, insisted that everything should be as normal as possible, however abnormal the conditions.' He sucked in his breath. 'Yes, we admired him for that. Terrific chap.'

She began to set out plate, knife, fork, napkin, opposite the disorder of her own half-finished meal. 'Would you like some beer or some wine? We have both.' She often found herself saying 'we', when she should now say 'I'.

'I'm not really a beer drinker. But don't bother about opening a bottle of wine just for me. Water will be terrific.'

'Oh, I'll join you in a glass. Why not?' She opened the door from the kitchen to the cellar. She had rarely been down there, not once since Roy's death. It was he who would fetch up the wine. After his death, it was Eric who would do so. 'Come and help me choose.' She switched on the light and began to descend the steps, with him limping, the handle of his stick over his arm, behind her. 'Are you sure you can manage? I didn't think about your foot.'

'Yes, I can manage, thank you.'

'White or red? Roy always said it was just chichi to insist on white with chicken.'

'Yes. I remember his saying that.' He was eager to confirm it. 'He used to prefer red with chicken. Didn't he?'

She nodded.

'Well, then, let's have a red.'

She held up a bottle. 'This?' She did not know it but Roy had been extremely proud of that Beychevelle 1966.

The young man squinted at the label with eyes, green and dark-ringed, which were set wide apart in his triangular face. 'Super.'

They remounted and, after the young man had opened the bottle, seated themselves, facing each other, at the kitchen table. He looked around him appreciatively, 'Cosy,' he said. 'Roy was wrong. I'd much rather be here than in the dining room.'

She nodded. 'I prefer it.'

He lowered his head and began to eat the food before him, picking daintily at now a leaf of lettuce, now a segment of tomato and now a shred of meat and then chewing meditatively, with an occasional smile at her. She watched him. Usually two strangers isolated together feel obliged to talk, however inanely; but, to her surprise, she was free of that compulsion. She was content to wait for him to start.

He stared out of the window at the grass, white with daisies, sloping up to a little spinney in which, when they were younger, the boys would often camp out on summer nights. 'This is a large property,' he said.

'Not all that large. But too large for me by myself – now that the boys are away.'

He nodded. 'School holidays. Roy was so proud of those boys.'

'Oliver was his favourite.' Roy had never seemed to her to be proud of Eric, despite his prizes, his performance as Hamlet and his poems and stories in the school magazine.

'Yes, Oliver was his favourite all right. But still . . .'

'I don't think he ever really understood Eric. Father and son were so unlike each other. When Eric played Hamlet at his school, he was so disappointed that his father showed so little interest. And yet, I sometimes think, perhaps Eric has taken his death harder than Oliver. He's so reticent, it's hard to tell.'

'Strangely, Roy told me about that Hamlet. He seemed to take pride in it then – when he told me about it. So perhaps he really took more pride in all Eric's achievements than he'd let on. That would have been typical of him.'

'Yes, typical.' She pushed the salad bowl towards him. 'Have some more salad.'

'It's smashing dressing.'

She did not tell him that the dressing had come, ready-

226

mixed, out of a bottle bought at Marks and Spencer. Roy would never have countenanced that. She supposed ruefully that she was going to pieces, without him to hold her together.

'You're on leave?' she said.

'Sick leave. Convalescing now. I'm on my way by car to the Officers' Home in Osborne – Isle of Wight. You've probably heard of it.'

'Oh yes. Years ago, Roy and I visited a friend of his there – a colonel he'd known in Korea.'

'Nice place. Very grand. Queen Victoria used to live there. Apart from Sandringham, there was nowhere she liked better – in her last years, after her old man died.'

Bridget wondered if, talking to other people, he would also refer to Roy as her 'old man'. The phrase somehow jarred.

'Where's your home?' she asked and then, when she saw his face suddenly dim and dissolve into a settled melancholy, she wished that she hadn't.

'My home? Well, it used to be near Norwich. But I don't really have any home now. I was an only child, you see, and my father died when I was nine. My mother had a struggle. Somehow gave me the best possible education – good prep school, Harrow. Then *she* died. So . . .' He shrugged, put out a hand and lifted up the bottle. 'May I?'

'Of course.'

'You'll have some more with me?'

She shook her head.

'You must.' He tilted the bottle, poured. He raised his glass, '*Saluti!*'

'*Saluti*,' she muttered. Like that 'old man', this 'saluti' somehow jarred. She could not imagine Roy saying 'Saluti' as he raised his glass to a colleague or, indeed, responding with a 'Saluti' if a colleague said it first.

He sipped, sipped again, then gulped. 'Lovely stuff.' He turned the label towards him and again stared at it. 'Roy certainly knew how to choose his wine.'

'Yes, he knew a lot about wine. I suppose it came from having had a grandfather in the trade. Funny he never wanted to go into it himself.' Funny and sad. If he had gone into it, he would never have been killed.

'Somehow one can't imagine a chap like Roy in the wine trade. He was all up and go.'

'There's some cheese if you'd like it. Only mousetrap. Or what about a peach?'

'The peach would be super.'

With the same delicacy with which he had sliced the tomatoes and cut slivers off his chicken leg, he now began to peel and cut up the peach, between knife and fork, without ever touching it. It took a long time, he was wholly absorbed.

Again, Bridget felt no need to keep a conversation going. She watched him, her arms crossed on the table before her and her eyes sad yet expectant.

He dabbed at his lips with his napkin, the peach eaten. 'Home-grown?' he asked.

'Oh, heavens, no. I expect it's from Italy.'

He thrust back his chair and stretched his long legs before him. The iron clanked.

'Do you want to hear about it or not?'

'About – about what?'

Suddenly, like a gust of wind revealing some object, a tin can or a fragment of glass, hidden in deep grass, so his question had revealed to her that dream, consolatory but seemingly lost beyond recovery, from which she had awoken. It had been of Roy, yes, she remembered it vividly now, but of Roy, not as he was, greying, paunchy and often irritable, in recent years but as he had been when first she had met him. He had been leaning from the window of a railway carriage and she had been looking up at him and their hands had been clasped. The train had started to move, he had clung on to her hands, she had begun to run beside the train. But she could not keep up, she began to falter, to fall, feeling his grip about to jerk her arms from their sockets.

Then he let go. He was shouting, 'I'll send you a parcel! I'll not forget! A parcel! A parcel!'

The boy leant forward, put a hand along her arm. It was a gesture at once intimate and totally devoid of any sexuality. 'About what?' he echoed. 'About his death.'

'You were there?'

He nodded, the green eyes suddenly darkening with the sympathy and grief which flooded into them. 'I was there. That's how I got this.' He indicated the leg in its plaster.

'Tell me,' she said. She leant forward. Waking, half-waking, dreaming, she had so often imagined his death. Now she would know.

He told her. Roy had insisted on accompanying the unit with an extraordinary, unnecessary gallantry; but he was so strangely calm that the boy had felt disturbed, it was as though the calm was one of acceptance of imminent death. The Argies (the boy used the word which Bridget could never bring herself to use) had been so eager to run that they had flung aside their weapons with no attempt to retaliate. Then had come the surrenders. White flags. When a white flag had appeared on a mound from which, all day, there had been accurately punishing artillery fire, Roy had gone forward with them. The Argies had machine-gunned him and, briefly, the unit had had to retreat. Tim himself had gone forward again under the protective fire of the British artillery and had found Roy, hoisted him on his shoulder and somehow, God knows how, staggered back with him. Roy was still alive but barely conscious. It was on that interminable journey back that Tim received the bullet that had shattered his ankle. But somehow he had managed to keep going, somehow he got back to British lines.

'Did he ever recover consciousness?' Bridget stared at him with a hungry intensity as, overcome by his story, he reached out again for the bottle and poured out from it into his glass.

He nodded. 'None of us realized how badly he had been wounded. I don't want to go into details.' He chewed on his lower lip, staring out at the lawn; he appeared to be on the verge of tears. 'I don't think he suffered, I'm sure he didn't. He was beyond that. But he - he mentioned your name. Repeated it, repeated it a number of times. And then he whispered to me, I could hardly hear him, I had to put my head down to his lips, he whispered to me in this faint but clear voice, he said, "Tell her, it's not over. Love conquers death and love casts out fear." '

Bridget stared at him in amazement. 'He said that?'

The boy nodded. 'Yes. That was what he said. I swear to God.' He repeated it, in a tone of wonder, as though he had only now heard it said to him. ' "Love conquers death and love casts out fear." '

'How strange!'

'Strange?'

'Well, I had this dream . . . And the message . . . It's what I've been waiting for during all these weeks.'

'You have?'

She nodded. 'Yes.'

Above their heads, the chimes of the front-door bell tinkled out. Tim started. 'What's that?' He sounded alarmed.

'The front door. Oh God, it must be Commander Cheston!'

The boy half-rose, reaching out for his stick.

'You don't have to go. I'll pretend I'm not here. I'll tell him I forgot.'

The chimes again tinkled. Bridget rose from her chair, went to the kitchen window and peered out around the curtain. She saw the Commander stomping up to the garden shed in which the mower was kept, take the lock in his freckled hand and make as if to attempt to pull it off. Then he thought better of that and stomped away again, in his unfashionably narrow grey flannel trousers and highly polished brogues. 'He's going, gone.' She felt extraordinarily happy and light-hearted as though she, and not the boy, had drunk more than half the bottle of wine. 'Let's go into the sitting room.'

'What about all this?'

'Oh, I'll see to it later. Plenty of time,' she added, a fleck of darkness drifting through the sunlight which now seemed to surround her. 'All the time in the world.'

In the sitting room, lying out on the sofa and smoking one after another of the cigarettes that Bridget kept for her guests, Tim talked chiefly about his own life, however much Bridget attempted to make him talk about Roy. He had wanted to be an actor, that was why he had been so interested when Roy had told him about Eric's success as Hamlet; but his mother had been so eager that he should go into the Army, the Michelmores had been soldiers for generations, his father had been a major in the Army until a wound, received in Malaya, had forced his premature retirement. He had intended to resist his mother's wishes but then, when she had died, he had felt unable to do so. 'If I owed anything to her – and I owed a lot – then I owed her that.' It was a good life, the life of a soldier, in comparison with the lives led by the majority of civilians. Lives of service. Honest. Decent. He had no regrets, none at all.

'That's what Roy felt. He often wished he'd remained a regular soldier himself. That's why he wanted one or other of the boys to go into the Army. Well, he was happy that at any rate Oliver decided on the Navy. He's at Dartmouth, you know.'

Tim nodded. 'Yep. Roy told me that. He said, "Well, if it couldn't be the Army, then the Navy's the next best thing." '

At last, as the sun lengthened across the unmown lawn, white with its daisies, Tim lifted his lame leg off the sofa, a hand beneath it, and then put down the other. 'If I'm ever to get to Osborne tonight, I ought to be on my way.'

'You could stay if you wanted.'

'That's very kind of you. But I told them I'd be there this evening and I think I'd better keep my word.'

She walked slowly beside him as he limped down the drive. 'I left my car in the lane, I didn't know if you'd want it in your drive.'

She laughed. 'Why shouldn't I want it there?'

'I hadn't realized how big your house was.' He sounded embarrassed. 'Of course, you have lots of room for parking. You could take twenty cars here and not even notice.'

'We've taken as many as fifty – when we've given parties.'

When they got to the gate, he raised his hand, the stick grasped in it, up to his cheek. He stared aghast down the lane. 'My God!'

'What's the matter?'

'My car. It's vanished. I parked it just there – under those trees. You don't think the police can have towed it away, do you?'

'Not from here. No. Why should they?'

'Christ, it must have been stolen! My brand new Polo! And – oh Lord – my jacket was in it, with all my cash and my credit cards and my cheque book . . . I never imagined in a place like this . . . One knows that in London . . .'

'You'd better get on to the police!'

'I suppose so.' He was suddenly fatalistic, 'Not that they'll achieve anything. By now, whoever took the car will probably be at least a hundred miles away.'

'Come in and telephone.'

'No, I might as well go to the station. They'll want all kinds of details.'

'It's quite a walk.'

'Is it? Well, I must say, in my present condition a walk would not be all that easy.'

'I could run you down.'

'No, no. You don't want all that bother. But could you – I hate to ask this – could you perhaps lend me your car?'

'Of course. I'll run in and get the keys.'

As she raced back towards the house, the thought came to her of Roy's Mercedes, unused since his death. It somehow seemed appropriate that this messenger from him, the bearer of the promised parcel, should drive in his car. It was the keys to the Mercedes, not her own Mini, that eventually she brought.

He gazed admiringly at the car in the garage. 'Roy used to talk about this car. How he loved it!'

She laughed. 'I sometimes used to think he loved it more than me.'

'Nonsense. No man could have loved anyone or anything as much as he loved you. I'm telling you that. You've got to believe me.'

He climbed into the car, adjusted the mirror, wound down the window beside him. He was wholly at his ease in it, clearly he had driven such a car or one like it before.

'Tell me the way,' he said.

She told him.

'Fine. I'll be back. As quickly as possible – though, knowing the way police stations work, I should guess that'll be a long time.'

Still exhilarated, she returned to the house and began to clear the table and stack the dirty crockery and cutlery in the dishwasher. She had a curious sensation that Roy, who had for so long been totally dead to her, had been suddenly resurrected. The boys had never wished to talk about him to her; her relatives and friends had been too embarrassed to do so. Only this stranger had been prepared to turn the key on that loft in which their shared memories had been gathering dust.

When she heard the car squealing to a stop outside the porch, she hurried out to it.

'Well?'

'Pretty useless. They're sending out a call to all the neighbouring forces. But, unlike this one, the car's not one anyone would notice or remember. And if he's a professional thief, well, he's sure to change the number. The funny thing is that only two or three days ago I was thinking that I must really get some kind of alarm.'

As he clambered out of the car, Bridget put out a hand to help him, her hand to his elbow.

'Thanks.' He smiled at her and, as he did so, she thought, in a totally asexual way, 'How beautiful he is! What wonderful eyes!' He held out the key. 'I'm going to have to do something extremely embarrassing now.'

'Yes?'

'I haven't got a bean.' He put his hand in his trouser pocket. 'Well, that's not strictly true. I have a few beans.' He peered down at the coins which he had taken out. 'To be precise, I have two pennies and three 10p pieces. But that's the lot.'

'I could lend you something.'

'Could you? Could you really? I'll send it back to you just as soon as I've been on to my bank in London and got things sorted out.'

'How much would you like?'

'As much as you can spare.' He laughed. 'Coutts's are a wonderful bank but they can seem awfully, awfully slow when one has an emergency like this.'

'I'll see what I have.'

They went back into the house and Tim sat in the hall, his hands resting on his stick, while Bridget ran upstairs and searched in her bag and in the desk drawer in which she also kept money.

She reappeared. 'I can manage forty-five. If you need more desperately, then I could go to the cash dispenser.'

'No, no, that'll be fine. At least it'll enable me to buy some basic things. All my luggage has gone too.'

'You could borrow anything of Roy's you wanted.'

'Oh, I wouldn't dream of it. No, no!'

'I'm sure he'd be only too happy to think of your doing so. Come upstairs and have a look.'

Eventually, with a show of reluctance, Tim had chosen a pair of pyjamas, two shirts, two ties, a blazer, three pairs of socks and half-a-dozen handkerchiefs. Bridget then pressed on him an electric razor ('But I can easily buy a cheap razor with blades'), some slippers, a spare toothbrush, found at the back of the bathroom cupboard, and an unused tube of toothpaste. She fetched down a suitcase and began to pack for him, while he looked on, smilingly grateful.

At the end he said, 'I wonder if you could do just one other thing? You've been so kind to me.'

'Yes, of course.'

'It's difficult to carry a suitcase with this.' He tapped with his stick on the plaster cast. 'I'm sure that someone will help me off the train and on and off the boat. People are so good about such things, aren't they? But I wonder if you could possibly run me down to the station.'

'Oh, yes, certainly.' Then on an impulse, thinking of this delicate boy – he seemed little more – humping Roy's semi-conscious body under murderous enemy fire, she suggested, 'Why don't you take the car? I never use it, I'm frightened of driving something so huge. I have my Mini.'

'But I couldn't possibly . . .'

'Please! You can return it on your way back from Osborne.'

'But I'll be there two weeks.'

'That doesn't matter. I'd been meaning to sell it. Eric wanted it – he's taking his test – which is why I hesitated to put it on the market. But a car of that size would be far too expensive for him to run. He'd be better off with a Metro or something of that kind.'

'Well, if you honestly think . . . It's marvellous of you.'

'It's only a way of making some small return for – for what you did for Roy. And for me too. I'll never forget that. Never.'

He heaved the suitcase off the bed. Then she insisted on taking it from him. 'You'll find it easier to get down the stairs without it to obstruct you. I can manage it. It's no weight at all. And I'm good at carrying things. Roy trained me on our hikes.'

'He even tried to train *us!*' He laughed. 'God, how we

sometimes hated that *keenness* of his – even while we loved him.'

She put the suitcase into the boot of the Mercedes, suddenly sad, after her previous exhilaration, that Roy's messenger would drive off now, that she would go back into an empty house, and that, except when he returned briefly to give back the car, she might never again see him.

He looked into her face, stooping slightly, with the tender concern of a parent looking into the face of an unhappy child. 'You've been so kind to me. So welcoming and hospitable. I'll write from Osborne – with my cheque of course – just as soon as everything is sorted out. But don't be too impatient. As I said, it may take a day or two.'

'Oh, don't worry.'

'At all events, I'll be back with the car and the suitcase and the other things this time two weeks hence.'

'Oh, don't bother about the suitcase and the things. Just be sure to bring back the car,' she answered in joke.

'Of course. Everything . . . Goodbye.' Then he did a startling thing. He moved shyly towards her, bent down and kissed her on the forehead. 'Thanks.'

She stood on the porch, one hand shielding her eyes against the late evening sun, as the car crunched round the half-oval of the drive and then gathered speed towards the gate. A hand came out of the window, it waved. She could not see him, with the sunlight flashing on the back window. She raised her hand, she waved it from side to side. Her hand felt strangely heavy, as though it were not a part of her.

The days passed. No letter came from Osborne. Could it be that he had not arrived there safely? Eventually she telephoned. A brisk woman's voice answered. 'Lieutenant Michelmore? One moment please.' A silence. Then, 'There's no one of that name here, I'm afraid.'

'Are you sure?'

'Yes, quite sure. I've just been through the list.'

'He'd have arrived, oh, on Monday of last week.'

'One moment, please.' Another silence. Then, 'No, I'm afraid we've no note of a Lieutenant Michelmore arriving that day – or since. I think there must have been some mistake.'

'You are the officers' convalescent home?'

'Yes, that's right.'

'And there's no other one on the island?'

'No, no other. Of course, there *are* a lot of private convalescent homes.' The woman was trying to be helpful. 'And a lot of hospitals and nursing homes.'

'Thank you. Yes.'

Bridget stood for a long time by the telephone, hearing, in memory, that grate of the iron on the flagstones at which she was now staring down. Grate, grate. Hard, remorseless. But surely no one, no one in this world, could be so cruel? Something must have happened to him, there must have been some mistake.

Ellen arrived, swaying up the drive as she pushed the pram before her. She had been lying out in the sun and her face, bare arms and legs were attractively tanned. She was talking to the child, fixedly staring up at her, as though he were an adult. Bridget could hear her through the open window, 'I must remember to call in at the cleaner's on the way back. I forgot yesterday and the day before that. I must remember. Otherwise Daddy's going to be cross with me.' Ellen was constantly forgetting things.

'What's the matter?' Ellen asked as soon as she saw Bridget's pale, unhappy face gleaming at her from the chair at the far end of the shadowy hall. 'Has something happened?'

Bridget put a hand on the telephone beside her, as though to assure herself of its reality and therefore of the reality of the conversation that had just taken place. 'I've had a shock,' she said.

'You look as if you had. What is it?'

Ellen, hugging the child to her with one hand, came over and put the other hand, firm and consolatory, on Bridget's shoulder.

Bridget told her.

Ellen, who had now perched, the child still held against her, on a chest in the hall, drew in her breath, her brows knitted. 'Well, I did wonder,' she said. 'But I didn't like to say anything.'

She was always amazed by the extent of Bridget's innocence and credulity. She was now in her forties, she had had three children, she had lived in Hong Kong, Singapore and Kuwait; and yet she believed anything that anyone told her, just as she believed in all that spiritualistic nonsense of hers.

'Oh, I wish you had!'

'I didn't feel it was really my place.' Once Ellen had attempted to argue with Bridget about a local medium, and that had been the only occasion on which the two of them had all but had a row.

'I wonder what I should do.'

'Go to the police! That's the first thing.'

'I find it so hard to believe . . . Almost impossible . . . I mean – he was so *convincing*.'

'Conmen always are. It's their profession, after all.'

Bridget still found it almost impossible to believe after she had been in touch with the police. Two plain clothes men drove round to see her and then, having heard her story, they suggested that she could go down to the station to look at some photographs. She turned over the pages of the album, thinking, in ingenuous amazement, as she looked at one perfectly ordinary face after another, 'But they all look just like anyone else!' At last she found his. He did not look just like anyone else. He maintained his delicate, aristocratic distinction even in the unflattering photograph, face turned straight to the camera, on the table before her.

The detective said, 'Yep. That figures.'

Later she learned that the man whom she thought of as 'Tim Michelmore' had a number of aliases but was really

Arthur Ainsworth; that he made a speciality of following up obituary notices in the *The Times;* and that he had been repeatedly convicted for the theft of expensive cars.

'Was the plaster cast also fake?' she asked the detective who told her all this.

He stared at this pretty, middle-aged woman, obscurely touched, as Ellen always was, by her air of forlorn, childish innocence. 'What plaster cast?'

'On his foot.'

He shrugged and looked down at the paper before him. 'There's nothing here about his being lame.'

Bridget went home. She did not care about the money, the clothes, the electric razor or even the car. But she was profoundly troubled by the chasm into which, once alone in the house, she found herself peering down with a giddy nausea. There were two realities and the chasm plunged between them. There was the reality of that consolatory dream which, unlike all her other dreams of Roy, was still vivid in her mind, of the boy's concern for her, expressed in that final kiss, and of that message that he brought back from Roy and all the other dead 'Love conquers death and love casts out fear'; and there was the opposing reality of her telephone call to Osborne, of the empty space in the garage, and of that photograph of a fragile, aristocratic-looking youth in an open-necked shirt staring defiantly into the lens of an invisible police camera.

She felt herself falling into the chasm, as one falls in a dream, on and on, silently screaming, and never reaching its bottom.

SEVEN

WILL BE?

Today the three women, Sybil, Lavinia and Bridget, will meet.

The term will start tomorrow at Sybil's school and she wakes up, far too late, in a state of irritability. We have left undone the things which we ought to have done and done the things which we ought not to have done and there is no goodness in us. There is no goodness in her staff, Sybil feels. Madge telephoned the previous evening to say that she would be arriving two days late, since she had to settle her mother into a new home in Worthing. 'Surely you could have done that sooner?' Sybil demanded acidly. Madge replied that, no, it was only the previous day that a row had blown up between her mother and the perfectly foul people who ran the home in which she had been living ever since their return from Morocco. 'It's highly inconvenient,' Sybil said, adding, with an illogicality unusual to her, 'I do think you might have given me more notice.' At that Madge shouted down the telephone, 'But I didn't know until yesterday evening! As I told you, it was only then that the whole row blew up.'

The bursar has failed to have the water heater serviced, though Sybil has repeatedly reminded him; the windows are in need of cleaning; and there are deadheads on the roses. If the staff do not set an example of efficiency to the girls, then they cannot expect it of them.

Sybil brushes her teeth with such violence that the gums start to bleed. She might be cleaning out the water heater, scouring the windows or slashing at the deadheads. One can rely on no one, one must do every fucking thing oneself. She spits into the basin, as though to void herself not merely of the saliva and toothpaste streaked with blood but of the acid bubbling within her. Then she remembers. Mrs Lockit is coming to see her this morning.

What can the woman want? On the telephone she was, by turns, cagey and coy. No, she wouldn't like to say what it was that she wanted to discuss. Yes, it was a matter of some importance – to both of them. It would be easy enough to come along to the school, because, by a strange chance, she would be going for an interview for a housekeeper's position in the neighbouring town and gathered that there was a bus stop right by the school gates. Dreadful creature!

Eleven days ago, Henry died of a heart attack. He had been out to a party given by some friends down the hill from the Village and, when he left, it had started to pour. The friends had suggested either that he should wait until one of the other guests could give him a lift or that they should telephone for a taxi. Henry replied that Mrs Lockit always had his supper ready at seven-thirty and that, as a matter of principle, he never took taxis. He would walk. He walked too fast and collapsed outside a pub, where he lay for some time, in a moribund condition, the rain pelting down on him, because at first every passer-by assumed him to be drunk. Eventually, two elderly women, returning from Evensong, had stooped over him and peered. They had realized that he was not drunk but extremely ill. He never regained consciousness.

Reading his obituary in *The Times,* Sybil wondered whether she should make the journey to Brighton for the funeral. Hugo would have wanted her to do so; but she had never cared for the old boy, so scratchy, snobbish and stingy, and there was so much to do at the school before the new term. She eventually appeased her conscience by ordering far too elaborate a wreath just as, in the past, before Hugo's marriage, she had appeased her conscience for having refused to allow Hugo to invite Henry to join them on a cruise of the Greek Islands by bringing back, at enormous expense and inconvenience, an outsize tin of Kalamata olives. On that occasion, Henry had said ungraciously, 'Oh, what a kind thought! I never eat olives, as Hugo should have told you, they always give me wind. But they'll come in useful for my next Village party! No doubt, if he could now speak to her from beyond the grave, he would say of the flowers, 'Oh, what a kind thought. Flowers always give me hay fever, but I'm sure they'll be appreciated at the hospital to which they will eventually go.'

After a hurried breakfast, Sybil clears away into a drawer the sheets of paper, covered in automatic writing, which have been lying under the blotter on her desk, and then settles down to examine the untidy draft of the timetable prepared by the Senior Mistress. Each timetable of the previous Senior Mistress was, as Sybil would often tell her, a real work of art. If this timetable is a work of art, it is of a kind produced by one of the less gifted girls for her O Levels. Sybil grimaces, picks up a red biro and begins to slash in a number of deletions and emendations.

She is still doing this when there is a knock at the door and the timorous little Filippino girl, who arrived only two days before to act as parlourmaid, comes in to announce, in an almost unintelligible accent, that there is a visitor to see her. Sybil looks at her watch. It must be Mrs Lockit. 'Show her in.' The girl looks bemused. 'Bring – her – here,' Sybil says loudly and slowly, as though addressing a deaf-mute. The girl scuttles off.

Mrs Lockit eventually appears, without the girl, who has left the door to the study open.

'Hello, Mrs Lockit.' Sybil rises and holds out her hand across the desk. But Mrs Lockit, who has never visited the school, is peering around her. Then she asks, 'What nationality might she have been?'

'Who?'

'The one who let me in.'

'Filippino.'

Mrs Lockit shakes her head, as though in disapproval, selects, not the chair intended for her by Sybil, opposite her own at the desk, but another one, by the fireplace, and then, having deposited handbag, string bag and Marks and Spencer plastic bag, seats herself, legs wide apart and fingers interlocked. Her hat looks like a coal scuttle, trimmed with grey net. Beneath it, her eyes are cunning and wary. 'I never thought to see you at your school.'

'I never expected to see you here either.'

'Big.'

'Over four hundred girls. Quite a responsibility.'

'But you like responsibility.' It is plainly not a compliment.

'I hope you got the job,' Sybil says, moving round the desk and taking the chair originally intended for her visitor.

Mrs Lockit pulls a face. 'Turned it down. They should have told me, instead of dragging me all this way on a wild goose chase. Just the one room, no central heating, no bathroom or kitchen to myself. "There's been some mistake," the old girl said to me. "You bet your life there has!" I told her.' Mrs Lockit smiles to herself at the memory of this exchange between a frail widow, no longer able to look after herself, and her sturdy self, so competent to do so. 'Still and all,' she goes on, 'it's given me a chance to see the school. Otherwise, we'd have met in that flat of yours in London.' She does not think much of the flat, so poky and bare.

'What did you want to discuss with me? Not the school, I'm sure.'

Sarky! Mrs Lockit draws in her chin and adjusts the folds of her pale blue crimplene skirt over her ample thighs. 'Your brother,' she says.

'My brother?'

'In a manner of speaking.'

246

Sybil waits. She feels vaguely frightened.

'Those experiments of his with my two nephews. I didn't approve of those.' She shakes her head. 'Not at all.'

'You didn't seem to discourage them.'

'Well, it was difficult – to discourage them. I mean – my sister living in such circumstances.'

Again Sybil waits. Her vague fear intensifies.

'She needed the money. Not to put too fine a point on it. But those boys, they oughtn't to have deceived him. No, that was wrong and I'm sorry now that, as soon as I learned what they were up to, I didn't put a stop to it. But there it is.'

'Deceived him? How exactly do you mean?' Sybil manages, for all her inner turmoil, to appear calm.

'You didn't believe all that thought-transference malarkey did you? A woman with your education!' She chuckles, enjoying the look of shock that, temporarily suppressed, is now appearing on the handsome face of the woman opposite her. 'They used a dog whistle,' she explains, 'or something similar – with a bulb attached. Cyril could hear it, most kids can. But your brother couldn't, Sir Henry couldn't, you couldn't, I couldn't. No, they oughtn't to have done that. A joke's a joke but I didn't approve of that.'

'Did Sir Henry learn about this?'

'Of course.'

Sybil is bewildered. 'He never told me. I wonder why.'

Mrs Lockit shrugs. 'There were probably other things he didn't tell you either.'

Fear grips Sybil's heart. 'Such as?'

'Well, it's one thing to tamper with children's minds – as, in a sense, your brother was doing, wasn't he? But to tamper with . . .' She draws down the corners of her mouth. 'If it hadn't been for Sir Henry, I'd have gone to the police when I came to hear of it. But I wanted to spare him a scandal. And then, of course, when your brother died like that, there no longer seemed any point.'

'I don't know what you're trying to say, Mrs Lockit,

but I absolutely refuse to believe that my brother behaved incorrectly towards either of your nephews.'

'Incorrectly!' Mrs Lockit laughs. 'That's one word for it. I like that!'

Sybil gazes out of the window at the lawn and, beyond it, the straggling rosebushes, with their deadheads. She sees a figure first somersault and then hurtle down a sheer cliff of cement. She shuts her eyes, she puts a hand up to cover her mouth, as though she were about to vomit. She no longer suspects, she knows now. Hugo killed himself.

In a quiet, steely voice, she asks, 'What precisely do you want?'

Mrs Lockit shifts her weight in her chair. 'Your brother was generous to the boys.' She smirks. 'He had reason to be. Now that you've got all that money of Sir Henry's – which was intended for him – well, I think your brother would have liked some of it to come the way of Cyril.'

Sybil rises, her beautiful hands, with their tapering fingers and carefully kept nails, clasped before her. 'Money? What are you talking about?'

Mrs Lockit is disconcerted. 'The money that old Sir Henry left.'

'Sir Henry left nothing to me.'

'To your brother.'

'He intended to make my brother his residuary legatee.' After a bequest of five hundred pounds to Mrs Lockit, of another five hundred pounds to a former colleague, and of pictures to some half-dozen friends, Henry willed his whole fortune, far larger than anyone had ever imagined, to Hugo. But Hugo was dead. 'But, as you will know very well, my brother predeceased him. Died before him,' she adds, as though contemptuously assuming that 'predeceased' is a word unintelligible to Mrs Lockit.

'But surely the money then comes to you and his wife?'

'It comes to neither of us.' Sybil is delighted by the ignorance which has led Mrs Lockit to assume that a sister and spouse should have equal rights to a dead man's estate. She

248

is even more delighted at Mrs Lockit's discomfiture. She smiles, suddenly she is radiant. 'I'm afraid you've been misinformed. Neither I nor my sister-in-law get a penny of that money. It's sad, in a way, because my sister-in-law and her children could have done with it. It would be no point in your asking her for help. And there is absolutely no point in asking me.'

Mrs Lockit frowns, biting her lower lip between teeth which are as small, white and sharp as those of a ferret. Then she says, 'There are things that could come out that you wouldn't want to come out.'

'Nothing could come out that would worry me in the least – or worry my sister-in-law. You can go and tell your lies to the police, you can even get your nephews to corroborate your lies. But the police aren't going to be interested in a dead man. And the newspapers aren't going to be interested in a dead man. No one's interested in a dead man.'

She stops at that. She suddenly realizes what she has said in that last sentence. No one is interested in a dead man. Corollary: a dead man is interested in no one.

Mrs Lockit heaves herself up to her feet. She looks oddly diminished, as though, in the few minutes in which Sybil has defied her, she has suddenly suffered some long, wasting disease. Her face is no longer ruddy, but yellow. She stoops and effortfully picks up handbag, string bag, plastic bag. The straps of the last, which is crammed full, bite into her pudgy wrist. 'I'll be on my way,' she says, raising an invisible white flag. Then she gazes at Sybil with a reluctant admiration. 'Well, fancy that about the legacy. You and his wife must have been pretty sick about that.'

Sybil shakes her head. 'Not really. We'd have liked the money, of course. But one's never disappointed if one fails to get something which one wasn't expecting anyway. Is one?'

Mrs Lockit edges nearer to Sybil. 'I wonder if I might ask you for a favour, mam?' She has never called Sybil 'mam' before.

Sybil nods graciously; but mixed with the sweetness of her triumph is the bitterness of defeat. Hugo loved that boy, Hugo killed himself. 'Yes?'

'I suppose you couldn't spare me a fiver? The fare was more than I expected and I find myself short.'

The impudence of it delights Sybil. It would also have delighted Hugo and Henry, since it would have confirmed their low opinion of humanity in general and of women in particular. 'Of course,' Sybil says. She takes up her bag, removes her wallet from it and pulls out a five-pound note. 'Are you sure that'll be enough?'

Mrs Lockit hesitates. Then she says, 'Oh, yes, thank you. Ample.'

'Good.'

Sybil presses the bell beside the fireplace.

'Who gets all that money then?' Mrs Lockit asks.

'What money?' Sybil deliberately pretends not to follow.

'Sir Henry's.'

'Oh, it goes to a nephew. His closest living relative. An accountant in Brussels. I met him once,' Sybil smiles. 'Would you like to see the solicitor's letter? I have it somewhere here.'

Mrs Lockit shakes her head. 'I'll take your word for it.'

Lavinia wakes early.

Last week she visited her doctor, an occurrence rare for a woman of her health and stoicism, to ask for a prescription for some sleeping pills. Her doctor, an amateur actor and constant theatre-goer, always allows her all the time which she wants, and even himself protracts their interviews when she is eager to end them, despite all the impatient patients in his waiting room. 'Well, it's understandable, your not being able to sleep, after what you've been through.' An elderly, precise man, who has come belatedly to an interest in what he himself calls 'the mind factor in diagnosis', he leaned across his desk, his cuffs white against hands brown from the use of a sunlamp. 'What form does your insomnia take? I mean, do you have difficulty in dropping off or do you wake too early?' 'I drop off at once.' The phrase perfectly describes her sense of literally falling, from a great height, into some deep and dark tarn. 'But then at three or four or five I'm wide awake again.' He nods. 'That figures. If you can't drop off, it's usually a sign of anxiety. If you wake too early, a sign of depression. You're depressed.' 'Yes, I'm depressed,' she agreed. 'You ought to be working. You owe it to yourself, you owe it to us, your public.' 'Perhaps. But I don't want to work.' She owed it to Stephen not to; but she did not say that. The doctor shook his head, in reproof, and then drew his prescription pad towards him. 'Have you seen this *Don Quixote* at the National?' 'No. I haven't been to the theatre for a long time.' 'I'd forgotten what a boring novel it really is. But I like the penny-two-farthings.' Since Lavinia not only no longer went to the theatre but did not even read reviews of plays, she had no idea that what he meant by 'the penny-two-farthings' was the antiquated tricycles which did service for Quixote's horse and Sancho Panza's ass.

Lavinia took one of the pills but none the less she has woken at nine minutes past six. She feels muzzy and faintly sick, as though after too many glasses of sherry on an empty stomach, but she knows that she will not be able to fall asleep again and so she gets up. Today is the day when, in Sybil's flat, she will be meeting that woman whose journalist husband was killed in the Falklands. In her present state Lavinia, who usually has a remarkable memory, cannot recollect the woman's name. That annoys her. It is as though, in the middle of a long run, she had suddenly dried.

When she has dressed, she has no appetite for breakfast; and so, having drunk a cup of coffee, black and unsweetened – though she no longer acts, she is still careful of her figure – she decides on a walk. It is such a beautiful morning and she always enjoys wandering through streets deserted except for cats, paperboys and milkmen. As she passes Henry's house, she looks up at the windows. The curtains are not closed, there is no single indication that he is not still there; and yet the house gives back a dead reverberation. She thinks of those terrible Village parties of his, cheap glasses half-filled with what the neighbours on the other side would call 'kitchen sherry', a few bowls containing salted peanuts and potato crisps, and Lucy, Mrs Lockit, clearing everything away and thumping corks into bottles with the palm of her grubby hand at the stroke of seven-thirty. The giant dahlias are in bloom. Ugly flowers, so stiff, gaudy and scentless. But Henry loved them, telling her more than once, 'Silly snobbery of people who affect to despise them!'

She walks on, her step amazingly buoyant, in her simple skirt, blouse and sandals, her legs and arms bare. A youthful builder in paint-stained dungarees, walking past on the other side of the road, whistles at her, not realizing that she is a woman in her forties. She enjoys that whistle, as she has always enjoyed the applause when she has walked on to a stage, the staring and nudging when she has gone into a shop or entered a railway carriage, and the jostling, smiling and asking for autographs outside the stage door.

The front, like the streets, is all but deserted. An elderly man, his face purple and streaked with sweat, jogs past her slowly, his elbows tucked close into his sides and his feet shuffling. Far out, on the edge of the sea, there is a woman with a small mongrel dog. The woman stands motionless, a hand raised to her eyes, as she stares out towards the red-streaked horizon. The dog scrabbles with agitated paws in the sand by a groin. Then the woman raises a hand to her mouth.

Distracting Lavinia's attention, two fishermen in cloth caps and cardigans on this day of an Indian summer, glide past her, silent and dignified, on old-fashioned bicycles with high handlebars, their rods on their shoulders.

After that, she hears someone calling her name. 'Lavinia! Hey, Lavinia!'

She turns. Far behind there are two male figures in open-necked brilliantly patterned short-sleeved shirts, blue denim shorts which look as if their owners had themselves ripped off their legs to truncate them, so ragged are their ends, and multi-coloured sneakers. One of them, who has the stocky physique and battered face of a fly-weight boxing champion, Lavinia recognizes. The other, who is like some emaciated bird, she has never met. She waits for them to catch up with her.

'Lavinia love! I was going to telephone you this morning. Aren't these coincidences just amazing! I was saying to Drew, I must see Lavinia Trent before we go, and blow me if there, in front of us, was Lavinia herself!' He turns to the young man, who is standing shyly a few paces behind him. 'Lavinia – this is Drew Schultz. Drew – Lavinia.' The young man, who is American, holds out a hand from which a gold bracelet, with an identity disc on it, dangles. He has a small gold stud in his right ear. Above it his hair sweeps thickly away, like a black wing. As Lavinia and Drew shake hands, the other man, who is called Eddie Moran, tells her, 'Drew is the most brilliant designer. I first came across his work at Louisville and I then persuaded him to come over here.'

'With no difficulty I may say,' the American puts in, smiling at Lavinia.

'Let's get ourselves a coffee some place.' Eddie is not American but, constantly commuting across the Atlantic, he tends to use Americanisms and even a vaguely American accent. 'We passed a café with some tables out of doors.'

Lavinia looks at her watch. 'It's not yet eight. Nothing will be open. You're up very early.'

'Always am. So's Drew. Successful people usually have three characteristics in common. They eat fast, they dress fast, and they wake up early in the morning.'

'You could come back with me. I might even grill you a kipper.'

'God forbid!'

'Well, make you some toast then.'

'Fine!' Eddie links his arm in hers.

'Where are you staying?' Lavinia asks.

'Oh, with the Naylors – as always. It's sometimes hard, they bicker so much, but they'd be deeply, deeply hurt if I went some place else. Do you see them?'

'Not for ages. I'm losing touch.'

'Bad girl!'

Drew lags behind them from time to time, to stare out towards the empty beach and the sea; then he hurries to catch up. 'It's so beautiful here,' he says at one point. 'Just beautiful. I envy you living here.' But, in fact, he is getting bored and is eager to return to the bars and clubs of London. Eddie is so much older than he is, he talks about nothing but himself and the theatre, and that remorseless voracity for food, gossip, work, money and fame no longer turns him on, quite the contrary.

Lavinia makes coffee in the kitchen, while the two men sit at the round table in the bow-window, looking alternately at her and at each other. Eddie is conscious of a dead resonance from the empty flat beneath him, once inhabited by Stephen, just as earlier that morning Lavinia was conscious of a dead resonance from the next-door house, once inhabited by Henry. Eddie used to wonder if Stephen might not be gay; but the boy was so far from being his type that he never investigated.

'You look terrific,' Eddie says, as Lavinia puts a cup down before him. 'Don't you agree, Drew?' Drew nods and then mumbles 'Thanks', as he takes the cup that Lavinia is now holding. 'Seeing you ahead of me, I thought, "Wait a minute now, wait a minute, who's that young girl?" And then I realized – God, it's Lavinia!'

'Not young, not a girl. A middle-aged woman.' Lavinia sits, coffee cup in hand, beside them.

'What I wanted to see you about . . .' Eddie throws out his legs and then spreads them far apart, so that the denim pinches the flesh, covered with reddish hair, of his muscular thighs. 'You know about this season of mine.'

Lavinia nods.

'First London, then Broadway. Jean and Terry are coming in on it. But the point is – I also must have you.'

'Me?'

'Yes, sweetie, you. I want you for my Beatrice.'

'Oh, it's too late for that.'

He does not understand her. 'Too late! What *are* you talking about? The best Beatrice I ever saw was Diana Wynyard's – I was a schoolboy at the time – and she was not so much in the first flush of youth as in the first hot flush of middle age.'

Lavinia shakes her head. 'Sorry. I've retired. Positively last appearance. You know that, Eddie.'

'But, Christ, it's so stupid, it's so bloody stupid!' Suddenly he is genuinely angry and indignant, not pretending to be so. 'You know the parable of the talents. What you're doing is wicked, apart from being stupid, bloody stupid. If people are damned for wasting their talents, then you'll be damned.'

Lavinia enrages him even further by responding with a sweet, gentle smile and a murmured, 'More coffee?'

'I don't want any more of your fucking coffee! I just want you to say, if not yes, then you'll think about it.'

'Sorry, Eddie.'

'Stephen's death wasn't your fault. You were a terrific mother to him, everyone in the business knows that. So why should you go on punishing yourself in this way for it? It's just masochism, that's all.'

Lavinia shrugs and looks away from them both, out into the garden. Those terrible photographs and cuttings shower down on her, as though they were razor-blades. Her flesh recoils, smarts, oozes an invisible blood.

'You're so obstinate!' Eddie cries out, not realizing that this is what people always say of him. 'There are times when I really hate you.'

Drew is shocked; but then, throwing back her head, Lavinia begins to laugh and at that he knows it to be all right.

'Well, we'd better be on our way. Jean and Terry will

255

probably be wondering what has happened to us.' Eddie pushes himself up from the table. He is not a man to waste time. Mission unaccomplished. 'Think about it,' he says. 'Please. Think about it, I beg you.' He puts a hairy arm round her and she feels his moustache on her cheek as he kisses her.

Drew says, 'Well, it was a real privilege to meet you, Lavinia. It's something I've always wanted. And thanks for that coffee.' To Lavinia's surprise, he then leans forward and, his hands on her shoulders, gives her a kiss first on one cheek and then on the other. Unlike Eddie, who smells of sweat, as though he had just emerged from a boxing ring, Drew smells of Caron Pour Un Homme.

Though Eddie tells her that they'll let themselves out, Lavinia goes with them to the door. Drew says, 'You have a lovely home here!' at which Eddie shouts, 'But she shouldn't be sitting around in a lovely home! She ought to be acting!' The two men go down the steps and, as they do so, Lucy, Mrs Lockit, emerges from her basement, in one hand a capacious handbag and in the other a string bag and a Marks and Spencer's plastic bag. Eddie and Drew stare at her hat and she stares at their bare, sunburned legs. Then she calls out, 'Good morning, Miss Trent! You're up bright and early.'

'Well, so are you!'

'I'm on my way to an interview for a job. And also to call on a friend. The other side of London, near Maidenhead.'

Lavinia never for a moment suspects the 'friend' to be Sybil.

'Well, have a good day,' she says. 'I hope the job works out.'

'I'm not in a hurry,' Mrs Lockit says. 'I'll only say Yes when I'm sure it's absolutely what I have in mind.' Henry's nephew has already been taking legal advice about dislodging Mrs Lockit from the basement. Then she says, 'Aren't you ever going to let that flat of yours? It seems a shame to leave it lying empty. Particularly with this housing shortage.'

'I'm thinking about it,' Lavinia answers coldly. But this is a lie. She cannot bear the idea of that dead resonance of the basement suddenly clearing and sharpening. There is a troubled spirit there and she does not want him troubled yet further. She often goes down there and wanders from workroom to kitchen, from kitchen to bedroom, from bedroom to bathroom, from bathroom to lavatory, as she did on that day when she found that figure, clad only in a pyjama jacket, dangling from a pipe.

'Bye, Lavinia!'

'Goodbye, Lavinia. And again – think about what I said to you.'

'Goodbye, Miss Trent.'

Lavinia hears none of them. She turns and goes back into the house.

'You're prepared to let a stranger and a conman have it, but you won't let me. That's fine, just fine.'

'I lent it to the stranger and the conman. A car of that size will be no good to you. I'll sell it now and on your birthday I'll give you a smaller one.'

Eric scowls down at his eggs and bacon. 'But *that's* the car I want. Don't you understand? I want Daddy's car.'

Oliver looks at his mother, raises his eyebrows and shrugs his shoulders. It is his way of saying: Don't give in to him, I'm on your side.

'A car like that costs a fortune to run. How do you imagine you're going to pay for the petrol? And a garage has only to see a car like that to up its price for repairs. Don't be silly, Eric.'

'I plan to work part-time as mini-cab driver. I met this chap. He does it at weekends. He never pays tax. Clears, oh, a hundred and fifty, two-hundred quid on just a Saturday and Sunday.'

'And how are you going to be a mini-cab driver if you're at the university?'

Eric looks petulant. 'I'm not all that sure I want to go to university. What's the point? At the end of it all, you're unemployed just like anyone else.'

Bridget wishes, yet again, that Roy were here to cope with this boy who is in every way beyond her: beyond her intelligence to reach, her love to encompass, her authority to dominate. 'Well, you must do what you think best,' Bridget says with a grudging sorrowfulness. What he thinks best is less and less what she thinks best.

'There is no point in Daddy and Mummy spending all that money on your education if, at the end of it, you throw everything up,' Oliver remarks priggishly.

'Oh, mind your own fucking business!'

Roy would have ordered Eric to leave the room for that. Bridget says nothing. The boys are now always fighting among themselves but she has learned that it would be as foolish to intervene as in a scrap between two young bull terriers. She can only look on, terrified and appalled.

She has no more appetite and so she gets up with her plate and scrapes its half slice of toast, butter and marmalade into the sinkbin. She flings what is left of her coffee after it and then switches on the grinder. If she had more courage and less self-restraint, she might have flung the coffee into Eric's sallow, sullen face.

'I'm going up to London today,' she announces. 'Ellen will get you both some lunch.'

'Again!' Oliver will miss Bridget. Since Roy's death, they have warily edged closer and closer to each other.

'Yes, I'm afraid so.'

'Don't tell me you're off to attend another of those spook-sessions of yours.'

'Spook-sessions?' She pretends not to understand.

But Eric knows that, of course, she understands, as he continues, 'It's useless, Mummy. Don't you realize? *Useless.* Daddy's dead and your father's dead and that's the end of it. If, somehow, they *have* survived – in some never-never after-life – why should either want to be called back to a world as bloody as this?'

His vindictiveness is not really directed at her but at the circumstances of the death of the father, obtuse, reactionary and domineering, whom he loves only now that he has vanished. But Sybil flinches as though from a blow.

Oliver says, 'Perhaps they would want to come back in order to comfort Mummy.'

'Oh, you don't believe that crap!' Eric sees the look of anguish on his mother's face and suddenly he is penitent. In a now gentle voice, he asks her, 'Well, where are you going in London?'

'I'm meeting a friend. Sybil Crawfurd. And she's going to introduce me to Lavinia Trent – who's a friend of hers.'

'Lavinia Trent!' Eric is more interested in the cinema than the theatre; but his girlfriend has a passion for the theatre and the opera and, unwillingly, he often has to accompany her to them. 'She played Cleopatra here two or three years ago, didn't she?'

Bridget nods. 'But I didn't see it. You know how your father felt about Shakespeare.'

Eric knows. He feels the same. 'It would be interesting to meet her,' he says.

'Well, once I've met her, perhaps you will.'

'Ask her down,' Oliver suggests.

'I might. If we get on. It's easy enough from Brighton.'

She goes upstairs. Her plan, long deferred, is to sort out Roy's clothes for Oxfam. She has asked the boys if they would like, if not the shoes, shirts, pyjamas and under-clothes, then the ties, suits, overcoats, raincoat, handkerch-iefs. But they have recoiled from the suggestion with a kind of superstitious dread, just as she now, having pulled open a drawer on neat piles of shirts and pyjamas in cellophane envelopes, recoils. The last time that she opened this drawer it was in order to lend to the man whom she still thinks of as Tim Michelmore a pair of pyjamas. Though the police now have the man in custody, she does not have any of the clothes which she passed on to him. She does not want them, she has never asked the police if eventually they retrieved them, as eventually they retrieved the car, all bruised and scarred as though from a war.

It is strange. Ever since 'Michelmore' played on her what that military-looking detective, with the reddish bristling moustache called 'a diabolical trick', she has had no more dreams. Each night's sleep is a temporary death. She dies, she is totally extinguished and then, reluctantly and painfully, she endures a resurrection. Perhaps Eric is right. Why should anyone want to be summoned back from the dead to a world as bloody as this?

She stands by the open drawer, with one of her hands resting on the pile of shirts which she was about to lift out. Her face, as intent as if she were listening for something, some whisper, some rustle, some call from afar, is reflected in the mirror on top of the chest-of-drawers. Beside the mirror there is a photograph of herself and Roy at their wedding in Chichester Cathedral. He was then still in the Army and they are walking out under an avenue of crossed swords. Suddenly she is reminded of childhood games of Oranges and Lemons: Here comes the chopper to chop off your head. She takes up the photograph, tosses it on top of a pile of shirts and then, raising a knee, pushes the drawer shut on it.

Looking at herself in the mirror – so much has happened to her, both outside and within, and yet, to her amazement, her appearance has not changed – she thinks yet again, as she has often done, of that extraordinary visitation. She thought that she was entertaining an angel when (if that military-looking detective is to be believed) she was entertaining a devil. Or are the two things one? He knew so much about her: her past life, her inmost nature, her secret feelings and thoughts. The military-looking detective had remarked that that went without saying, conmen always managed to give that impression. Eric spoke of 'empathy'. She was not sure what that meant. Empathy? she queried and he answered, 'What novelists have. Conmen and novelists have something in common.' She still looked bewildered and so he went on, 'He imagined you as you really are.' But that merely complicated things yet further for her.

She hears Ellen arriving downstairs. Eric and she are talking. Eric laughs at Ellen for her fads but secretly he admires her and is attracted by her. He would not mind going to bed with her, he once confessed to Oliver, who was shocked – 'But, Eric, she's *ancient!*'

As Bridget makes her bed, she thinks of the day ahead of her. She will go to the National Gallery, not to any particular exhibition, but to moon vaguely around. She has come to enjoy that sense of anonymity in a crowd. Sometimes in the National Gallery, the Victoria and Albert Museum or the London Museum, she has had some unexpected, interesting encounter, usually with a foreigner as lonely as herself. There was a Japanese professor, terribly ugly, who talked to her incomprehensibly about his work on enzymes while treating her to tea and far too many cakes at a café crowded with elderly people reading Polish newspapers; there was a jolly girl, a schoolmistress, from the Hague, who was interested in UFOs; there was a middle-aged English woman, stout and woebegone, who tried to persuade her to go with her to, of all things, a thé dansant. There is appeasement and assuagement in such contacts, too fleeting to leave any more mark than a butterfly which momentarily alights on a leaf.

The bed done, Bridget looks at her watch. It will soon be time for her to leave to catch her train. She goes to the door. Then she remembers something. Crossing to her desk, she takes up some sheets of paper (pointless, pointless, but Sybil has insisted that she bring them), folds them roughly and stuffs them into her handbag.

Bridget goes down the stairs, to where, in the hall, Ellen is hoovering briskly, a silk scarf knotted around her hair to make a bandeau. The baby, plump and silent, is on the sitting-room carpet. Ellen kicks off the hoover, 'Hello!' she says. 'I hear you're off to London again. You've become a terrible gadabout.' Roy used to say, 'If you're not careful, that girl's going to become altogether too familiar.' Bridget has not been careful, the girl is too familiar. Bridget does not care; in fact, she prefers it that way.

Yes, she says, she's going to London to see a friend; and then she adds that she has made a steak-and-kidney pie and would Ellen please heat it up in the oven for the boys and also cook them some frozen beans. Ellen disapproves of meat-eating and frozen foods but she nods. 'There's also some yoghourt,' Bridget adds. Ellen approves of that, though she wishes that the boys would eat it with brown, instead of white, sugar.

'Where *are* the boys?' Bridget asks.

Ellen says that Oliver is still reading the paper in the kitchen and that Eric has gone out. 'Gone out? Where?' Bridget asks. It is odd that he should have gone out without saying goodbye to her. Ellen replies that perhaps he is in the garden.

'Goodbye, darling.' Ellen puts a hand on Oliver's shoulder. He looks up at her, a fledgling to its mother, his mouth slightly open. He has been reading the sports pages of the *Telegraph*, while stuffing himself with slice after slice of bread piled high with honey. Something vibrates, high-charged and perilous, between them, like a high-voltage current along a filament so delicate that there is the constant danger of a fuse. Bridget feels it passing back and forth between her ageing fingertips and the youthful bones beneath them. 'Be good,' she says, though he is never anything else.

Oliver smiles up at her, strangely dreamy. 'Be good too.'

'I never have the chance to be anything else.'

She kisses him on the forehead, says goodbye to Ellen in the hall and then goes out into the garden. Eric is nowhere in sight. 'Eric!' she calls half-heartedly. No voice answers. She goes over to the garage and is surprised to find the door

open. The cars are side by side. She merely glances at the
Mercedes in the gloom and then walks over to her Mini,
which she will leave in the station car park. It is only when
she has inserted the key in the lock of the door and is about
to turn it that she realizes that Eric is sitting in the driving-
seat of the Mercedes. She walks over and opens the door.
She stares at him; he stares back at her with a defiant
insolence.

'What are you doing in there?'

'Sitting.'

'How did you get in?'

'Took the key from your desk.' It was from this same desk
that Bridget took the money that she gave to 'Michelmore',
in addition to the money from her handbag.

'You'd no business to do that.' Eric shrugs and looks
away. 'That desk is private.' Eric does not answer. Has he
examined the sheets of paper now in her handbag? She
wants to be angry but she cannot summon up the spirit.
'You're not to drive this car,' she says.

'Who says I was going to drive it?'

'Without a licence . . .'

'Who said I was going to drive it?' he repeats.

She slams the door of the Mercedes shut and goes over
to the Mini, climbs in, and with trembling hands, attaches
the safety belt. He is sitting at the wheel of his father's car.
He is looking like his father. He has talked to her like his
father. It is another, perhaps even stranger kind of
resurrection.

She drives out of the garage, stops the car and turns her
head sideways so that mother and son are looking at each
other. She winds down the window, she smiles tremulously.
'Goodbye, darling.'

Hands on the wheel, he stares through her.

Sybil will take down the Crown Derby tea service which
belonged first to their mother and then to Hugo and which

Audrey has now given to her as a keepsake. She will set out three cups, three saucers and three plates on a silver tray given to her to celebrate her twenty-five years as head-mistress of the school.

Bridget will pay for the lunch that she has eaten at a table with three strange women, each of them silent, in the restaurant at Peter Jones and will then wonder whether, since service is included, she ought to leave a tip and, if so, where. She is never good at such things; and none of the other women has yet given her a lead.

Lavinia will spray some scent on to her palm and, as she is sniffing at it, will suddenly realize, oh lord, she's going to be late. She will say to the shop assistant that yes, she'll take that bottle. The shop assistant will later tell another shop assistant that she has just sold Lavinia Trent a bottle of Prince Matchabelli Cachet.

Bridget and Lavinia will travel up in the lift together. Each will guess who the other is and each will be on the point of saying 'Aren't you . . . ?' But they will each be silent, avoiding each other's gaze. Lavinia will press the bell and then Bridget will say, 'I thought we might be bound for the same destination.' Sybil will open the door, handsome and formidable, and will introduce them to each other, even though that is no longer necessary.

Sybil will go into the kitchen to make the Earl Grey tea in the Georgian silver teapot which also belonged first to her mother and then to Hugo. She will be scrupulous, as always, about warming the pot. Meanwhile, in the tiny sitting room, Bridget and Lavinia will be talking about the glorious Indian summer, the terrible unemployment figures, and the relative costs of houses in Brighton and Chichester. Lavinia will say that Chichester is so much less squalid than Brighton; Bridget will say that Brighton is so much more lively than Chichester. But neither would wish to live in the other place.

Sybil will come in with the tray and Bridget will try to help her. Lavinia will know better. Sybil will say, with a hint of irritation, 'No, no. Do sit down. I can manage, thank you.'

'Lovely tea! Just what I wanted after a morning of shopping,' Lavinia will exclaim.

'Earl Grey,' Bridget will say. She has, Sybil will privately think, a genius for stating the obvious.

The women will begin to talk of the work of the Institute. They will talk of physical mediums, readers of the Tarot, palmists, psychometrists, metal-benders. Then they will talk of themselves.

Sybil will be first. She will talk with a total, innocent frankness, surprising in a woman so self-contained and sophisticated, about her relationship with Hugo. 'I've never been so close to anyone in my whole life. I've never loved anyone so completely. Often we didn't have to say things to communicate. We just *knew*. That's why it was such a shock to me when he announced, just like that, that he'd decided to get married. It was the only important thing in his life of which I'd had no previous inkling. That,' she will add cryptically, 'and one other thing, later . . . We used to say to each other that whichever of us died first, would make some sign to the other. Hugo always kept his word. Never, ever did he break a promise made to me. So, if he could possibly get through to me, however arduous the process, then he would do so. No doubt of that. None at all. But *has* he got through? Has he?'

Neither of the other two women will be able to answer that quietly anguished question, even though she will repeat, 'Has he? Has he?'

Bridget will speak next. 'I never knew how much I loved Roy until I lost him. There were times – I suppose there are such times in every marriage – when I used to ask myself why ever I had married him. He was everything to me, the children hardly counted, but I was never everything to him, though I know that, of course, he loved me, there was no one else, only his career as a war correspondent, about the best there was. I had that vision about my father's death–'

265

she will forget that Lavinia, now puzzled but not wishing to interrupt her, knows nothing about it '– but when it really seemed that there was this, this messenger from him, he proved to be just a conman.' Again she will forget that though Sybil knows all about 'Michelmore', Lavinia does not. 'Sometimes I feel that, yes, he's there, he's trying to get in touch with me. And then at other times, there's this deadness. Nothing.' She turns to Sybil. 'Of course there was that automatic writing of yours – the goose walking over the grave, the white flag turning black. That *may* be something. It *may* be. And there are all those vague messages through mediums at the Institute. But nothing, nothing certain.'

Lavinia will talk less freely. She will hold something essential back. She will not be able to talk of Stephen's self-mutilations or of that time when the schoolboy game of self-asphyxiation proved almost fatal. But, almost as hard, she will confess her failure as a mother. 'I kept telling myself that every decision that I took and every thing that I did was for him, only for him. But, of course, I was wrong. It was all for myself. He was merely the excuse for my egotism, just as an animal, a dog or a cat, can become the excuse for the egotism of others, with their "I'd love to stay but must get home to put out the dog" or "I'd love to help but I can't leave the cat." That was all he really was to me – a dog or a cat. To be loved when it was convenient to love him and always to be fed and brushed and taken, if necessary, to the vet. It's terrible to think of what I did to his life – or half-life. That's why I want, want so much, to believe that it's not all *finished* for him. That's why I decided that as, as a kind of reparation, I must give up my acting. I had sacrificed him to it. Now it to him.'

The three women will stare at each other.

Then Sybil will take up again. Bridget will now find her somehow frightening. Lavinia will decide that Sybil is being extraordinarily, well, sybilline. 'We are such different women, until today we've never been really close. But somehow death has united us in a way in which life has

266

never done. The silent majority of the dead? But there's also the silent majority of the bereaved. Yes?' She will look at the other two, they will nod. 'These cross correspondences,' she says. 'They exist. I'm sure they exist. But who directs them? Is it Hugo, as part of an elaborate, tremendously difficult way of proving to me and so to you and so to everyone that, yes, the dead do go on into a world of light, yes, they do look down on us or up at us or across at us, yes, they do speak, however much in riddles, to each and every one of us? Or is it some universal intelligence? Or is it, well, just me? Or you?' She will turn to Bridget. 'Or you?' She will turn to Lavinia. None of them will be able to reply. 'The rationalists always have an answer.'

They will talk of other things but now they will have talked themselves out and those other things will merely be scribblings in the margins of their previous discourse.

Bridget will eventually say, 'I brought you some more of my writings. And drawings. Do people often produce automatic drawings?'

Sybil will nod, 'There was a boy who produced automatic pictures which many people, even art critics, declared to be indistinguishable in style and execution from masterpieces by people like Picasso, Manet, Degas, Monet.'

Bridget will scrabble in her handbag and will throw down some sheets of paper, as she rises. 'Mustn't miss my train,' she will say. 'The boys will be waiting for their supper.'

Lavinia will also get up. 'I ought to be leaving too. I have to be at the Barbican by six-thirty.' Then Lavinia will glance down at the sheets of paper scattered across the table. One of the pencil drawings will catch her eye. Then another will catch it. And another. She will examine them, without the others – Sybil is finding Bridget's umbrella for her – realizing that she is doing so.

One of the pencil drawings will show cars piled up on top of each other with, in the foreground, a single blood-stained boot. Another will show a child lying back, its mouth wide open in a rictus of agony, while its abdomen gapes. Another will show a woman, a mask obscuring her face, who dangles, trussed up like some chicken, her pudgy face blue, from a meathook embedded in a cracked, white ceiling. Another will show a muscular oriental, his head shaved . . .

Each drawing will be a miniature, amateurishly slapdash reproduction of those terrible photographs and newspaper cuttings that she had first resolved to burn, so long ago now, in the grate of the sitting room of her Brighton house, and then, having burned a single photograph, had instead hoarded, mysteriously checked, far back in the drawer of her desk.

She will decide to tell the other two women every detail of Stephen's past? She will hold out the sheets in trembling hands? She will exclaim with joy and terror, 'But this is incredible!' as all three of them stare down at the drawings in her hand?

She will decide that she cannot speak anything so unspeakable about her own, her only child? She will look away from the sheets, as though they were no concern of hers? She will mumble, artfully concealing her joy and terror, 'I think I must have brought an umbrella too?'

The other two women will stare at Lavinia, Sybil with a boldness which might be mistaken for hostility and Bridget from under lowered lids, one of which will twitch as though a tiny worm were wriggling beneath it. They will be bewildered and surprised that Lavinia, usually so graceful and self-possessed, should be standing before them like some gauche, embarrassed teenager, her legs wide apart, her head on one side, one shoulder hunched, and her lower lip drawn in between her teeth. Then that bewilderment and surprise will quicken into a breathlessly uncomfortable expectation. They will each know that Lavinia, for some unaccountable reason, is hesitating whether to divulge something of extreme importance to them. Their attention will tighten and tighten as though an invisible hand were remorselessly turning a screw; but at the moment when it will seem that the screw

268

must either snap off or split the material into which it is being driven, Lavinia will turn away from them.

'Well . . .' Her voice will be all but inaudible. 'Goodbye, Sybil. Thank you for the tea.' Her body will swivel slowly, away from her hostess, to face her fellow guest. 'Goodbye,' she will muttter, staring downwards at Bridget's tiny feet in their impractical court shoes. Clearly, it will not be her intention that the two of them should travel together, or even leave together. She will then jerk away, one elbow high, as though she were pulling herself free of a hand attempting to restrain her. She will walk towards the lift, Sybil and Bridget both watching her in silence, and she will tug at its door, her face screwed up as though at an effort almost too much for her. Without looking round at them, she will enter, clash the door closed, and vanish from their sight. Though not even she now knows this, they will never see her again.

Sybil and Bridget, facing each other by the open front door, will have nothing to say. But, in the silence which will prolong itself on and on between them, each will no longer surmise but will know, know with total certainty, that Lavinia possesses the key for which they have been searching. It is there. If she wished, she could hand it to them, as easily as she could hand to them the front-door key to her Brighton house, which she keeps in her bag. Each will feel a sudden joy buffeting her, similar to the wind which will suddenly whirl up the stairway as Lavinia opens the door to let herself out into the darkening evening. It will be a joy so violent that each will, for a moment, wonder if it will cause her to lose consciousness. Each will even know the reason for the joy. There has been a cross correspondence which, unlike all the other cross correspondences, defies all rational explanations. Lavinia knows the nature of that cross correspondence, even if she may never reveal it or even confirm the fact of its existence.

Bridget will gulp, her mouth open, as though in an atmosphere so thin that she is in danger of asphyxiation. Her lips will show a blueish tinge under their lipstick. That tiny worm will wriggle even more frantically as she lowers her lids. Sybil will press a palm to her breastbone, the fingers splayed. It will seem to her as if some huge bird, imprisoned within her, were beating its wings in an effort to get out.

'Well, Sybil . . .' Bridget's speech will be slurred. 'Thank you.'

'Thank you for coming.'

'Strange woman.'

'Strange,' Sybil will repeat, with the dazedness of someone coming round from a deep sleep or an anaesthetic. Then she will give herself a little shake. 'Be in touch,' she will say.

Bridget will nod.

Lavinia will walk down the Bayswater Road, towards Marble Arch, and though it will have been her intention to take a taxi to the Barbican and though many taxis will pass her, she will not raise a hand. She will walk on and on, faster and faster, and all the time she will feel joy cascading into her, like rainwater into a cistern previously choked with dry mud. It is true, it is true! But she couldn't, no, she couldn't, have revealed to the two tremulously expectant women, much less to the world at large, her own and Stephen's shame. Never, never for one moment. No.

Sybil will go into her bedroom, the used tea things, which she usually carries into the kitchen and washes as soon as her guests have left, ignored at this moment of choking, dizzying rapture. She will pick up Hugo's silver-backed hairbrush, which she has kept, she does not know why, beside her own on her dressing-table ever since his death ('You won't mind if I have it, will you, Audrey? It used to be our father's'). She will draw from the hairbrush a single pale hair – she will not remember ever having seen it there before – and then, dropping it to the floor, she will stand by the open window, feeling the chill of the autumn evening like a caress on her forehead, cheeks and bare arms. She will chuck the hairbrush across on to her bed and, suddenly, like a bride, she will turn to the door she has shut behind her,

270

will raise both her arms and will cry out, in a voice of grief appeased and happiness regained, 'Oh, Hugo, Hugo, Hugo!'

Bridget, on an impulse, will turn towards Holland Park instead of making for Kensington High Street underground station. She will enter the park and, though the sky is darkening and the air is growing chill, she will wander, by narrow, erratic paths, deeper and deeper into its tangled heart. She will see a child, with another, smaller child on his handlebars, bicycling in the distance. A jogger will loom up at her, his mouth agape on to the grey, icy air, and then he will vanish. A dog or the ghost of a dog will patter past, in obedience to a far-off whistle.

She will approach a small, secret pond, on which some ducks float so motionlessly that they might all be dead; but they will not be dead, at any moment they could be aroused to clamorous life. They, the water and Bridget will now be equally still. She will grip the iron railing tighter, she will stare into the bushes massed on the other side of the pond and then, suddenly, it will seem to her as if the bushes are alight, the flames whirling around them and up from them and towering higher and higher, even though not a single leaf or twig is consumed and the ducks do not stir. Bridget will whisper out of her contrition and longing, both now appeased, 'Oh, Roy, Roy, Roy!'

Eventually Lavinia will walk out of Brighton Station, while the people surge towards her or surge past her, importunate, restless, distracted wave on wave. She will be oppressed by the alternating frenzy and desolation of their unavowed need. She will know that need, since for so many months it has been her own. She will know it so well.

She will go into her cold, empty house – day after day she will have been waiting for a man to come to repair her central-heating boiler – and she will trudge up the stairs to her bedroom, go to her desk and take out an envelope. She will pluck the fan of pleated paper out of the grate of the sitting-room fireplace and then she will take down a box of matches from the chimneypiece. She will place the stiff

271

photographs and the limp newspaper cuttings in a crisscross pattern on the bars, she will strike a match, she will put the match to one of the photographs.

Acrid and grey, the smoke will prick her nostrils.

Then, when the last scrap of newspaper has been reduced to a palpitating cobweb before it disintegrates, she will suddenly realize the enormity of what she has done. She will press the fingertips of both hands to her mouth, she will rock back and forth, and in agony she will sob out, 'Oh, Stephen, Stephen, Stephen!'